Castillo nodded gravely, and Jenna felt she could almost read his thoughts. Because she was thinking the same thing . . . something nobody wanted to say out loud, at least not yet.

But if they conclusively determined that Mr. Charles Flood had been drowned in chlorinated fresh water before being dumped into the ocean, then things would grow even more complicated. With a single murder, the killer was usually a friend or relative of the victim. With two killings that were similar, the investigators could search for connections between them, like Jaffarian and Sullivan having both been patients of Dr. Cosgrove.

Once the number rose to three, and with no other solid leads, it became far more likely that there *were* no connections between the victims. That they had been selected at random by someone who just wanted to draw blood, someone who just wanted to end lives.

Jenna was sure they had all suspected it earlier. Already they had given him a name—The Baptist—as if they had already been certain what they were looking for. Not someone on a revenge kick, or anyone with a money motive. They could no longer pretend this was an ordinary homicide case.

No. There was little doubt now. They were after a serial killer.

# christopher golden
# and rick hautala
# LAST BREATH

A *Body of Evidence*
thriller starring Jenna Blake

**SIMON PULSE**
New York London Toronto Sydney

This book is a work of fiction. Any references to historical events, real people, or real locales are used fictitiously. Other names, characters, places, and incidents are the product of the author's imagination, and any resemblance to actual events or locales or persons, living or dead, is entirely coincidental.

〰〰

SIMON PULSE

An imprint of Simon & Schuster Children's Publishing Division

1230 Avenue of the Americas, New York, NY 10020

Text copyright © 2004 by Christopher Golden

All rights reserved, including the right of reproduction in whole or in part in any form.

SIMON PULSE, Series logo, and colophon are registered trademarks of Simon & Schuster, Inc.

Designed by Russell Gordon

The text of this book was set in Dante MT.

Manufactured in the United States of America

First Simon Pulse edition October 2004

10  9  8  7  6  5  4  3

Library of Congress Control Number 2004104486

ISBN 0-689-86526-0

Dedicated to the memory of Bill Relling

All my love and appreciation to my wife, Connie, and to our children. You've got a long way to go before college, kids, but I'm hoping your experiences are slightly less exciting than Jenna's. Special thanks to Lisa Clancy, without whom there would be no Jenna Blake, and to Michelle Nagler, who took to her like an old friend. Thanks are also due to the usual suspects, who keep me walking that fine line between sanity and insanity: Tom Sniegoski, Jose Nieto, Amber Benson, Bob Tomko, and, of course, Rick Hautala, who gets his wish in the next book. My gratitude to Allie Costa and Ashleigh Bergh for their help and friendship. And, finally, much thanks to Dr. Maria Carlini, for her knowledge, assistance, and enthusiasm.

—C. G.


I would like to thank my *enkeli,* Holly . . . for being incredibly supportive and loving during these times when "there's always something." I also want to express my love and appreciation to my sons, Aaron, Jesse, and Matti, for being who they are . . . relentlessly. Words can't capture the gratitude I feel to my "brother in ink," Chris Golden. Thanks for inviting me—once again—to share Jenna's world. And finally—but absolutely not least—I want to say "Thank you" and "God bless" to my dear friend Bill Relling, who died much too young. I will treasure all the years we shared as friends and co-writers and can honestly say that I'm a better person for having known you.

—R. H.

# Prologue

At night the big tank at the New England Aquarium glowed with an otherworldly light, and the sharks prowled the water with dark menace, as though they were making plans for the next time some diver was foolish enough to drop in there with them. Keith Manning had always been afraid of sharks, but in the two years since he had taken the job as a security guard at the aquarium, he dreamed about them almost every night. Their teeth. Their dead-looking, killer's eyes. In the dreams he never quite made it to shore, or to the pier, or up into the boat, before he felt those teeth slicing into him. Then he would wake up, eyes wide, a phantom pain in his leg where those dream teeth had caught him, and he would sit there for several minutes, wanting to make sure the dream had passed before allowing himself to go back to sleep.

But that was the problem with sharks. They lurked.

And when you least expected it, they would move in again, as silent as shadows. The dream sharks were no different.

Keith never talked about his dreams. Gage, the guy he was partnered with most nights, would have given him no end of crap about it, and when he was working with Tina D'arcy, he never brought it up because he figured it wasn't the most manly thing, having nightmares about sharks, especially when he worked with them all week.

It was a Tuesday night, just after one A.M. Gage was on the desk, and Keith was walking the floor. They switched off by the hour, all night long. There was always a lag in the transition, five or ten minutes when they would shoot the breeze, but not more than that. Both of them were Patriots fans, but beyond that, they had little to talk about. Gage was twenty-four, and Keith forty-two. They got along all right, but Keith didn't think of Gage as his friend.

The aquarium was built around a massive central circular tank, with a walkway that wound around it. The other exhibits in the main building were built into the walls, and another walkway—this one squared off—rose at a more gradual pace as it made its way along those outer walls. Between the squared and the circular walks was a gap through which visitors could look down upon the penguin pool on the first floor. The offices and other rooms were locked off, but there were other exhibit areas outside the main building, particularly the otters and sea lions, and those had to be checked as well.

Every time it was his turn to do the walk-through,

Keith followed the same pattern. He knew he should vary the routine, but it wasn't as though the aquarium was likely to come under terrorist attack, and there was nothing to steal. The only sort of disruption might be the occasional *Free Willy* nut who wanted to steal the sea lions or something, to free them from captivity and return them to the ocean.

Freaks.

Even that sort of thing had only happened a few times, though. So Keith stuck to his routine. He found comfort in it.

He started at the outer wall on the ground floor and worked his way up, then came down the circular walk around the central tank. His gaze would drift to the glass almost of its own accord, and he would watch the fish and eels and the massive sea turtles. And the sharks, of course. He would watch the sharks. During the day they were surrounded by people staring at them, but late at night when it was just Keith, and Gage or Tina was at the desk, he always felt as though they were staring at him, like he was an intruder.

After walking the main building and returning to the first floor, he picked up his key ring, stopping the metal jangling that accompanied his every step, and opened the rear door. There was a short alley behind the aquarium that took him past the exterior tanks, and he gave them the usual cursory examination as he took a pack of Camel cigarettes out of his pocket, tapped one out, and placed it between his lips. The aquarium was built on a wharf that backed Boston Harbor.

Keith used his lighter to fire up his Camel and took a long drag, the orange tip of the cigarette crackling as it burned in the darkness. He let the ocean breeze refresh him, took in long gulps of the salty air, and did not let himself be bothered by the irony of alternating between that fresh sea breeze and unfiltered nicotine blasts. He liked to watch the lights of the boats out on the harbor and imagine where he would strike land if he could fly out over the water and just keep going as long as there was ocean underneath him.

Halfway through the cigarette, he sighed and turned to his right, going over to the gangplank that led up to the entrance to the performance ring where they had the dolphin show. There was a fence and a metal gate, and he checked the lock, but he didn't think about it further than that. Nobody was getting in there, and the dolphins weren't kept in there overnight, anyway.

As he turned to head back, the radio at his hip crackled with static and then Gage's voice:

"Keith. Are you on the floor?"

He unsnapped the radio and thumbed the button to reply. "I'm in back. Why? Something wrong?"

There was a momentary pause before Gage responded. "Just thought I heard something. Nothing on any of the cameras, but . . . I don't know. You'd better come back inside. Have a look . . . crap! The camera covering the rear door is out."

Keith swore under his breath, his pulse quickening. Most nights on this job were quiet. He hated the ones that weren't.

He hurried back to the rear door, slipped inside, and locked it behind him. The keys hanging from his belt jangled, and he unclipped the ring and slid it into his pocket to quiet them. He paused inside the door and looked around for any sign of an intruder.

Nothing.

Quickly, he began to make his way toward the front of the aquarium, scanning left to right for any movement that did not belong. He heard footfalls coming quickly toward him and glanced up to see Gage hurrying over, glancing around.

"I think I caught a shadow on one of the cameras, someone moving just out of range," Gage whispered. "Up top."

Keith nodded. He pointed at the outer walkway and gestured for Gage to go that way, then he started toward the circular path around the central tank. He couldn't believe this was happening. In the two years he had been on the job, they'd had only three break-ins, and none of the intruders had gotten more than twenty feet into the aquarium before he had taken them down. The cameras and alarms should have alerted them. It didn't make any sense. He couldn't understand how anyone could have gotten into the aquarium without tripping an alarm, unless they had been there since closing, hiding somewhere. . . .

He froze on the concrete walk.

*Or unless some idiot left the back door unlocked while he had a cigarette.*

Again he cursed to himself, realizing what it would

mean if this turned out to be the real thing. His job was on the line.

*Stupid, friggin' moron!* he thought, furious with himself.

He could hear Gage moving up the outer walk. Keith shook his head, filled with self-recrimination, and started up the inner circle again. He ran around and around the central tank, eyes darting to his left as he checked each observation window. His stomach began to churn, and he grew dizzy. Blinking, breathing through his nose, he forced himself not to slow.

*Damn it,* he thought. *Damn, damn, damn!*

He was halfway up when he glanced into the tank.

The shark was there, gliding through the water, and though it slid past him, its eyes seemed to track him. Still dizzy, he allowed himself just a moment's pause, watching the shark.

Then another shadow moved in his peripheral vision, but it was not inside the tank.

Even as Keith looked up, a gloved fist struck his temple and he stumbled backward. Fingers grabbed his hair, but he was still off balance and could not keep his feet. He felt himself turned, twisted, and propelled forward. At the last moment he tried to put up his hands to stop himself, but it was too late. His face collided with the glass of the tank, which was so thick, it might as well have been steel.

Keith went down hard, darkness swimming at the edge of his vision. He must have blacked out, because it seemed only seconds later that an alarm blared, echoing all through the aquarium. He forced himself up onto his hands and knees, shaking his head and trying to put it all together, to figure out what the hell had just happened to him.

Static on his radio. "Keith! Keith, where the hell are you?"

Still shaky, he staggered to his feet and grabbed his radio. "Here. I'm here. Son of a bitch jumped me. Slammed my . . . Jesus, slammed my head into the tank." He swayed on his feet and reached up to touch his forehead. There was no blood, but the bump was already enormous, and he hissed with pain as his fingers grazed it.

The alarm continued to blare, making his head hurt even worse.

"Well, whoever it was, is gone now," Gage practically snarled. "The glass is all broken out of the back door."

That explained the alarm, at least.

"I don't get it," Keith said into the radio. "What the hell was the guy doing in here?"

Even as he said it, he turned and glanced into the tank where the internal lights created a haunting ocean landscape of phosphorescent blue and green. The fish seemed skittish, but with the alarm sounding, he could not blame them.

Keith froze.

Floating in the tank was something that did not belong there. Not at all. Many of the larger fish had begun to swim around it.

It was a man. A dead man, whose face was pale and whose eyes bulged and stared at Keith with the same dead gaze the sharks had. A moray eel snaked around the dead man's legs, and several of the fish had begun to nibble at his fingers. One swam in front of the corpse's face as if studying a single dead eye, trying to decide whether or not to nibble at it.

Then there was further motion in the tank. Some of the fish were skittish and swam off. Keith looked up to see what had spooked them, and a shudder of dread went through him.

The sharks were coming.

But this wasn't a dream. Keith couldn't wake up from this.

All he could do was watch.

# chapter 1

On the last day of classes, Jenna Blake sat in the second row in the basement of Bransfield Hall and tried to contain her excitement. At the podium at the front of the classroom, Professor Georges had begun to remind them of some of the major points he had lectured on during a semester's worth of Europe from 1815. The distinguished gentleman had a trademark twinkle in his eye, a love of his subject that he communicated to his students. He was the best teacher Jenna had ever had, and though she had decided that her goal was medical school, she hoped she would be able to take another class with Professor Georges before she graduated.

Today, though, much as she adored him, it was all she could do to pay attention to his words. Her knee bounced under her desk. The sunlight that fell through the rectangular windows high up on the walls splashed into the room. It was the second week of May, and the breeze that blew in through those transomlike windows

9

was warm and carried the scents of spring.

Jenna felt herself bursting with good feeling, wanting the class to be over. She glanced at the clock and counted down. It had been a long year, filled with both the best and the most terrible moments of her life, and she felt that she had grown up in so many ways. At least, most of the time. Right now, it felt like junior high all over again, watching the clock, thrilled to be finishing her freshman year at Somerset University in Massachusetts.

Guiltily, Jenna tried to focus on what Professor Georges was saying. She tapped her pen against her bouncing leg as though music were playing in her head. She was wearing a light green tank with spaghetti straps, and tan shorts that barely covered her hip bones. Even that felt a little exposed to her; she could never wear some of the things a lot of the girls on campus wore. Not that she was shy about her body; she just didn't like the idea of giving every guy who passed by a free show.

The minute hand on the clock ticked into the upright position. Professor Georges glanced over a moment later, saw that it was two o'clock exactly, and then nodded and smiled at the class.

"Well, that's all, then. It's been a pleasure having you all. I'll look forward to seeing you next week for your final exam. I will maintain my regular office hours every day until then, so please don't hesitate to drop by or e-mail me."

Everyone began collecting their notebooks and laptops. Jenna stood up, slid her pen into her pocket, grabbed her books, and headed for the door, grinning.

There was a cluster of students near the door, thanking Professor Georges, but Jenna decided that could wait until the final. She moved past them, navigated some traffic on the stairs, and then took the rest of them two at a time. A moment later she was pushing through the front door and leaving Bransfield Hall behind.

Somerset University had begun on top of a hill in the city of the same name, so the oldest buildings were atop that hill, lined on either side of a stretch of green lawn and tall, enormous old shade trees. This was the academic quad, one of the most peaceful spots on campus. As Jenna started back toward her dorm, she looked around at the students stretched out on the grass, some of them already studying for finals, others simply enjoying the warmth of the late spring day, its scents, its breeze, its sunlight or shade.

Yes, finals were yet to come, but there was the unmistakable feeling of victory in the air, of achievement. They'd made it through the year. Jenna felt like cheering. Not in a cheerleader-y way, 'cause that so wasn't her.

Well, maybe today it was.

A song popped into her head, apropos of nothing, and she began to sing Amanda Marshall's "Sunday Morning After" softly under her breath. As she walked toward Sparrow Hall she reached up with her free hand and pulled off the elastic that had held her auburn hair in a ponytail and let it fall free across her back. Her hair was longer than she had ever worn it, but that was one of the things she was going to take care of this afternoon— it was time for a radical cut.

"Jenna!" someone called.

She glanced to her left and saw her ex-boyfriend Damon Harris crossing the lawn with his two closest friends, quiet Anthony and charming, flirtatious Brick. All of them were headed in the same direction, toward Sparrow Hall. She met up with them on the path ahead.

"Hey," she said to Damon, with whom she had remained friends. They were in the same dormitory, on the same hall, and that had provided some intense moments when she regretted their breaking up. For the most part, though, they were both okay with it.

He smiled at her. "Hey."

"Hey, Lady J," Anthony said.

Jenna gave him a quick hug. He towered over her, and she always felt tiny when he was around, though she was far from short.

Brick shot her an admonishing look. "Oh, fine. Is that how it is? I see. Uh-huh."

He wasn't as handsome as Damon, but Brick had charisma to spare. Most guys who behaved the way he did would have gotten slapped. Brick usually just got a roll of the eyes or, if he was lucky, a flirty giggle. Jenna opted for the eye roll.

"Relax. You know I save the best for last," she said as she hugged him. Brick hummed softly, as though he had just tasted something delicious, and Jenna whacked him on the arm.

"Unbelievable, huh?" Damon said as they all turned toward Sparrow Hall again. "Last day. You done with classes?"

"Just finished," she confirmed.

"Where you living next year?"

"Yoshiko and I are going to room together again. We found a pretty big double in Whitney House," Jenna explained. "What about you?"

Damon gave her a sidelong grin and cocked his thumb at Ant and Brick. "I'm living downhill in Talbot Hall with these two clowns."

"Oh, that's sure to be a study-fiesta," Jenna said, mock-serious.

Brick let out an exaggerated gasp. "You wound me, girl, you really do."

But Jenna wasn't paying attention anymore. They were approaching Sparrow Hall now, with its many-gabled roof and Gothic exterior. On the front steps she spotted her roommate, Yoshiko Kitsuta, and Yoshiko's boyfriend, Hunter LaChance. They were her best friends, and they were waiting for her.

Yoshiko saw her coming and raised one clenched fist in a victory pump. "Yes!" she cried as she ran to Jenna. The girls threw their arms around each other and did a few quick bounces. Hunter was a Southern boy, and a bit more laconic, but he gave Jenna his easy smile and nod-ded.

"Time to celebrate," Hunter said in his slow, Louisiana drawl.

"Oh, most definitely," Jenna agreed.

Damon and his friends said hello and good-bye as they went into the dorm, and Hunter and Yoshiko were polite enough. Even though Jenna insisted the breakup had been mutual, they were her best friends and they felt it was sort of their job to never let Damon completely off the hook for possibly hurting her feelings.

"So!" Yoshiko said excitedly, putting one hand on her hip. "Are you ready?"

Jenna laughed and stared at her. This was the same shy girl she had met the previous fall? It seemed hard to believe. Yoshiko's silken black hair was much shorter than Jenna's, but where once it had seemed to represent Yoshiko's conservative side, now it only accentuated the ways in which she had loosened up over the course of the school year. Today, she wore low-rise black denim jeans and a cropped top that showed off her belly. Earlier in the year, she wouldn't have been caught dead wearing that shirt.

Though he had been raised a bit on the conservative side himself, Hunter didn't seem to mind at all. He was a thin, lanky guy with a boyish face, a look he had been trying to counter all year by keeping his blond hair buzzed very short. But in blue jeans and a tight, solid green T-shirt, he still looked like the boy next door to Jenna.

Today, though . . . today was their day to get crazy. And Yoshiko wanted to know if she was ready.

Jenna arched an eyebrow. "Honey, I was born ready."

Yoshiko smiled softly. "I'm glad one of us was."

"Come on, roomie," Jenna said, sliding an arm around her. "You can do it. A little adventure in your life. And then dinner at House of Blues."

"Oh, I'm *in*," Yoshiko assured her. "I just can't *believe* I'm in."

"Me either," Hunter said, arching an eyebrow as he glanced at Jenna. "I don't know how I let you talk me into these things."

"Come on!" Jenna protested, spreading her arms and spinning around once. "This is a day to celebrate. We've all changed this year. We're more ourselves now than we've ever been—maybe than we'll ever be! Don't you want to go home and have people be able to see that you're not the same person who left for school last August?"

"Easy for you to say," Yoshiko noted. "You're not even going home."

Jenna laughed. That much was true. Yoshiko was returning to Oahu, Hawaii, and Hunter to Louisiana. Jenna, on the other hand, was searching for an apartment near campus to sublet for the summer so she could keep working over the break. Her mother wasn't happy about it, but she seemed to be trying her best not to interfere.

"Hey, my dad's just getting back from his sabbatical. I want to spend time with him," Jenna said. "And my job isn't like delivering pizza. I'm kind of part of a team, y'know? I can't imagine leaving that behind for ten weeks."

"I guess," Yoshiko said, her smile turning playful. "But you're taking the job awfully seriously for a girl who wants to get wild."

"Hey! I can have facets! So, are we doing this or aren't we?" Jenna demanded.

Yoshiko crossed her arms and leaned against Hunter. "We're just waiting for you to go dump your books."

Jace Castillo strode down a quiet corridor at Massachusetts General Hospital, his irritation fueled by frustration. After seven years in narcotics with the Boston Police Department, he had made the move over to homicide, and he'd been regretting it pretty much from day one. He had expected, when he made the move, that there would be less of the territorialism and political crap that had marked his career in narcotics. Now, he realized that he ought to have known better. Homicide wasn't any better. It was just different. They dealt with dead people instead of drugs.

"Jace, just don't shoot him, okay?"

Castillo laughed softly and glanced over his shoulder, slowing to allow his partner, Terri Yurkich, to catch up with him. Then they fell into step side by side. They were detectives, out of uniform, but Castillo was sure anyone seeing them at that moment would have read "cop" off of them in an instant. Terri was as tall as Jace and in better physical condition, and the two of them walked with that unmistakable air of command particular to police officers and soldiers.

"Jace?" Terri prodded.

"Okay, I won't shoot him," Castillo assured her. "Much as I'd like to."

She smiled. Jace grinned. He couldn't help it. There was no sexual tension between them at all, which was good, but in the time since he'd joined the homicide unit he'd taken a real liking to his partner. Most of the time she was serious, but sometimes her blue eyes and angular face brightened like a summer day. That was nice. She was smart and clever and paid incredible attention to detail. He was glad Terri Yurkich had his back.

They rounded a corner. The second door on the left was the main office of Mass General's pathology department. Castillo did not bother to knock. He tried the knob and found it unlocked, which meant someone, at least, was in there. Grim satisfaction filled him as he pushed the door open and went inside with Terri trailing right behind him.

They walked into the outer office of the pathology department. There were two desks, but only one of them was occupied. Castillo had seen the woman behind the desk before but could not remember her name. She was an attractive, older Latina whose eyes narrowed as he and Terri entered. Though she did not rise from her chair, she seemed to exude a kind of ominous energy that would have deterred almost anyone from trying to bypass her and enter the warren of offices and labs beyond her. "May I help you, detectives?" she asked.

"Dolores, isn't it?" Terri asked.

Even as the woman nodded, Castillo silently thanked his partner for remembering her name.

"Yes," Dolores said. "But Dr. Vieira isn't in today. He's attending a seminar in—"

"We know," Castillo replied. "We want to see Dr. Hallett."

Dolores arched one eyebrow, and she started to reach for a phone. "I'll just see if he's in."

"That's all right," Castillo said. "We can look for ourselves."

"Now, just a minute!" Dolores protested.

Castillo ignored her, but as they passed, he heard Terri trying to mollify the woman.

"This is part of an ongoing investigation, Dolores. Don't worry. We'll be in and out in no time."

They walked out of the reception area and into a short corridor that ended with a heavy metal door. There were several labs beyond that door, but Castillo wanted to check the offices first. The first two were empty, but when he poked his head into the third one, he found Mark Hallett sitting at a desk with a pile of paperwork, signing his name to a form.

"Dr. Hallett, hey, what good luck to catch you in the office," Castillo said.

The young pathology resident was startled at first, and then he looked uncomfortable. He was thin and pale and had a goatee that didn't suit him, and he did not rise to greet the detectives. Castillo watched him, arms crossed, the same way he had sweated out a thousand suspects on the street or in an interview room. Terri stood in the doorway behind him, her hands at her sides. A lot of cops would have leaned against the door frame, trying to be casual, but Castillo appreciated that she did not. They were in no danger from Hallett, but Terri hadn't been his partner long, and he was pleased to see that by instinct she kept her hands free.

"Detective Castillo," Dr. Hallett said. "You could have

called. I would have been able to tell you that Dr. Vieira isn't available."

Castillo gave up all pretense of good humor. "I know that. Dolores up front just told us that. And you could have told us the same thing if you'd actually answered your phone today. You might even have called me back and let me know. So where does that leave us? When is Vieira coming back?"

Dr. Hallett's pale face was slightly flushed, and he dropped his gaze, unwilling to meet Castillo's eyes. "He's in upstate New York and won't be back until the day after tomorrow."

"I see." Castillo glanced at Terri, and she rolled her eyes. Then he turned back to Dr. Hallett. "I'm going to pretend, Dr. Hallett, that you've been so wrapped up in your paperwork here that you haven't been hearing your phone ring, and you haven't listened to your voice mail. Maybe the hospital's even having trouble with voice mail.

"So here's what all of my messages say. The night before last, someone broke into the aquarium. When that someone left, a dead man was floating in the big tank. The biggest piece of chum those fish have ever seen. We've ID'ed the DOA as Nicholas Jaffarian, a computer software salesman. Now, if I were the kind of guy to make assumptions, I'd assume Jaffarian died of drowning in a goddamned fish tank. But I'm not that kind of guy, Dr. Hallett, because I'm a homicide detective, and we're not supposed to make assumptions. We're not supposed to have to make assumptions, because the medical examiner is supposed to be able to tell us how and when the victim died."

Castillo uncrossed his arms and took a step closer to the doctor's desk. "But you can't tell us what we want to know if you don't listen to your voice mail, can you?"

Hallett was an odd-looking guy, with too much nose and too little chin. He was almost birdlike, particularly when he twitched the way he did now, reaching up to scratch the back of his head as though he could pretend the detectives weren't even there.

"It's . . . well, it's complicated," Dr. Hallett said.

In the doorway, Terri grunted a quiet little "hunh."

Castillo glanced back at her. "Hunh what?"

"He got all the messages," she said. "He was trying to put us off until Vieira comes back."

The moment she said it, Castillo knew it was true. He had been unable to understand how Dr. Hallett could have been so careless. Now he realized it hadn't been negligence at all.

He rolled his eyes. "Talk to me, Doctor."

With a sigh, Dr. Hallett gazed up at the ceiling and raised his hands. "Fine. Fine, all right?" He picked up a pencil and began to tap it on the desk as he stared at Castillo. "I'm doing my residency, okay, but I'm not an M.E. I can do your basic autopsy, and I like to think I'm pretty observant. But I need more than that here. Your DOA shows signs of a struggle, but the bruises aren't as fresh as they should be if it was the struggle that landed him in the fish tank. I think cause of death is probably drowning, but I'm not going to make that call until Dr.

Vieira is back. It doesn't help that the sharks took a few chunks out of the guy. The whole thing is a mess. I don't want to put anything on record without Dr. Vieira backing me up."

"I can respect that," Terri said, entering the office at last. She loomed over the doctor's desk. "You know your limitations. That's important. But what the hell are you doing, stalling a case? Call the chief county M.E. Get him over here, or ship the DOA to him. We need *answers*, Dr. Hallett. Now. The trail's already a day and a half cold. We're looking into Jaffarian, but we need to know if there's anything in the autopsy that could help us."

Castillo watched Hallett as Terri spoke and saw the way the young doctor twitched when she mentioned the chief county medical examiner. A ripple of disgust went through him. "He knows, Terri," Castillo said.

His partner stepped up beside him. "What do you mean?"

Castillo nodded toward Dr. Hallett. "The chief M.E. for Essex County is Walter Slikowski, who works out of Somerset Medical Center. Mass General's always bringing him in to consult. He's a legend. But Vieira's only been the M.E. here for a couple of months, and I'm betting Slikowski's reputation has got Vieira's nose out of joint."

He stared at Hallett. "Dr. Vieira instructed you to wait for him to return. He told you not to call Slikowski, didn't he?"

Dr. Hallett hesitated a moment, then nodded reluctantly. "Dr. Vieira wanted to handle this personally."

"Of course he did," Castillo said sharply. "But listen to me, Doctor. Our job is difficult enough without you and your boss obstructing us, interfering in a police investigation."

The doctor's eyes widened. "Now, wait a minute, nobody's—"

"Nobody's interfering? Bullshit! What if the autopsy results give us information that could have led us to the killer? Every second you keep this DOA on ice is another opportunity for the guy who murdered him to shore up his alibi, or hide a little deeper, or get away, or maybe do it again. So to hell with your boss. Pick up the god-damned phone and call Walter Slikowski and get him over here *now*. I don't care if you have to beg."

Dr. Hallett stared at him with wide eyes, then glanced at Terri, and then at Castillo again.

"Go on," Castillo said, crossing his arms once more. "We'll wait."

The days leading up to finals were so crammed with work and studying that by Thursday, the afternoon she'd spent in Harvard Square with Yoshiko and Hunter began to seem like the last bit of fun she would ever have. So much for her wild side.

Thursday was also Jenna's last day of work at the M.E.'s office until after finals, which were scheduled to begin the following Wednesday. But that morning, when she arrived at his office, Dr. Slikowski instructed her to do nothing but man the phone and use the time to prepare. Jenna had argued that they had voice mail for that, and that he shouldn't be paying her just to sit there and study, but the M.E. insisted that he didn't want to cut into the hours she had planned to work, and he wanted her to get as much study time as possible. Dr. Walter Slikowski—whom his friends called Slick, a nickname he barely tolerated—had become a sort of mentor to Jenna. And a friend. But he was also the boss, so she didn't argue.

She knew how lucky she was to have an employer who was looking out for her best interests. And how fortunate she was to have a job she loved.

Somerset Medical Center included both a hospital and a medical school, the entire facility separated from the undergraduate campus only by Carpenter Street. Back in the fall, when Jenna had first begun to work for Dr. Slikowski, crossing Carpenter Street had seemed like stepping into another world entirely. None of her classmates had any business over there unless they needed to see a doctor. SMC didn't seem like another world to her now, but the feeling of leaving her classmates behind whenever she went to work still lingered. And the truth was, she didn't mind. Some people thought Jenna's job working as a diener—a pathology assistant—for the Essex County M.E. was bizarre, but it was a part of her life now. Part of what defined her—even to herself.

It had begun as nothing more than a way to make some money working part-time during school. Now it had become the foundation for all of her ambitions for the future. Her father was a professor of criminology at Somerset University, and her mother was a surgeon back home in Natick. In a way, forensic pathology incorporated the specialties of both of her parents. And yet she wasn't doing it for them. Jenna had come to college hesitant to think about a medical career, because she hated the sight of blood and the idea that someday a patient's life might depend upon her. The job of the medical examiner was something else entirely. It wasn't the patient's life that was in the M.E.'s hands, but the peace of mind of those the deceased had left behind.

Jenna believed in the nobility of the work that was done in Dr. Slikowski's office and laboratory—so much so that she had gotten herself too involved with a number of cases, putting herself in danger more than once in the nine months since she had been hired.

Today, she had to ignore the files that had outstanding paperwork and the audiotapes from the autopsies of the previous two days. Dr. Slikowski made audio notes and still used tape because he did not trust digital recording devices to not erase themselves accidentally. The M.E. was only in his mid-forties, but he often behaved as though he were much older. His reluctance to trust new technologies was a perfect example.

On that Thursday, she sat at her desk in the outer office she shared with Dr. Albert Dyson, a pathology resident at SMC, and she studied. Jenna had come back from lunch to find that Dyson and Slick were downstairs working in the autopsy room, so she was on her own. The door to the M.E.'s interior office was open, and the afternoon sun reached all the way to the door, throwing a splash of warm sunshine on the carpet. Erratic jazz saxophone played softly on the sound system in Slick's office, but in the otherwise quiet space, the music filled every corner. Thanks to her employer's love of jazz, Jenna had developed a fondness for it herself. Of late, Slick had been in a jazz horns phase, mostly listening to Miles Davis, but she was pretty sure the tune piping out of the speakers at the moment was Sonny Rollins.

A piano played underneath the sax, and Jenna smiled, her fingers miming the tapping of piano keys right along with the music. How many times had she seen guys play air guitar? Well, she preferred air piano. Once upon a time she had played regularly, though mostly for herself. But college had gotten in the way. The only pianos on campus were in the music rooms in the basement of Coleman Auditorium.

And Jenna didn't go there.

Not ever.

There were bad memories associated with the pianos down there, and she didn't love music enough to ignore them. Still, sometimes she missed it.

"Come on, Blake, you're procrastinating again," she whispered to herself. She laughed softly at how true that was, then sighed and tried to focus on her medical anthropology notes again. It wasn't the first final she had, but it was the one she was the most worried about.

Just as she had begun to focus on the notes, trying to really understand what she was reading and to make the connections necessary to put it all together in essay form for the final, the phone rang. Jenna pushed a lock of hair away from her eyes and snatched it up from the cradle.

"Pathology. Dr. Slikowski's office. This is Jenna."

"Hello, Jenna. This is Dr. Mark Hallett at Mass General. Is Dr. Slikowski available?"

"I'm afraid he's not, Dr. Hallett. Can I help you with something?"

Even as she was speaking, however, Jenna heard other voices in the background of Dr. Hallett's call. She frowned as she listened to a brief commotion on the phone, and then another voice came on the line.

"Jenna, this is Jace Castillo. How are you?"

A little tremor of alarm went through her, and she frowned. Working with Slick had meant working with detectives for a number of different police departments in the area, but the Boston P.D. didn't call unless they had something really odd. "I'm all right, Detective Castillo. What's going on?"

"We've got a DOA down here that I'd really like Slick to take a look at. Homicide, obviously, but the circumstances are pretty weird."

Jenna heard a tightness in his voice that she understood immediately. "Let me guess. You can't send the body here without Vieira losing his mind."

"Exactly," Castillo said. "And he's out of town."

*Out of town.* And Castillo obviously didn't trust the resident who had made the phone call, and whose name Jenna had already forgotten. She could tell from the detective's tone that time was an issue, so she didn't bother to ask if he could wait. "Dr. Slikowski's in the middle of an autopsy right now, Detective," she said, glancing at the clock on the wall. "I'm not sure how much longer he'll be. Let me interrupt him, and one of us will get back to you shortly."

Castillo thanked her, and they hung up. Jenna lifted the phone up again and began to dial the extension for the autopsy room, but quickly hung up again. She had not seen Slick or Dyson since Monday, and at the moment she really did not feel like studying medical anthro. With a guilty smile, she got up and left the office, tapping her pocket to make sure her key card was there.

Jenna went down the busy corridor past administrative offices. There were several people on the elevator as she rode downward, including a woman with two children, all of whom looked as though they had been crying. Her heart went out to them. In a way, it was more difficult to see the patients' families than the patients themselves. She wondered about the person they had come in to see—perhaps the kids' father—and what he was in the hospital for. Something pretty frightening, from the look of the family.

They got off on the first floor, and Jenna was alone on the elevator as it continued down. Moments later the doors slid open again, and she stepped off into the basement. There was an inescapable antiseptic smell down there, and although more administrative offices were on this floor, it felt to her like the people who worked in the basement were intruders in Dr. Slikowski's realm.

She strode quickly down the long corridor, her shoes tapping out a rhythm on the floor. Just past the door to the morgue was the autopsy room. Once upon a time, she had been unnerved by that room, but no more. It was the place where the real work got done.

When she entered, Dr. Slikowski had his latex-gloved hands deep inside the open chest of the subject on the gleaming metal table. The medical examiner was confined to a wheelchair, but the table could be lowered to just above his knees. It had been built to accommodate him, but that was one of the things that made it difficult for him to conduct autopsies at other hospitals.

The room looked like some kind of torture chamber. A large light on a swiveling metal arm blazed down brightly upon the pale flesh and gleaming viscera of the corpse on the table. On the far side of the room was a stainless-steel table with many drawers set into its base. There were hanging scales and others on the counter, a locker full of surgical gowns and masks, a computer with a plastic splash guard over the monitor, and above the table a massive vent and a camera setup. But what finished the picture of the place as a torture chamber were the tools.

Even now, Dyson was at the long counter using a scalpel to take samples of the dead man's lungs. He turned as Jenna walked in. "Hello, Jenna," Dyson said. Even his rich olive skin took on a sickly hue under the cold lights of the autopsy room. "What's up?"

Dr. Slikowski glanced at her, arching an eyebrow. The light gleamed off his wire-rimmed glasses. He was a thin man, his hair graying in a gradual, salt-and-pepper scattering, and at times the fine bones in his face gave him a sort of severe expression that he did not intend. Jenna knew him well enough not to take it personally.

"Good afternoon," Slick said, the two words almost an inquiry in themselves. "What brings you down to see us?"

By now, Dyson was already moving around the table and equipment to get a better look at her. "Well, well," he said. "Did you come down just to show off your new haircut?"

Jenna smiled. On Tuesday afternoon when she had gone into Harvard Square with Yoshiko and Hunter, part of her mission had been to change her look. She had worn her hair the same length pretty much since junior high school. The cut she had gotten was much shorter, hanging just to her shoulders, but it framed her face in a way that she thought—hoped, at least—made her look older.

Slick, of course, only frowned. Jenna would have been surprised if he had even noticed that her hair was different.

"Unfortunately not," she said. "I have a message for you and thought I'd stretch my legs."

She explained about the call from Detective Castillo. Slick listened patiently and then glanced over at Dyson. "Al, could you finish up here?"

"Of course."

Dr. Slikowski leaned to his right to speak more clearly into the microphone that was beside the autopsy table. "As previously noted, subject endured a great deal of internal injury, evidenced by significant quantities of blood in the chest cavity. Dr. Dyson will continue the autopsy from here, closing the chest and handling the cranial examination."

Slick removed his bloody latex gloves and rolled his wheelchair away from the table. He tossed them into a hazardous-waste receptacle and glanced over his shoulder at Jenna. "Are you rushing off somewhere after work, Jenna? I don't want to keep you from your studies."

"I've got time. The first one isn't for almost a week."

"Care to join me?"

Jenna nodded. The tone of Castillo's voice, the tension in his tone, had intrigued her. "I'd be happy to."

"All right. Just give me a minute or two, and we'll be off."

As Slick washed his hands, Dyson walked over to Jenna, smiling again. "You look great," he told her. "Really. But I wouldn't have guessed you'd go for such a radical change."

Jenna grinned. Dyson was like a big brother to her, and his reaction was exactly the sort of thing she had wanted out of her new look. She felt different from who she had been a year before, and she thought that the way she looked should reflect that. Hunter's hair was already too short, but he had gotten some darker highlights put in, and Jenna thought he looked cute. Yoshiko hadn't had a haircut, but that wasn't really why they had gone into Harvard Square in the first place.

"Radical?" Jenna asked. "Me?"

Then she lifted up her shirt just high enough for Dyson to see the little silver ring that dangled from her newly pierced belly button.

His eyes went comically wide. "Why, you rebel, you," Dyson said, teasing her fondly.

"Nope," Jenna replied, lowering her shirt to cover her belly again. "Just evolving. Happens to everyone. I'm a work in progress."

Dyson gave her a knowing look. "Aren't we all?"

There was a tension in the autopsy room that made Jenna's skin crawl. Neither the presence of the drowning victim on the steel table nor the fact that they were about to cut the man open bothered her at all. But being in that room with Slick, Detective Castillo, and Dr. Hallett—feeling the hesitation, even resentment, that Hallett was giving off—made her extremely uncomfortable. The irony wasn't lost on her.

Not that Dr. Hallett was being uncooperative. Far from it. With Jace Castillo breathing over his shoulder and the county medical examiner in his presence, there was no way Hallett's boss could fault him for letting Slick do the autopsy. But it didn't make Dr. Hallett any less stiff.

The awkwardness of the situation was compounded by the fact that Mass General did not have an autopsy table designed to be used by a man in a wheelchair. Slick could see over the top of the body, but only just. To do more than observe would be especially difficult for him here. Even as Jenna watched, he bumped his chair up against the table—only one of three in the sterile steel and glass and linoleum room—and studied the victim.

"I'd be more than happy to assist you, Dr. Slikowski," Dr. Hallett said.

Jenna stiffened. It was only logical that Hallett should assist. He was the path resident here, and she was just a diener. This was his autopsy room, really. On the other hand, Slick would not have brought her along if he had not wanted her to be involved. Jenna had no idea what to expect. There were politics involved, interhospital diplomacy, that sort of thing. She prepared herself for the likelihood that she would be excluded.

For what seemed an uncomfortably long time, Slick regarded Dr. Hallett. Then he shifted his gaze over to Jenna, and at length glanced back at Hallett.

"Given the physical limitations of your facilities, Doctor, I will need your assistance with the initial incision and the removal of the rib cage. Beyond that, if you don't mind, I'll work with Miss Blake. We have a certain rapport."

*She shoots . . . she scores!* Jenna thought, trying hard not to smile, savoring Slick's last comment: *"We have a certain rapport."*

The look of mild irritation that flashed across Dr. Hallett's face was unmistakable. She had no sympathy. The guy might be more than competent, but he came off like an arrogant ass. "Of course, Doctor. Whatever you prefer," Hallett said.

Slick and Jenna already had gowns, gloves, and surgical masks on. Detective Castillo stood well back from the autopsy table, so he didn't bother with the sterile precautions. He had opted to remain as an official observer, though his partner, Detective Yurkich, had driven out to the North End of Boston to interview the deceased's friends and neighbors. Jenna was surprised Castillo hadn't just gone with Yurkich. The two were a good team, though Jenna thought them incompatible. The tall, blond woman was silent and serious, where Castillo was darkly handsome and charismatic. Not that what Jenna thought mattered. She had learned from observing Danny and Audrey that what made cops good partners was trust.

Now that she considered it, she figured Castillo had stayed behind just in case Dr. Hallett gave Slick a hard time. But it didn't seem like there was anything for Castillo to be concerned about. Dr. Hallett went to a cabinet and withdrew a gown for himself. As he put it on, Slick glanced at Jenna, reached out, and turned the recorder on.

"Autopsy number 00549073, subject is Nicholas Jaffarian. Thirty-three years of age."

Jenna looked the body over, clearing her mind of any preconceptions, just as Slick had taught her. She knew the man had drowned, knew the circumstances of the discovery of his body. But she had learned not to take anything for granted. Even so, it was hard to erase from her mind the knowledge of what had happened to him when there were bite marks in his flesh, places where the sharks had nipped at him. Three of the fingers on his left hand were missing entirely.

"Just be glad we made a solid ID," Castillo said.

Curious, Jenna glanced up at him.

Castillo shrugged. "When a body's been underwater for a while, the skin on the fingers and toes starts to" —he made a face— "peel off. Makes it difficult to get clear prints."

"Difficult," Slick replied without looking at the detective. "But not impossible. As long as there's one finger where the dermal papillae have not been destroyed, we can pull a print."

Jenna felt her lips pull into an expression of distaste, but she did not allow herself the "eeeew" that normally would have slipped out. Not with Dr. Hallett there, watching them curiously. She was relieved that the Boston P.D. had already made their ID.

The M.E. looked over at her. "Jenna, what is the scientific name for fingerprint identification?"

*Aww, come on!* she thought. *A quiz, now?* But the truth was, she loved the challenge.

"Dactyloscopy. Give me a hard one next time." She grinned.

"How many points of comparison in a fingerprint are needed to establish proof of identity?"

Jenna winced. That was a trick question. But what was the answer?

Castillo nodded his encouragement and mouthed the word: "Twelve."

"Don't help!" she chided him. "Right. Twelve, for evidence in a U.S. court of law. Europe requires sixteen."

Clearly impressed, Dr. Slikowski nodded his approval. The matter was dropped, and they returned to work.

Slick carefully examined fiery red marks on the back and sides of the dead man's neck, speaking to the recorder as he worked.

"There are bruises on the victim's neck and throat that indicate a struggle. Bruise pattern indicates human hands made them—not a rope, wire, or other strangulation tool. Based upon their placement, it appears that the assailant held subject from behind, probably while holding his head under the water. Preliminary hypothesis only."

Jenna smiled to herself. *Preliminary hypothesis.* Slick would never even have made the observations unless he was almost completely certain. He never jumped to conclusions. If he said it was murder by drowning, that was what it had been.

"Dr. Hallett," Slick said, "please give Miss Blake an autopsy chart."

Hallett did as he was asked, and without waiting for instruction, Jenna began noting on the chart all of the various marks and bites left by the sharks and other aquarium creatures. She noted the bruise marks as well.

Dr. Slikowski conducted this autopsy as he conducted every autopsy he ever did: step by precise step. They had already photographed the body front and back with its clothes on, then cut the clothes away and run another complete series of photographs.

The M.E. adjusted his wheelchair so he could get a

closer look at the victim's neck. "The assailant was not bare-handed," Slick declared.

Jenna frowned. "How can you tell?" she asked, curiously.

Slick indicated a network of small, broken capillaries beneath the skin that looked like a tangle of tiny red threads. "Do you see the lines here . . . here . . . and here? He was wearing some kind of protective gloves. My guess would be latex medical examination gloves. Also, there's not even a hint of a fingerprint on those bruises, and the margins at the edge of the bruised area are too distinct."

Dr. Hallett had been hanging back up until this point, but now he rounded the autopsy table to observe more closely from the opposite side. He bent to take a better look at the bruises.

"Great," Castillo said. "Latex gloves. Not a lot to go on."

Jenna glanced back at the detective. "Why not?"

Castillo sighed. "You can buy them at any pharmacy, not to mention every cop and crime scene collector has a box in their car." He shoved a hand into his back pocket and withdrew a white latex glove. "Hell, I've got one here. And in the glove compartment. Probably in every jacket I own."

Slick cleared his throat, drawing Castillo's attention. "My apologies, Detective. I'll try to find you a more helpful clue."

Castillo raised an eyebrow, and one side of his mouth twitched into a thin smile.

"Come here, Detective Castillo," the M.E. instructed.

As Castillo approached, Slick gestured at the corpse. "Do not touch the body, but please place your hands around the victim's neck as you would if you wanted to strangle him."

Jenna raised an eyebrow. Castillo looked more like he wanted to strangle Dr. Slikowski than the deceased. The detective stepped over and spread his hands out over the bruised area. As he did, Slick bent in and began to measure the bruised impressions on the victim's neck.

"It would be better to turn the body over," he said, frowning. "We'll get more accurate measurements when the autopsy is completed and the cadaver has been closed. For now, though, it's safe to say the killer has somewhat smaller hands than you do, Detective."

Slick glanced at Jenna. "Would you oblige me?"

As Castillo moved out of the way, Jenna grimaced and took his place. She had latex gloves on, so though Castillo had not touched the corpse, she hesitated only a moment before wrapping her hands around the cold, dead flesh on the table before her. She laid her fingers across the dead man's throat, white latex gleaming beside dark bruises. Her stomach did a flip-flop. In her mind she pictured what it must have been like being held under water. Being choked. Losing all her air. "Oh," Jenna said, flinching and pulling away.

Slick raised an eyebrow and looked at her in concern. She shook her head to assure him she was all right, nothing was the matter. He let his gaze linger on her a moment and then nodded, taking her at her word.

"Miss Blake's hands, as you can see, are smaller than the killer's." With a single, arched eyebrow and just the hint of a smirk at the upturned edges of his mouth, the M.E. looked at Castillo. "There you go, Detective. A more substantial clue. All you need do is bring in anyone with hands smaller than yours and larger than Jenna's."

"Thank you *so* much," Castillo said dryly.

Slick rolled his chair back a foot or two from the table and nodded toward the pathology resident. "Dr. Hallett. Feel free." Then he glanced at his assistant. "Jenna, scrape the nails, please."

Dr. Hallett offered them a weary smile. Jenna did not want to, but she found herself dredging up a certain amount of sympathy for the man. Here he was, essentially being forced to perform in a way that he probably thought he had graduated from when he had gotten out of med school.

Hallett examined the body, making several observations of his own that mainly had to do with muscle tone. Jenna swabbed underneath the victim's fingernails. If Jaffarian had scratched his assailant during the struggle, there might be shreds of the killer's skin under his nails. She sealed the scrapings in a sterile test tube, labeled and dated it, and set it aside in the refrigeration unit to send out to the state lab later for DNA analysis.

Once the preliminaries were done, Jenna stood back as Dr. Hallett set to work. He started by cutting a large Y incision on the victim's chest and abdomen, then peeling back the skin to expose the ribs and internal organs. The sound of the bone saw cutting through the sternum set her teeth on edge, but she leaned forward with rapt interest as Hallett spread open the dead man's chest. Leaning close, he examined the chest cavity and made a few preliminary slices into one of the lungs.

"Evidence of blood in the lung tissue," he said tonelessly. He turned his head so the microphone would pick up his voice, but Jenna nodded as if he were speaking directly to her, not for the official record.

Slick maneuvered his wheelchair for a better view.

"Ruptured blood vessels in the chest cavity. Internal bleeding," Slick observed.

"More evidence that he put up a struggle," Dr. Hallett replied.

Dr. Slikowski watched as Hallett's hands moved carefully. With precision he cut deeper into the chest and abdomen, spreading the ribs wider as he prepared to remove the heart, lungs, trachea, and esophagus.

"Please remove the organs individually," Slick instructed.

Hallett frowned above his mask, his brow furrowing. "That's not standard procedure, Doctor. Mind if I ask why?"

"A whim," Slick said, glancing at Hallett over the wire rims of his glasses. "I get them every now and then. There are some question marks in this case. In drownings, the organs often provide clues. I want to take it slowly."

Dr. Hallett nodded. "All right. Any preference of order?"

"Let's have the stomach first," Slick said. "Then the

lungs. Set the stomach aside, please, and we'll examine the lungs. They may hold answers."

As she had done many times now, Jenna would weigh each organ and then section it, taking a sample of the tissue for further analysis.

Dr. Hallett bent to his work. When he sliced through the duodenum with the tip of his scalpel, a sudden sharp smell caught Jenna's attention. It wasn't much—just a whiff that was barely detectable over the strong odors of lab chemicals and the hideous smells of the dead. But it was strong enough to get her attention. "What's that smell?" she asked, squinting at Dr. Slikowski.

Slick hesitated for a moment, sniffing the air through his surgical mask with a perplexed expression. "I—I'm not sure I know what you mean, Jenna," he said. He cast a quick glance at Dr. Hallett and then back at Detective Castillo, but neither of them seemed to have noticed anything unusual.

"It smells like . . . chlorine," Jenna said, snapping her fingers. Before she could say anything else, she covered her surgical mask with her gloved hand and sneezed once, sharply.

"Bless you," Slick said.

"Sorry." Jenna looked sheepishly at her boss and then at their observers. "I'm not really allergic to chlorine, but sometimes it makes me sneeze."

Dr. Hallett bent slightly above the autopsy table and breathed deeply in and out several times. He shook his head. "I don't smell anything."

Slick leaned closer to the cadaver. Lowering his face,

he sniffed once loudly, then straightened up. In his wheelchair, he was much closer to the corpse of Nicholas Jaffarian than anyone else. "No, it's there. You're absolutely right," he said with a quick glance at Jenna. "It smells like chlorine bleach." Even though he was wearing a surgical mask, Jenna could tell that he was smiling.

After clearing his throat, he spoke carefully so the recorder would pick up his words. "Miss Blake has detected traces of chlorine in the victim's stomach. As chlorine is basic, stomach acid will likely have neutralized it, negating any test. Let's have a look at the lungs. If there's water there, that will be a purer source to test from."

He nodded toward Dr. Hallett.

Leaving the stomach on the tray, the pathologist went back to the corpse and removed the dead man's lungs. He handed the organs to Jenna. She carefully lowered them into the basket scale to get an accurate weight reading, then marked the result, in grams, on the chalkboard on the wall beside the refrigeration unit.

Dr. Slikowski wheeled himself over, took the lungs, and placed them into the dissecting pan at the foot of the autopsy table. Using a fresh scalpel, he sliced into the tissue. The dark organ split open like a ripe fruit, and the powerful smell of chlorine filled the room as water spilled out.

"Do we have a sample of the water from the aquarium tank?" Jenna asked.

Slick shook his head from side to side, his eyes

focused intently on his work. Finally, he glanced up at Jenna. "No. We don't. Normally we wouldn't have needed one. Now, though . . . I want to get one, but first let's get readings on the chlorine levels in the water from the subject's lungs. Free chlorine, combined chlorine, and total chlorine residuals."

Jenna looked at him, absolutely stumped. "Sorry. I have no idea how to do that." Her cheeks flushed. She hated having to admit she was clueless in front of the others in the room, especially Hallett.

"What've you got, Doc?" Castillo asked.

Slick glanced at the detective. "I'm not quite certain yet."

Dr. Hallett had been watching Slick's examination of the subject's lungs. He had learned better than to do anything without Slick's say-so. Now, though, he raised an eyebrow and glanced at Jenna. She expected to see some attitude there. After all, he was a resident, and what the hell was she? A nineteen-year-old college girl with premed intentions. Sure, she had hours and hours of practical experience, had assisted in dozens of autopsies, but Hallett didn't know that.

He surprised her, though.

"Let me take care of that," Dr. Hallett suggested, without an ounce of condescension.

Jenna didn't know why his demeanor had changed. Maybe Hallett had seen that she was capable; or maybe he simply had decided to rely upon the trust Slick obviously put in her. Either way, she was relieved.

Dr. Hallett slid open the bottom drawer in one of the

lab tables and, after a moment, pulled out the test kit they needed. Jenna stepped aside to let him approach the body, watching intently over his shoulder as he dipped the narrow strip of light blue paper into the water that had spilled from the dead man's lungs. When Dr. Hallett removed the paper, it had turned to light pink. After comparing it to the chart on the side of the bottle, he turned to Dr. Slikowski. "This registers in the 4.5 to 5 range on their chart."

"Can you convert that to parts per million?" Slick asked, frowning.

"With a different test, I can," Hallett said. "But this color closely matches what the manufacturer says is on the high side of optimum for a swimming pool."

"But they don't chlorinate the water in a fish tank," Jenna said, puzzled by this turn of events. "I had goldfish when I was in junior high, and I had to be very careful about dechlorinating the water."

"You're absolutely right," Slick said with a nod of the head. "The staff at the aquarium would monitor the water and maintain it as close as possible to the natural environment of their fish."

"So that means . . ." Jenna let her voice fade away as she followed the logic of the puzzle.

"Yes?" Slick asked, now looking intently at her. This was typical of their relationship. He wanted her to work it out for herself. "So that means . . . what?"

"It means he probably didn't drown in the New England Aquarium."

"Strike the *probably*," Slick said.

"He was already dead when he went into the tank."

"That doesn't make any sense," Dr. Hallett said, frowning.

"Agreed," Castillo piped in, but he leaned against a table, arms crossed, and studied them curiously. "That's where we found him, though."

Jenna stared at Slick, hesitating to be the one to articulate the logical conclusion. At length she turned to Castillo. "Maybe so, Detective," she said. "But he didn't die there. He was murdered somewhere else. Drowned, most likely, in a swimming pool, perhaps. The subject was dead some time before your perp broke into the aquarium and dumped the body."

"Why the hell would anyone need to drown someone twice?" Dr. Hallett asked, mystified.

"I'm not sure why he would want to, but it will make our job more difficult. The composition of the water would normally yield many clues. There are contaminants in water specific to every region: purity, fluoridation, etcetera. We will probably still be able to determine if it was an indoor or outdoor pool by looking for pollen and bacteria, for the presence of insect traces, debris from plants—that sort of thing. If it's an indoor pool, we might have traces of debris from ceiling tiles or paint chips.

"Mixed with the water from the aquarium, all of those elements are going to be far more difficult to isolate."

Jenna stared at him. "Wow, does that sound like a lot of work."

Slick smiled slyly. "Not to worry, Jenna. That's what residents are for."

Dr. Hallett seemed about to protest when Slick held up a hand. "Relax, Dr. Hallett. We'll take care of this out of my office. Dr. Dyson is more than capable of doing the analyses that are required here."

*Poor Dyson!* Jenna thought.

Castillo glanced at the body, but his gaze shifted back to Slick. "I still don't get why the killer would have drowned the guy in a pool and *then* dumped him in the tank. Do you think he wanted the sharks to eat the evidence?"

A shudder ran through Jenna as she contemplated the idea of the hungry sharks ripping into the dead man's flesh. But instantly she pushed the image, and the idea, away.

"I don't know. He must have known there were security guards at the aquarium. And he certainly would have known that the sharks couldn't destroy everything. Why not just bury the body somewhere, or dump it into the ocean?"

"Perhaps you're giving the killer too much credit," Dr. Hallett said.

Castillo frowned. "No. I think Jenna's right. So far, our investigation tells us that the perp knew the routine the security guys kept to. This was planned. It wasn't to get rid of the body. Not a stunt like this."

"A stunt," Jenna said. "Are you thinking whoever did it wanted to draw attention to it? Wanted to be outrageous?"

"Sure," Castillo said. "Someone does something like this, chances are he's trying to make a statement."

Jenna was bewildered. "A statement about *what?*"

"Ahh," Dr. Slikowski replied with a light chuckle and a thoughtful nod. "That's the core of the puzzle, isn't it?"

Castillo regarded them darkly. "Yeah. Yeah, it is. Problem is, when a psycho wants to make a statement, and nobody gets it, he's only going to say it louder the next time."

Jenna did not like the sound of that at all.

*What a cute couple they make,* Jenna thought later that night as she spotted her father, Frank Logan, with his fiancée, Shayna Emerson, at a candlelit table in the far corner, away from the windows. Kobe's Place was a little Thai restaurant on Washington Street in Boston that Jenna had found only recently.

As she strode toward Frank and Shayna, she smiled. Even from a distance she could see that their semester-long sabbatical in France had added a little more gray to her father's beard. They had spent the last two weeks on the Riviera, and her father was tan and trim, thinner than when he had left, but he looked very healthy. Even Shayna, who was usually as pale as paper, had gotten a little sun. Jenna wasn't a big supporter of tanning. The whole "cooking-your-skin Big Cancer Party" was not her thing at all. But she wasn't so fanatical about it that she couldn't admit that a little color in the faces of a couple of academic workaholics was a good thing.

Frank Logan beamed the moment he saw his daughter

wending her way between the tables. He stood up to greet her.

"Sorry I'm late," Jenna said. She hoped her father and Shayna would like what she'd done with her hair, but she had made sure to wear a long, loose-fitting shirt that was not too tight. She wasn't quite ready to let them know about the navel-piercing.

Her father pulled out a chair for Jenna, and after hugs and kisses all around, she sat down, grateful for the opportunity—finally—to be off her feet. The autopsy of Nicholas Jaffarian had gone far longer than she had anticipated, partially because Mass General was not set up for a man in a wheelchair to conduct one. Slick had to coordinate his own work with Jenna's and Dr. Hallett's. Add to that the strange circumstances of Jaffarian's murder, and . . . well, she was just pleased to be sitting down.

Even though both her father and Shayna taught at Somerset, Jenna found it curious how seldom her path crossed with theirs. Of course, they had been in France all spring on sabbatical, so she hadn't seen them at all for several months. They had returned home just a few days ago, and other than picking them up at Logan Airport, this was the first opportunity she'd had to get together with them.

"So, are you studying hard for finals?" her dad asked as he settled back in his chair and raised his wineglass to his mouth. A waiter came over to the table and filled Jenna's glass with water. She smiled her thanks and took a sip before answering her father.

"You better believe it." She let out a puff of breath

that lifted her bangs from her forehead. "Study and work. That's all I seem to do."

Just the mention of work made her realize that some aspects of the disturbing autopsy—especially the gaping holes where the fish had bitten off chucks of the dead man's flesh—were still bothering her. A little shiver ran through her, and she saw that her father had noticed. Not wanting to have to elaborate, she turned to Shayna. "So did you get that French lace ring pillow you said you saw in Rouen?"

"I got something better," Shayna said, smiling almost wickedly as she reached into her purse and withdrew a box wrapped with gold foil. She carefully removed the top and folded back the pink tissue paper inside to reveal a cream-colored leg garter with lacework that looked like spun sugar. It seemed so delicate that it might dissolve if she breathed on it.

"Oh, my. That's *gorgeous*." Jenna gingerly lifted the garter from the box and inspected it closely. "It's too bad you have to throw away something as beautiful as this."

"Someone's going to have to catch it before it hits the floor," her father said with a laugh, "because most of my friends who will be there won't be able to bend over to pick it up."

Shayna raised one eyebrow. "Who knows, Jenna? Maybe you'll catch the bouquet when I toss it."

"No way." Jenna smiled weakly and shook her head as she replaced the garter in its box. "Someone else can catch it. I'm not going to move a muscle."

Shayna carefully folded the tissue paper over the

garter, closed the box, and slipped it back into her purse. "You never know when love will strike," she said, glancing lovingly at Frank.

"So, it's like getting hit by lightning, then?" Jenna asked.

Her father smiled. "Yeah. Actually, it's a lot like that. But I guess you know that already, don't you?"

Jenna chose not to respond to that line of inquiry. "Have you finalized the date? Is everything set?"

"Everything? I don't think everything will be set until we close the door on the honeymoon suite," Shayna said. "There's even more planning involved than I expected." She cast a quick glance at Frank. "But we've settled on the last weekend in October."

"We tried to get it as close to Halloween as we could," her father said.

For a moment, Jenna thought he was serious; then she saw that he was smiling.

Shayna frowned at him and gave him a good-natured swat on the arm. "Very funny." Then she focused on Jenna again. "There's a full moon on Saturday, the twenty-sixth. We found the perfect little inn overlooking the ocean in Magnolia. If the sky is clear, we'll be able to see the full moon reflected over the water."

"Jenna doesn't want to hear about her old man's romantic notions," her father said, shifting in his chair. He seemed a bit embarrassed, and Jenna thought it was adorable—a side of her father she had never seen before.

"So," he went on, "from the sound of some of the e-mails you sent me, you've had quite a time while we were out of the country . . . especially in Florida during spring break."

"I've learned a lot," Jenna replied with a solemn nod. "If you'd told me a year ago my life was going to be like this, I . . . I never would have believed you. Sometimes I wish I could just skip right over the rest of my under-grad studies and go right to med school."

Shayna frowned. "Don't ever wish your time away, Jenna. It goes by much too fast."

"Oh, I'm not," she said. "Not really. I love it here. I wouldn't want to leave my friends behind. But there's just a part of me that feels like . . ." She paused, trying to find the words. "Working with Dr. Slikowski has taught me so much, not just about pathology, but about, well, work and life. About what it means to *be* something. I'm a girl. A student. My job is to study, to learn—all of that. But this whole year I've had a kind of sneak preview of what it's going to be like when I'm all done with the studying, and I've got a purpose. A real purpose.

"I'm not ready to give up on just being a girl and hanging out with my friends. But I feel like I've got this insight none of them have. And I like it."

Frank reached across the table and gripped her hand, giving it a tight squeeze. "I'm awfully proud of you. I just hope you're not working so hard with Walter Slikowski that you're neglecting the things you actually get graded for studying."

Jenna smiled. "If finals go well, I've got a shot at mak-ing the honor roll. Happy?"

"Very," her father assured her.

"You really are pulling off a remarkable balancing act, Jenna," Shayna said. "You remind me of a student I had the year before last. He was paying for his tuition at Somerset by working full-time as a clerk at a law firm in Boston."

"Full-time?" Jenna said. "How did he pull *that* off? With class schedules and everything?"

"I don't know. But he got in his forty hours a week and still had a 3.67 average for the semester."

"Wow," Jenna whispered. She had thought her schedule was overwhelming, but it was a breeze in comparison.

"So, what are your plans for the summer, honey?" Frank asked.

Jenna took a deep breath and then plunged in. "Well, I thought I'd stick around this summer. You guys have been gone a while, and who knows, maybe you'll need help with wedding preparations. Mom's all right with it."

She smiled and looked intently at her father for a moment. Her father and mother got along all right. Their divorce had been so long ago, they both seemed to be very much over it. Still, she always felt just a twinge of discomfort whenever she mentioned one of them to the other.

"So, you're really staying because you don't want to spend the summer away from your job," her father said knowingly.

Jenna shrugged. "Well, there's that, too. And I can certainly use the money." She rushed on before he could voice any disapproval. "Of course, I still have to find a sublet. You wouldn't believe what people want for rent, and some of the places are just . . . ohh." She shivered with disgust. "They're like a closet in the basement of some frat house or something."

Shayna's face suddenly lit up. "You know, I think I might be able to help. There's a graduate student in the English department named Virginia Rosborough. I think she's looking for one or two people to sublet with her while her roommates are gone for the summer."

"Seriously?"

"I'm pretty sure. Do you want me to find out if she's got anyone yet?"

"Definitely. That'd be great." Jenna tried not to get excited. She was all too aware of how tough it was to find decent housing anywhere near the university, even during the summer months. Any lead was a good lead.

"Virginia's taking my American Renaissance seminar this summer. In fact, she has an appointment to see me tomorrow morning. I'll ask her then."

"Thank you," Jenna said. "That would be such a load off my mind."

"She's a bit of a stick, though," Shayna said.

"A stick?"

Shayna shrugged. "She's just . . . she's a very serious student. She doesn't have a whole lot of personality."

"It'd just be for a couple of months," Jenna said. "I'd really appreciate it if you'd ask her for me."

"Absolutely."

"So," her father said, "you find working with Slick

and Al Dyson so interesting, you can't even leave for a few months?" He chuckled and took another sip of wine. "I remember when I first suggested that job to you. You didn't seem all that interested."

Jenna shrugged. "People change." She felt a twinge in her belly and glanced around for the waiter. "And I. Am. *Starving.*"

"I'm glad you chose this place," Shayna said as she unfolded the menu and started to scan it. "I've had enough French cuisine to last me—"

"Until our next sabbatical," Frank interjected. He had also been scanning the menu, but he looked up at Jenna with a twinkle in his eye. "Do you have any suggestions?"

"Absolutely," Jenna replied. "I came here with Yoshiko and Hunter a couple of weeks ago. You have to try the Masaman curry. Get it with chicken and at least three stars."

"Three stars? Won't that be too hot?" Shayna asked, her brow furrowing with concern.

"Oh, come on, honey. Live a little," Frank said, giving her hand a playful tap. He closed the menu and placed it to one side. "Masaman curry it is, then," he said, raising his wineglass and draining it.

Jenna laughed, allowing a bit more of the tension she'd been carrying to seep out of her. It felt so good to see her father and Shayna again. She hadn't realized until now how much she had missed both of them. Even better, if this line that Shayna had on an apartment worked out, she'd be all set for the summer. She could put some money down right away, and maybe then her mother would stop the subtle pressure she was putting on her to spend the entire summer in Natick.

*Ah, yes,* Jenna thought as she settled back in her chair and took a sip of water. *Life is good.*

"Oh, sure. They look good now, but just wait. Come September, they'll break our hearts like they always do."

Michael Sullivan's Irish accent always seemed to get thicker the more beers he downed. Tonight, after five or six cold ones in Angelo's, a small, quiet neighborhood bar on Dorchester Avenue in Boston, he was starting to sound like a former resident of Belfast. His head was spinning a little, so he gripped the brass rail with both hands to steady himself. The large-screen TV to one side of the bar was on, and Clyde, the bartender on duty tonight, had it tuned to the Red Sox game from Anaheim. Pedro was on the mound. He was pitching everything in the book, and no one was hitting him. It was the bottom of the eighth, and the Sox were leading seven to nothing.

"Last call, Mikey," Clyde said as he wrung out a damp rag in the sink and then started wiping down the bar. "If you want, you can stay and watch the end of the game while I clean up, but I can't serve anything past one o'clock."

"No sweat," Michael said.

He covered his mouth with one fist to stifle a belch as he heaved himself off the barstool. Fishing his wallet from the back pocket of his jeans, he took out a twenty-dollar bill and dropped it onto the bar. "Keep the change."

Clyde shot him a quick glance and nodded before scooping up the bill and sliding it smoothly into his pocket. Michael felt unsteady on his feet as he hiked up his pants by the belt. When he walked over to the door, he tripped on the threshold and had to grab the wall quickly before he fell.

"Whoa. Take it easy there, pard'ner," Clyde called from behind the bar. "You want me to call you a cab?"

"I'm a cab," Michael said as he shook his head and waved. He chuckled at his joke and wondered why Clyde didn't find it as funny as he did. "I'll be fine."

A tiny voice somewhere in his head was telling him that he shouldn't stay out late like this so many nights. It wasn't fair to either Darcy or the kids. But he countered that voice by telling himself that he worked damned hard at the Boston docks to provide for them, and his wife and kids shouldn't begrudge him a little time to do something he enjoyed.

"Catch ya later," he called out, his voice slurring. He grunted as he shouldered open the door and walked out into the warm, spring night.

He'd brought his Red Sox jacket with him, expecting the temperature to drop later, but the city seemed to trap the heat of the day like a closed oven. Slinging his jacket over his shoulder, he started toward home. His apartment was about a mile away, and as he walked, he thought maybe it would have been wiser to let Clyde get a cab for him. Then again, a walk would do him some good. It would help clear his head. No sense getting home with too much of a buzz. That would just give Darcy something else to get angry about.

Michael had just turned into a dark alley that cut over to Spring Street, a shortcut he'd used since he was a kid growing up in this part of the city, when he frowned and drew to a stop. A cool prickly feeling rushed up his back, and he was sure it wasn't just a fitful breeze. A familiar feeling had come over him; a childhood feeling. The feeling he would get when he woke up in the middle of the night when everyone else was asleep. The feeling that outside those black windows, someone was watching him.

*Drunk and paranoid*, he told himself.

Only problem was, he didn't believe that. He hadn't heard any footsteps behind him, and he hadn't seen any suspicious shadows flitting in and out of sight, but he was positive someone was there.

*When did they pick me up?* he wondered. He was so buzzed, he hadn't been paying attention. It could have been anytime since he left Angelo's.

Michael didn't feel any fear. When you're born and raised in Dorchester, you get your street smarts fast or else you end up tasting a lot of pavement. Ever since he had been a kid, Michael Sullivan had been one of the fastest and toughest guys in his neighborhood. He took great pride in that.

His fists clenched at his sides, he turned and looked back at the lighted end of the alleyway. The harsh glow of streetlights lit up Dorchester Avenue like daylight, but here in the alleyway, he was lost in darkness.

"Anybody's there—show yourself. I'll kick yer ass for ya," he called out. "You picked the wrong mark tonight."

There was no response. Not even an alley cat or a rat, scuttling to safety. Michael was just starting to turn around to continue his walk home when a quick scuffing of feet came up behind him. Something hard slammed into the back of his head. His knees buckled, and he dropped to the pavement without a sound.

He was down, but he wasn't out.

Bright light exploded and spiraled across his vision, and there was a high-pitched ringing inside his head that blocked out every other sound. He tried to see who or what had blindsided him, but the alleyway pulsed and wavered with thick shadows. He had the impression he had suddenly plunged deep underwater.

Something sticky and warm washed down the side of his face. He raised his hand and touched it, only distantly aware that it was blood . . . his blood.

"Have you been baptized?" a voice asked. It filled the night like a roll of thunder.

"Wha—what?" Michael mumbled, rolling his head from side to side. He could feel his scalp grinding against the pavement.

"Have you been baptized in the water?"

Michael was too stunned, too confused to make sense of it. He groaned when he felt hands—strong hands—slip under his armpits and lift him. He was too weak to resist. His shoes scraped and chattered on the rough pavement as he was carried deeper into the alleyway.

Then the hands let go, and he dropped hard enough to hurt. His head bounced once on the asphalt, and a yellow shower of stars filled his sight.

Through the stars, he saw a figure, leaning over him, but it was too dark to be distinct. All he saw was the outline of a head, framed against the glowing night sky. Fingers rubbed the blood that was gushing from the wound on the side of his head.

*Blessing me?* Michael wondered. *Is this a priest? Is that what this baptism question was about? Was I out? How long? . . . How bad is it? How much blood?*

Michael felt an edge of frantic fear. He was too groggy to make sense of any of this. He felt a single finger press against his forehead and draw a line straight down between his eyes. Then the finger drew another from side to side, making a cross on Michael's forehead.

"Have you been baptized in the blood?" the voice asked.

But by then, he only half heard the words. He had lost too much blood, and he was beginning to lose consciousness again. Slowly he drifted down . . . down . . . until he settled into impenetrable quiet and absolute darkness.

# chapter 3

Professor Emerson—*Shayna,* Jenna reminded herself. *You can't keep calling her Professor if she's going to be your stepmother*—Shayna had been as good as her word. On Friday she had given Jenna a phone number for the grad student she had mentioned who had a room to sublet, and by Monday, Jenna found herself making the trek to check it out. Not that it was a very long trek.

Virginia Rosborough's apartment was on the third floor of the house at 49 Walker Street, a little more than half a mile from campus. It wasn't the most upscale neighborhood in Somerset, but it would be an easy walk to the hospital for Jenna. Even before she saw what the place looked like on the inside, she was desperately hoping things would work out.

Someone—she assumed it was Virginia—had buzzed her in when she pressed the doorbell. Her knees felt a little rubbery after going up two flights of stairs, and she noticed that her hands were sweating. She took a deep breath when she reached the door of the top-floor apartment.

She knocked lightly, and almost immediately the door opened inward. A young woman looked out at her. She was shorter than Jenna, and scarily thin. She was barefoot and wore loose-fitting tan shorts and a dark blue spaghetti-strap T-shirt. Her blond, shoulder-length hair was pulled severely back, leaving a few strands of bangs hanging down over her forehead. Her glasses were large and round, giving her pale face an owlish look. Jenna didn't see how this woman could be mistaken for anything *but* a graduate student in English.

"You must be Jenna," the woman said without smiling. She took a single step out onto the landing and held out her hand for Jenna to shake. "I'm Virginia Rosborough."

"Yes, hi. Nice to meet you, Virginia."

"Please, come in," Virginia said with a tight nod. She stepped to one side to allow Jenna to enter the apartment first.

"Oh, it's gorgeous," Jenna said, genuinely impressed as she entered and looked around. Virginia shut the door behind her and threw the deadbolt.

The living room was a bit on the small side, but it was cozy and tastefully decorated. There was a plush love seat and a coffee table by the bay window that looked out onto Walker Street. Hanging from the ceiling above it was an array of houseplants. Jenna recognized one, a spider plant, but none of the others. Only one picture was hanging on the wall: a framed Dalí print. On the coffee table, arranged neatly, like in a doctor's office, were several recent issues of *Vanity Fair, The Atlantic Monthly,* and *Harper's.* A bookcase on the side wall was stuffed with textbooks and literary novels. There were no Larry McMurtry or James Lee Burke books, or anything else that Jenna would have read in her spare time. There was also none of the casual chaos that marked a typical student's room. Everything was neat and orderly except for the desk beside the door that led into the kitchen. There, an opened laptop was almost lost beneath sheaves of papers and piles of books and scholarly magazines.

"It's so comfy," Jenna said, instantly wondering if she sounded as young and naive as she thought she might. After all, she was still a freshman, and this was the big time—a graduate student's apartment.

"Well, don't get too comfortable," Virginia muttered. "It's just until classes start again."

Jenna flinched, insulted and a bit hurt. Before she could respond, though, the sudden sound of rushing water—a toilet flushing—issued from the doorway behind her. It was loud enough to startle her. She'd had more than one unpleasant surprise during her freshman year, so sudden noises tended to make her jumpy. Seconds later, a thin guy wearing faded and torn blue jeans and a well-worn FLAMING LIPS T-shirt wandered into the living room. He wore only socks on his feet, and one of them had a rip in the toe that would have driven her nuts but which he didn't seem to notice at all.

"Hey," he said, nodding but not quite making eye contact with Jenna.

"Jeffrey. This is Jenna Blake," Virginia said, sounding almost matronly now. "She'll be renting the third bedroom for the summer. Jenna. This is our other roommate, Jeffrey Tilton."

"Jeff," the guy said with a quick nod.

As he held his hand out for her to shake, all Jenna could think was how Virginia had introduced her as if everything was already agreed to. And as far as she was concerned, it was. She didn't care if the bedroom she'd be using was nothing more than a broom closet. It was almost impossible to find a decent sublet in the area, particularly this late in the game. She was lucky to have found a place she could afford, so close to campus and the hospital. That it was so nice inside was just a bonus.

She was determined to stay here this summer, even if it did mean sharing the place with a guy. It was one thing having boys on one wing in the dorm, but it was quite another to be sharing the same space, even the same *bathroom*, with a male. Jenna felt a little intimidated, having been raised in a household after her parents divorced with just herself and her mother, and it was definitely not what she had been expecting.

But she would adjust.

"I think I might've seen you around campus some," Jeff said.

Jenna felt uncomfortable that he never looked directly at her, even when speaking to her. He kept cocking his head and shifting his gaze to one side or the other, his eyes unfocused—almost as if he were blind.

"Maybe," Jenna said with a smile.

She felt a little bit bad that she couldn't say she had ever noticed him, too, but Jeff seemed like the kind of guy who worked at disappearing into the woodwork. Compared to anyone's high school, Somerset was a huge place, and in her first year there, Jenna was already comfortable with the small circle of close friends she'd made: Yoshiko, Hunter, Damon, Brick, Ant, and a few others. This experience of living off campus for the summer would be good for her even if all it did was widen her circle of friends and expand her horizon a little.

"So why aren't you going home for the break?" Jenna asked brightly. "Are you taking a few courses?"

Jeff almost seemed to flinch at her question, and he ducked his head lower, staring at the floor.

"Sorta," he said, his voice so low, Jenna almost couldn't hear it. "I—ah, I don't really get along all that well with my folks, and since I'll be a senior next semester, I figured"—he shrugged and slapped his hands against his thighs—"I might as well just stay here."

Jenna could see that this was a sensitive subject for him, and she felt another, stronger wave of pity for him. She heaved a silent sigh of relief when Virginia interrupted, saying, "Would you like to see the bedroom?"

"Sure thing," Jenna said.

As Virginia led her away in one direction, Jeff wandered off in the other without a word.

*Kinda weird*, Jenna thought, but she instantly put Jeff

out of her mind when she saw what would be her bedroom. It was small, as she had expected, but there was a double bed against one wall, a bureau and desk against the other, and a closet with the door partway open—enough for Jenna to see that it was spacious enough to store her things so she wouldn't have to take everything home to Natick. The window looked out at the street below. "It's perfect," she whispered, as much to herself as to Virginia.

"I'm glad you like it. And I hope you'll understand that there are a few rules for the apartment. No parties. No overnights with boyfriends or whatever. You'll need to buy your own food and toiletries. Clean up after yourself. And no blaring your music. When I'm here—which isn't very much—I need to focus."

*Wow,* Jenna thought, *she's like the evil stepmother in some fairy tale.*

Virginia's tone was icy. Jenna wondered if she ever loosened up or if she was always like this. Either way, it didn't really matter. All she was looking for was a place to stay for the summer, and this place was perfect. She had gotten very lucky to have Yoshiko as her roommate freshman year. If Virginia wasn't destined to be her friend, she could handle that.

"I'll take it . . . if you're offering," Jenna said, trying not to say the wrong thing. She'd never rented an apartment before. It was such a . . . she hated to think it, but, it *was* such a grown-up thing. And though she was an adult now, working and living in an adult world, sometimes she still felt a bit like a kid.

"I just need someone to help me cover the rent until my roommates return for classes in the fall," Virginia said dismissively. It was clear from her attitude that she wished this wasn't the case. "Since you have Professor Emerson's recommendation, I suppose that's good enough for me."

Jenna stuck her hand out, and they shook hands again.

"This is perfect," she said, clapping her hands together. "And don't worry. I'll be the model roommate. I'll move my stuff in after finals."

"As long as you have your first rent check to me by the end of the week, you can move in whenever you want," Virginia said over her shoulder as she walked out into the hall and started back to the living room.

"No problem," Jenna said, following along a few steps behind her. "I'll drop it off tomorrow."

Once they were back in the living room, Jenna realized that, as excited as she was, she didn't have anything more to say to Virginia. Jeff was nowhere to be seen. After a brief, awkward silence, she headed toward the door.

"Aren't you forgetting something?" Virginia asked.

Jenna shot her a quizzical look and watched as she reached into a coffee mug on her desk and picked up a metal ring with two keys on it. She smiled tightly as she handed them to Jenna.

"You have to be able to get into the building." Virginia's haughty tone irritated Jenna, but she smiled as she looked at the keys.

"The round one opens the front door, and the square one opens the apartment door," Virginia said matter-of-factly. "I'll be at the library most days until my summer seminar starts, so—please—make sure you lock up after yourself."

"Don't worry, I will," Jenna said. "I have your number. I'll call if I have any questions."

"Please. Do," Virginia replied tonelessly as she went to the door and unlocked it. With a quick nod of her head, Jenna went out into the hall clutching the keys tightly in her hand.

*I can't believe it!* she thought, resisting the urge to whoop with joy as she bounced down the stairs.

Less than a week after finals had begun, eight days after she had arranged for her off-campus summer sublet, Jenna closed a blue test booklet and flattened it with her hand as she eased back in her seat and took a deep breath. Tapping her chin with her pen, she considered— one last time—what she had just written. As far as she could tell, the test had been easy . . . maybe a little *too* easy. She was suddenly concerned that she had made a terrible mistake and not even realized it.

*Finals aren't supposed to be this easy, are they?*

But she had studied hard for all of her tests, and she'd been ready. If anything, she had overprepared—if such a thing was possible. She looked at the clock and saw that there was still almost half an hour to go. She didn't like the idea of being the first person to turn in her test, but she didn't feel the need to read all of her answers one last time either. She'd gone over them more than enough already, and she was confident that she had nailed this one.

The legs of her chair chattered loudly on the floor as she stood up and walked slowly to the front of the room. A few students glanced up at her, and she cringed, knowing that—this time, at least—she was *that* student: the one who finished first and made everyone else suddenly nervous about the answers they were giving. She could practically hear people in the room thinking, *How can she be done already?*

Taking a deep breath and holding it, she walked down to the front of the classroom and handed the blue book to the graduate assistant who was monitoring the test for Professor Dribben. The assistant accepted the test with a slight nod of the head, then placed it casually on the desk beside her and went back to her own reading. Feeling an almost wistful sense of finality, Jenna went back to her desk, collected her things, slung her backpack over her shoulder, and walked out of the room. She was careful to ease the door quietly shut behind her so it wouldn't bang and distract the other students.

Her shoes clicked on the linoleum, echoing loudly in the hallway as she made her way to the front door. She shouldered the door open and stepped out into the sunshine on the steps of Ballard Hall. Throwing her arms out wide, she closed her eyes and took a deep breath, luxuriating in the warm, spring air as she spun around in a complete circle.

*I did it!* she wanted to shout. *That's it! I'm done! My freshman year is over!*

The mixed feelings of relief and exhilaration and trepidation were almost too much to handle. It was a bit disorienting. She didn't know if she wanted to laugh out loud or cry or shriek and jump up and down for joy, but she restrained any impulse to cut loose. As she looked across the quad, a sense of incredible, indescribable well-being swelled up inside her.

*This is college, girl,* she told herself. *Act like an adult.*

Still, she couldn't help but skip down the steps before starting up the walkway, heading back to Sparrow Hall. The last day of finals, and the campus already seemed sort of deserted. Her friend Roseanne had already finished up and gone home for the summer, as had Damon and Brick. She thought Ant was still on campus, but he would be heading home to Buffalo soon as well. Fortunately, Hunter and Yoshiko hadn't left just yet.

*Everyone's leaving, scattering to the far corners of the world,* she thought a little wistfully. *Everyone except for me.*

In the midst of her excitement about having put the final touches on her freshman year, she was surprised by the sadness that welled up inside her now. It reminded her of the way she had felt after high school graduation last June. The end of her freshman year at Somerset wasn't as final as graduation, of course. But she had left her high school friends behind to start living her life, and staying on campus to work with Dr. Slikowski felt much the same. Everyone else was going home. Jenna took a step into the postcollege world every time she went to work, and those experiences made her different, in a way.

Hands down, this past year had been the best and the worst year of her life. There had been so many things happening so fast, she wondered, sometimes, how she had ever handled them all. The death of Melody LaChance—Hunter's older sister and one of the best friends Jenna had ever had—haunted her most of all. It left Jenna with a sadness that she thought might never leave her.

But good things had happened too.

She had learned so much about subjects she never would have thought she would find interesting. Twice, she had fallen in love. With Damon, of course, though she wasn't sure it had ever been real love. And with Danny Mariano. Leave it to her to fall for a handsome police detective thirteen years older than she was. That was a whole big complicated *thing,* but at least she and Danny were still friends. Good friends.

In the previous nine months, Jenna had discovered so much about other people, and—most importantly—about herself. Working in the morgue with Slick and Dyson had given her a unique perspective that, she was sure, none of her classmates had. A perspective most people *never* got.

"Oh, cut it out," she whispered to herself. *No more ruminating. It's a fantastic day, with every reason to celebrate.* "Stop thinking so much, Blake. Just enjoy."

Finals were over, and her grades would be what they would be.

"Was the test that bad? It's got you babbling to yourself?"

Jenna jerked to a stop when she heard Yoshiko's voice. "Huh?" she muttered, turning to find her roommate striding right up to her, just a few feet away.

"I thought you might be having a stroke or something," Yoshiko said with a smile. "I called your name three times, and you didn't even hear me."

"Really?" Jenna said, shaking her head, momentarily dazed. "I guess I didn't. That must have been zombie-goofball Jenna. She who is Not a Freshman, Not Yet a Sophomore."

"So how was Dribben's final?"

Jenna shook her head. "Not bad at all. I finished early."

"Obviously," Yoshiko said with a laugh. "You said you wouldn't be done until three o'clock. I came over to meet you, but you'd already left."

"I was the first one done," Jenna said. "Unless I really messed up on something, it wasn't all that hard. So did you get all your stuff stored in the cellar over at Whitney House?"

Yoshiko nodded. "Hunter helped me get it put away, but carrying all those boxes"— she winced as she raised the bottom hem of her T-shirt— "I think my piercing might have gotten infected."

Jenna leaned forward and studied the red ring of infection below Yoshiko's navel. It looked tender. "Yikes," she said, resisting the impulse to probe it with her fingertip. "You'll have to keep putting antibiotic on it. Does it hurt?"

"Not really," Yoshiko replied unconvincingly.

Jenna felt a little guilty. It had been her idea, after all, to get pierced. "If you take care of it, I'm sure it'll heal fast," Jenna promised her.

Yoshiko arched an eyebrow. "Says the girl whose medical experience consists entirely of patients who *never* healed."

"Hey!" Jenna cried, and she batted Yoshiko on the arm.

The two of them shared a laugh, then fell into step together, heading back toward Sparrow Hall.

"Hunter's last exam isn't over until five o'clock," Yoshiko said. "I told him we'd hook up with him then and head into the Square for dinner. After all, this is our last night together."

"Don't say it like that," Jenna chided her.

"Well, it's true," Yoshiko said. "But it isn't like we're not coming back."

Yoshiko was right, of course. But there was such a ring of finality to those words, *our last night together.* It was, though, the last chance they'd have to hang out together before her friends left for the summer. It called for another trip to Harvard Square. Yoshiko wasn't going to get an argument from her on that.

While they were waiting for Hunter to finish his last final, the two girls walked down to Jenna's new apartment. She had been wanting to show it to Yoshiko since the previous week, but they had been studying so much that they hadn't found the time. When they arrived, Jenna was relieved that Virginia wasn't around.

"Oh, man, this is *incredible,*" Yoshiko said when Jenna unlocked the door and let her in. She *ooh*-ed and *ahh*-ed about the setup as they walked slowly through the apartment, carefully checking out each room. "We have to get a place like this for our junior and senior years."

"You think?"

"Absolutely!"

"I don't know. I kind of like the idea of staying in Whitney House." Jenna shrugged and shook her head. "Let's see how everything goes this summer. A place like this is pretty expensive, you know."

"Not if you have three or four roommates."

"Oh, yeah? And just who were you thinking of inviting to share an apartment with us?"

Yoshiko winked and gave her a knowing smile that looked positively devilish. "You never know, do you?"

Jenna laughed. She had known that she was going to miss Yoshiko this summer, but she was just beginning to realize how much.

"Yo, Frankie? That you?"

Ken Arruda dropped the newspaper to his lap and looked up. His co-worker had left less than five minutes ago to pick up some coffee and doughnuts from Dino's in town. He shouldn't be back for another fifteen or twenty minutes, depending on traffic.

*Not unless he forgot his money,* Ken thought.

He sighed with irritation as he heaved himself up from his chair and stepped out into the hall. The steady thrumming of the chlorinators and filtration units vibrated the walls and floor of the Somerset Water Treatment Plant, what the locals called "the Filter Plant." Ken squinted as he looked up and down the corridor, but he didn't see anyone. "Frankie?" he called again. He didn't like the way his voice echoed in the narrow confines of the building. It sounded odd.

The air was cool and moist, and it was laced with the heavy odor of chlorine. Ken was new on the job, having been hired less than six months ago, but he couldn't help but think that no matter *how* long he worked there, he'd never get used to the smell of chlorine. It burned his eyes and nostrils and made him sneeze a lot. It was worse in the room where the chlorinators and filter tanks were kept, and he made it a practice to avoid going in there as much as possible.

*This stuff's gotta be bad for your lungs,* he thought. It was small consolation to think that Pearl, his wife, would be able to sue the town and maybe collect a sizable settlement if he died from some horrible lung disease.

Cocking his head to one side, he listened, positive that he had heard something. It had certainly sounded as though a heavy steel door had opened and then slammed shut.

*Be nice to have a gun or something,* Ken thought. What with all the worries about terrorists, there was a chance—slim, but still a chance—that someone might try to break into the plant and sabotage the water supply. He and Frank were the maintenance crew, and they always got to the plant a couple of hours before anyone else on the day shift. In the winter, Frank had told him they'd be there before the sun was up. Ken wasn't look-ing forward to that. The only other people there were a couple of techs who worked the graveyard shift. For them, that meant checking the levels once in a while, and reading or napping the rest of the time.

Nice work, if you could get it. It sure as hell beat mopping the place up when a pipe broke.

Ken's fists were clenched at his sides as he walked down the hallway, past the door that led into the room with the filtration tanks. He paused for a moment out-side the door and glanced into the room, but he didn't see anything out of the ordinary.

Still, he didn't like it.

He'd been working here long enough to know what sounds did and didn't belong, and what he had just heard—as faint as it was—just hadn't sounded right.

At the end of the hall, he leaned forward and peered out through the small, wire-mesh window set in the middle of the steel door. The parking lot was deserted except for his old Pontiac and a Jeep Cherokee that the two techs finishing up third shift always carpooled to work in. Frankie's pickup truck was gone.

"Everything's fine. No worries," Ken whispered out loud to himself, but he found little reassurance in the sound of his own voice. He didn't like the way it echoed in the hall beneath the steady humming of the pumps.

He double-checked to make sure the door was locked; then he started back to the maintenance office. Checking his watch, he saw that the techs would have to run another check on the chemical levels in about ten minutes. He was probably going to have to wake them up again.

Ken drew to an abrupt stop when he glanced down at the floor outside the filter room and saw the large wet spot on the tile floor. "What the heck?" he muttered as he bent down to check it out.

The footprint was clearly outlined with water, but it already appeared to be drying up. It could leave a streaky afterimage, though. The chlorine was concentrated enough for that. Looking carefully, he saw another three or four footprints heading toward the door.

*Frankie must have checked something in the filter room before he left*, Ken thought. *Must've had a repair or something.*

But Frankie hadn't mentioned anything like that to him. And even if he had been in that room, unless there was a leak or a burst pipe, his boots shouldn't have gotten wet.

It wasn't going to be long before the day shift started to arrive, and the real work at the plant would begin. Mr. Gustavson, one of the plant managers, was a stickler for keeping the place clean. There was no telling when some city councillor might drop by to inspect the place under the guise of a friendly visit. Maybe even someone from the FBI would stop in to check on their security procedures, such as they were.

Ken went to the maintenance closet and dragged out a mop and bucket. After wringing out the mop, he swiped it across the floor in several wide arcs, applying enough pressure to obliterate the footprints. He groaned out loud when he pushed open the door to the filter room and saw the trail of watery footprints that angled across the floor from the filter tanks. The thick smell of chlorine made him shiver and cough. Grumbling under his breath, he followed the wet path with his mop, wiping it away and leaving behind wide swatches of wet, glistening tiles.

"Guy's a freakin' slob," Ken muttered once he had reached the bottom of the metal steps. They led up to a low balcony that encompassed the three large filtration tanks. His heart skipped a beat when he looked up and saw a streak of wetness running down the side of the tank.

"What the heck was he doing in here?" he asked himself as he leaned the mop against the railing, gripped the rails, and started up the steps. His heavy work boots rang like hammers on the metal steps.

The hum of the filters and pumps was much louder now, throbbing in his head and vibrating deep in his stomach. But that was nothing compared to the shock he experienced when he saw the figure floating in the filter tank closest to the wall. His breath caught painfully in his chest, and his first thought was that he must be hallucinating from breathing all the chemicals in the air. He rubbed his eyes and shook his head, trying to convince himself that he was imagining this.

But there it was.

A body—it looked like a man—wearing a dark blue Red Sox jacket was floating facedown in the filtration tank. The motion of the water made him spin slowly in a circle.

*Sheesh, I guess I won't be drinking any town water for a few days,* was Ken's first thought, and then he turned and ran back to the office to call Mr. Gustavson on his cell phone. Someone had to call the police, too, but he figured it ought to be the boss, not a guy like him.

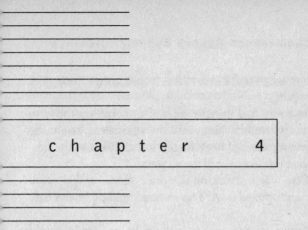

## c h a p t e r     4

On Thursday, when the time came for her to move out of Sparrow Hall, Jenna was more than ready. The previous afternoon she had gone to see Yoshiko off at the airport. Hunter had left early the same morning, insisting that Yoshiko not come along so that she didn't have to make two trips to the airport in one day. That was Hunter, though. Their little Southern gentleman.

With the two of them gone, freshman year really had come to a close.

Sparrow Hall was like some bizarre haunted house, just a few slackers left behind, still fumbling their things into vans, pickups, and station wagons. Jenna had packed most everything yesterday afternoon. She had two suitcases, a duffel bag, an old black trunk, milk crates filled with books and CDs, a TV, a DVD player, and a computer, all piled up in the middle of the room. She wasn't going to need all of that stuff at her sublet, but it didn't make sense to truck everything home just to bring it all back again.

Her mom had initially offered to come up today to help her move her things into the apartment, but at the last minute she had been forced to bail because the hospital had put her on call for surgery.

There was a knock on the door. Jenna smiled, went over, and opened it. Al Dyson was standing in the hallway.

"Dyson to the rescue," he said, his smile bright against his rich, olive skin.

Jenna gave him a hug, holding on a bit longer than necessary. "Thank you *so* much for coming," she said as she released him.

"What are friends for, huh?" he asked. He knit his brows as he studied her expression. "Hey. You okay?"

She took a breath and nodded, a smile fluttering to her lips. "Yeah. It's just . . . I don't know. Feeling a little blue, I guess."

"Blue? You've been listening to too many of Slick's jazz CDs. That's the problem," Dyson said, teasing.

Jenna smiled again, and it wasn't as difficult the second time. "It's just a weird time. The transition. Everyone's gone. I want to go home, but at the same time I don't. I know that doesn't make any sense at all. I was just feeling kind of lonely this morning."

"Which makes you doubly glad to see me, right?" Dyson said.

"Yes, Al." Jenna rolled her eyes, but Dyson was right. She was very glad to see him, to have a friend around.

"Hey," he said, his voice softer now, no trace of the banter between them. He put a hand on her shoulder. "It's totally natural. Feeling what you're feeling. And it isn't just today, or the end of the school year. College is all about transition. The whole shebang. Four years of it. From the kid you were to the person you're going to be. Going home can be nerveracking. Take it from me. But try to remember: No matter what changes in your life, you're not a different person than you were. There's just more to you now than there was before."

Jenna gazed at him a long moment. How was it that he always seemed to know the right thing to say? It was a talent she wished she possessed. But it wasn't really a talent. Dyson was speaking from the heart, and she knew that. "You're sure about that, huh?" she asked.

"Trust me," Dyson said, a kind of melancholy in his eyes that reflected her own. "The summer after *my* freshman year, I told my whole family and all of my high school friends I was gay. Totally came out of the closet. Kinda wished I'd kept my mouth shut until September or so."

"They didn't buy the whole 'You're not different, there's just more to you now' thing?" Jenna said, smirking.

Dyson wagged a finger at her. "Brat."

"That's me."

"Some of them did. My parents were pretty cool about it. But the aunts, uncles, cousins, and some of the idiots I went to my high school with—they weren't so open-minded. People have an image in their heads of who you are or who they think you're supposed to be, and they don't like it when you suddenly shatter that image."

Jenna shuddered. "Jeez. I can't live my life worrying about what somebody else's image of me is supposed to be."

"No," Dyson said, shaking his head. "You can't." The two of them smiled at each other, and then Dyson threw up his hands. "All right. If we're done with philosophy class, let's get on with this whole move thing. I am your loyal servant!"

"Cool," Jenna said. "I've always wanted one of those. Do you peel grapes for my refreshment?"

"Only on Mondays," Dyson snapped, and they both laughed.

It took them three quarters of an hour to get all of Jenna's things down to the street level and packed into the aging Toyota 4Runner that belonged to Dyson's boyfriend, Doug. Jenna had expected the third-floor apartment to be empty when she arrived, but when she opened the door, her key sticking slightly, Virginia appeared from the kitchen wearing an expression of mixed curiosity and annoyance. When she saw that it was Jenna, she offered a frosty smile. "Oh, hello. I thought you were moving in tomorrow."

"No," Jenna said slowly. "It was always supposed to be today."

"Oh well, that's all right, I suppose. Please try to keep it quiet, though."

Jenna nodded, thinking nasty thoughts. She suspected

her smile was probably as frosty as Virginia's. "Is Jeff around?" she asked, thinking that, unlike Virginia, her other summer roomie might actually offer to help.

"No," Virginia replied. "I have no idea where he's off to."

With some effort, Jenna carried the heavy suitcase into the apartment and set it down in the living room. She opened the door to her room just as Dyson came into the apartment with her duffel bag slung over his shoulder and her TV in his arms. Virginia arched an eyebrow.

"Hello," she said, her tone filled with expectation. This was her place, after all, and he—a stranger—had entered it unannounced.

Jenna made the introductions, but without much enthusiasm. "Al, this is Virginia. Virginia, this is my friend Al Dyson. Dr. Albert Dyson."

Her eyes widened slightly at the word "doctor." "It's a pleasure to meet you, Dr. Dyson."

"You too," Dyson said, paying very little attention to the ice queen as he staggered into Jenna's room and placed the TV on top of the bureau there.

The next trip in, Jenna carried two crates of books. Dyson struggled with her trunk, which he shouldn't have attempted alone. He was still somewhere on the stairs when Jenna set the books down in her room. She caught Virginia watching her speculatively, a sly sort of smile lifting one side of her mouth. "So, tell me about Dr. Dyson?"

Jenna couldn't help laughing. Dyson was like her

brother, and much older than she was, so she had never even considered him from that point of view. What was funny, though, was how much her snooty new roommate had perked up with Dyson around. It wasn't her place to do so, but she would have loved to tell Virginia that Dyson was gay. On the other hand, it was just as entertaining for Jenna to watch him not notice *her* at all. "He's just a friend," Jenna said. "We work together."

Virginia frowned. "Really? What do you do, exactly? Are you a candy striper or something?"

Dyson had managed to get the trunk inside, but it was much too heavy, and he let it fall onto the couch. Virginia actually flinched at this insult to her furniture. Panting, Dyson leaned against the couch, taking a rest before he moved the trunk the rest of the way.

"Candy striper," he said, chuckling to himself. "That's pretty funny. Slick's going to love that."

But Jenna wasn't amused. She didn't like talking about her job to people she didn't know very well. Most people thought it was a very strange, even unpleasant, occupation for anyone, least of all for a nineteen-year-old college girl.

"Slick?" Virginia prodded.

Jenna crossed her arms. "Dr. Slikowski. He's the chief medical examiner for the county. I work for him at Somerset Medical Center. Dr. Dyson is a resident there."

But obviously Virginia had not heard much past "medical examiner." Her mouth was open in a little O that made Jenna want to slap her.

"You work for the medical examiner? Doing what?" Virginia asked with obvious disdain.

"Answering phones. Filling out forms. Filing. And sometimes assisting with autopsies."

The look on Virginia's face instantly transformed from disdain to outright disgust.

"Hey, don't worry," Dyson said as he hefted the trunk again. "There isn't a body in here. We never let her bring her work home."

On their next trip down to the 4Runner, the two of them broke out into little fits of laughter.

Detective Danny Mariano gripped the edges of his seat as his partner, Audrey Gaines, rounded the corner of Spenser Street, cutting it tight enough that the right rear wheel clipped the curb. Danny always wore a seat belt—it was the law, after all—but today he thanked God for its invention. With a wary gaze, he stole a glance at Audrey out of the corner of his eye. Her arms were stiff, and she sat ramrod straight in her seat, her jaw clenched.

Audrey was the best cop Danny had ever known. She had taught him pretty much everything he knew about being a homicide detective. They were friends, too. Like family. They watched each other's backs. Today, though, Danny had the feeling Audrey would gladly have driven a knife into his.

She was wearing a tan jacket over a black turtleneck and black pants. Simple, yet elegantly cut. Even angry, Audrey was stylish. The tan jacket was set off by her ebony skin, but her dark eyes were hard and cold. He

CHRISTOPHER GOLDEN AND RICK HAUTALA

often thought that, as a girl, she might have been beautiful, but her years in homicide had done that to her eyes, filled them with things that would no longer allow her to be beautiful. "Look, Audrey," he began.

One hand shot up, palm toward him, waving him into silence.

Danny sighed and ran a hand through his short brown hair. He ignored the view outside the windows, the businesses and homes they were passing, and instead stared down at his black sneakers, at a grease spot he had gotten on his blue jeans at lunch, at his hands.

Again, Audrey cut the wheel. The tires squealed a little as she pulled into the parking lot of the Somerset Water Treatment Plant. As Danny looked up, Audrey tugged the keys from the ignition and popped open her door so quickly, it was like she was trying to escape from him. When Danny got out, she was already marching across the parking lot, her arms stiff at her sides. There were two black-and-white patrol cars in front of the building and one uniformed officer next to the black wrought-iron steps of the main entrance. "Audrey!" he called, almost angry himself now. "Come on!"

She paused. He saw her shoulders rise and fall as she took a deep breath. Then she turned toward him. "You coming?"

Danny smiled in disbelief. "Jesus, Aud. All I said was 'Happy Birthday.'"

Detective Audrey Gaines had turned forty-five today. She glared daggers at her thirty-two-year-old partner. "What's so happy about it?"

Danny sighed and smiled wearily. He knew that at least part of Audrey's cranky-birthday-girl attitude was just for show, but they had been partners long enough that he also knew some of it was for real. It happened every year. In the past, he had suggested she just lock herself in her apartment on her birthday, but for some reason she never tried that method of avoiding facing the passage of time.

*Misery loves company,* Danny thought.

As she went across the lot, cutting between the two black-and-whites, Audrey pulled a pack of cigarettes from her pocket, then fished in the same pocket for a lighter. She fired the cigarette up and clutched it between her teeth while she put the pack and the lighter back. Audrey had quit smoking months ago. *Guess it was too much to think she'd get through her birthday without hitting the nicotine again,* Danny thought.

She took a long drag, blowing out a plume of smoke as she trotted up the metal stairs to the door. She nodded once to the uniformed officer there, and he opened the door for her. The officer did not even look at her. And he sure as hell wasn't stupid enough to wish her a happy birthday.

Danny followed her and didn't dare give in to the urge to nag her about smoking. Nor did he bother to suggest that they might not allow smoking inside the plant, or that it was possible—not likely, but possible—that her smoke, or tapped-off ashes, could contaminate the crime scene.

"Ernie," he said, nodding as he entered.

"Detective," the officer replied.

Inside, another uniform pointed the way, and a moment later they were threading along a narrow corridor. The entire building hummed, but the deeper they went inside, the more that humming sound bored into Danny's chest and skull. It was a bone-grinding noise that set his teeth on edge, and he figured it was the kind of thing people either got used to if they had to be there a while or else it drove them nuts. He knew it wouldn't take long for it to drive him nuts.

The corridor opened into a much wider hall where a pair of steel double doors had been crisscrossed with yellow crime scene tape. Two more uniforms—Kreske and Suarez—were loitering in the hall in front of those doors, along with an overweight maintenance man who needed a shave, and a pair of anxious-looking men. Each of the latter two wore a jumpsuit that Danny assumed was the uniform for the people who actually worked in the plant, but their outfits were spotless. It was a water treatment plant, so he didn't expect them to be filthy, but at least they should be rumpled. The guys whose jumpsuits weren't rumpled had to be in charge.

Audrey, clearly having made the same assumption, approached the men. Danny went directly to the two uniforms. He glanced over at the maintenance man, who wouldn't meet his gaze. The guy shuffled a bit and, stuffing his hands into his pockets, leaned against the wall. His shift had likely ended a long time ago.

"What've you got?" Danny asked, addressing Suarez. Kreske had more seniority, but he was a moron.

Suarez glanced at his partner, but Kreske just snapped the gum he was chewing and nodded.

"There are three filtration tanks in there," Suarez said, gesturing toward the double doors. "Maintenance guy's name is Ken Arruda. Heard some noises, thought it was the other maintenance guy on duty. Went to check it out and found the body in one of the tanks."

"Stinks like hell in there. Nearly lost my breakfast," Kreske muttered. "Chlorine, man. My nostrils are burning."

Danny nodded his thanks. He was sure there was more that Suarez could have told him, but he wanted to hear it from the witness. Audrey was still talking to the administrative types, and from the way her voice was rising and the way she dropped her cigarette and ground it out on the linoleum with no trace of apology, he had a feeling they were pissing her off. They looked pretty uptight, but even so, Danny had pity on them. "You're Mr. Arruda?" he asked the maintenance man.

"Yeah. Yeah, Kenny. Ken. Look, can I get going soon? All I did was find the guy. I got a lot of work to do."

Danny nodded. "I'm Detective Mariano. Just give me a minute, Ken, and you can go."

Arruda seemed relieved at this.

"Tell me, in your own words, how you came to discover the body."

"Well, see, I heard something. Thought it was Frankie—"

"And Frankie is?"

"Frank Marshall. But not like the movie guy. We work together. He'd gone out to get us some . . . um . . . well, he'd stepped away a minute. So I thought when I heard the noise, maybe he'd fallen down or . . . I don't know what I thought. I went to check it out, and that's when I saw the footprints. I figured it was him, y'know. He's kind of a slob for a guy who cleans up after folks for a living. I got a bucket and mop and—"

"Hold on," Danny said, frowning. "What footprints?"

Arruda's eyes lit up. He sensed that Danny found this important, and it made him feel important too. "Just sort of wet, y'know? Coming out of the filtration room. I figured maybe he'd had to do a repair in there or something." The maintenance man shrugged and then pointed. "Just over there is where I saw the first one."

Danny strode several feet in that direction, only to be stopped by the man's voice.

"Oh, you can't see nothin' now, Detective Mariano," Arruda said, a note of pride in his voice.

For a moment, the meaning of this statement didn't sink in. It was water, after all. It wouldn't have left much trace once it evaporated. Maybe something, with all the chemicals in here, or some dirt or grime from the bottom of a shoe. But not . . . then it hit Danny. Arruda was a maintenance man. Before he'd found the body, all he had seen was a mess. Danny sighed and turned to stare at him. "You cleaned them up, didn't you?"

Arruda frowned, obviously not understanding why the detective's tone had changed. "Yeah. It's my job, isn't it?"

"Yeah," Danny replied. "Yes, of course it is." He did not bother to try to explain to the man that even if they couldn't ID someone based upon the dried outline of a damp footprint, there were things they might have learned about their perpetrator.

The maintenance man finished telling the story of how he had discovered the DOA. There was nothing else in the tale that Danny found remarkable.

"So can I go now?"

"Sure. Get back to work."

Arruda nodded, smiled, and then hurried off down the corridor, relieved to be back to his routine. Danny was always amazed at how many people could encounter something as horrid, as terrible as murder, and be more upset by how it impacted their scheduled lives than by the deed itself.

As Danny started back toward Suarez and Kreske, he saw Audrey shake hands with the men in the spotless jumpsuits. When she turned and saw him watching her, she rolled her eyes. Then she strode up to where Danny stood with the uniformed officers and gestured toward the double doors and the crisscrossed crime scene tape. "Open it," she said.

Kreske gave a sniff of contempt. There were cops on the Somerset P.D. who didn't like being given orders by Audrey Gaines—some because she was a woman, and others because she was a black woman. Kreske had already proven that he was never going to make detective. Hell, he was unlikely to ever make sergeant.

Suarez tore the yellow tape off the door and opened it for them. Though Audrey chose to ignore Kreske, Danny gave the officer a hard look as he went through the doors. Kreske averted his eyes long enough for Suarez to close the door behind them, and then Danny and Audrey were alone in the room with its massive water tanks, with only the awful thrumming of the filtration systems to keep them company.

"So what's the story?" Danny asked her.

For what might have been the first time that day, Audrey smiled. "Someone jimmied a side door. They assume the perp parked behind the Dumpster on the side. No alarm, because the maintenance crew was already in. Whoever it was got in and out with the victim without anyone seeing anything. The only way that works in my head is if the DOA was either unconscious or dead already. Not that any of it makes much sense, dumping a body here. Unless the suspect is a former employee, or the victim is, or both. Oh, and you're going to love this. Your witness, the maintenance man? He found the body sometime around eight thirty this morning."

"What?" Danny turned to her, not sure if he'd heard her correctly over the noise in the room. "The call didn't come in until almost eleven. What were they doing that whole time?"

Audrey's smile widened into a cynical grin. "It's a city facility, Danny. Arruda told his manager. The manager went to the director, who's pals with our dear mayor."

Now Danny felt his stomach do a little flip of disgust. "You're saying instead of calling the police, they called the mayor's office?"

"Sure," Audrey said, her face mock-serious. "Got to make sure they control the flow of information, that they handle the news properly, right?" She scowled. "When the director called us, he'd been told exactly what to say by some PR flack in the mayor's office."

The doors opened behind them, and the forensic team entered, carrying all of the gear they would need to study the scene, searching for fingerprints and other trace evidence. Audrey waved to them.

"I have no idea what to say to that," Danny told her, keeping his voice low, the words just between them. He sniffed and shook his head.

"Just wait. It gets better."

Danny stared at her.

Audrey pointed toward the tank in the center. "They didn't even drag him out to make sure he was dead. Nobody dared disturb the crime scene. It never occurred to anyone that while they were trying to figure out how they were going to spin it for the press, the guy might have still been alive and drowning."

"He was probably already DOA," Danny noted.

"True," Audrey agreed. "But they didn't *know*. They didn't check."

A tiny sound came from her throat, something between a sigh and a laugh, and she led the way up the metal stairs to the scaffolding that surrounded the tank. Danny followed. At the top of the steps, they paused, side by side, and stared down at the dead man floating on his belly, Red Sox jacket saturated with water.

Audrey made that same sound again. "Jesus," she said softly. "Happy birthday to me."

———————

On Thursday night, Jenna was safely ensconced in her bedroom—her *new* bedroom—and trying to get used to it. The old pumpkin pine floorboards creaked a little, and one of the windows—the one where she thought she might put a fan once hot weather came—didn't open. She didn't really feel at all at home and wondered if it was just displacement talking, or if it was because any time Virginia was in the apartment she felt as though she should hide under the bed.

*You know me,* Jenna typed, watching the words appear on her computer screen. *I try to get along with everyone. In my entire life there's only been one person I can think of that I disliked instantly, and that was what's-his-name, the teacher who kept pawing Moira at yearbook meetings. Mr. Auberge, or however it was spelled. But Virginia is so in need of an attitude makeover.*

She hit Return, using Instant Messenger. Less than thirty seconds later, a response popped up from Priya Lahiri, one of her best friends from high school.

*I can think of a couple of other things that might change her attitude. One of them she'd like. The other she wouldn't. But it doesn't sound like she's gotten either one in a long time, if ever.*

Jenna laughed and glanced over her shoulder at the door to her room. It was closed, but Virginia had gotten under her skin enough that she checked every minute or so, not wanting her words to be seen.

*Well, it's only for the summer. She says she's hardly ever here, anyway, so that's good.*

She sent the message. As she was waiting for a

response, there was a light knock on the door. Jenna's pulse quickened, and she clicked to close the Instant Messenger window. "Come in?"

The door opened, and Virginia poked her head in. She wasn't much older than Jenna, but her pinched expression made her look like an old shrew. "Jenna."

"Oh hey, Virginia, what's up?"

The grad student twisted her lips up as though she'd just tasted something sour. "Are those your dishes in the sink?"

Jenna raised her eyebrows. "Oh, yeah. Yes, they're mine. Sorry. I got sidetracked. Just give me a minute and I'll take care of it."

Utterly humorless, Virginia nodded, but her expression let Jenna know that the girl had doubts about her. "Fine. But don't make it a habit. I don't have a lot of rules in the apartment, and it's not exactly like this one's difficult. I clean up after myself. It's not a lot to ask you to do the same."

She remained in the doorway, awaiting some further response. Jenna was capable of dealing with rude people, but this was stretching her good nature to the limit. "I said I'd take care of it. I just need a minute to shut down my computer."

With a huff, Virginia pulled the door closed.

*You've got to be kidding me,* Jenna thought. *Who in the world is that uptight?* But, of course, she already had the answer. She was living with the most uptight person in the world.

There was another knock at the door and, teeth gritted, Jenna called for Virginia to come in. But it wasn't

Virginia. Jeff Tilton popped his head into the room. He was sort of gawky and quiet, but there was something in his self-deprecating way that Jenna found endearing. "Hey, Jeff. What's up?"

"Um, well, I was just going to watch a movie. Want to join me?"

Jenna hesitated. Did he mean in his room or the living room? Was he flirting, or just being friendly? This whole living-with-a-guy thing presented its own share of complications. "What movie?"

"*Memento.*"

"Sure," she said. "Yeah, just let me log off. And clean my dishes before I get thrown into solitary confinement."

Jeff smiled and shut the door. He really did seem like a nice guy, but she hoped that he didn't have anything but the movie in mind. She didn't have any romantic interest in him.

Her computer *pinged*, and she glanced at the Instant Messenger window that had just popped up, preparing to tell Priya that she had to go, that she would speak with her later. But the message wasn't from Priya. It came from fuzzydys, which was Dyson's online nickname.

*Hey,* the message said. *Hope you're settling in all right. Just saw that you were online and wanted to know if you still planned on working tomorrow.*

A second window popped up, this one with Priya's reply, but Jenna ignored it for the moment.

*Yes,* she typed back to Dyson. *Why?*

*Slick and I were both out this afternoon, but we've got a*

*present waiting for us in the morning from Gaines and Mariano. It's going to be an interesting day.*

Jenna felt a subtle charge slide underneath her skin as she typed: *Interesting in the Chinese curse sense . . . like 'may you live in interesting times'?*

Dyson's reply appeared within seconds. *Exactly.*

On Friday morning, Jenna was so involved with typing up a transcript of one of Slick's recent autopsies that she barely glanced up when she heard footsteps coming down the hallway. There was a light rap on the door, and as it swung open she looked to see who it was. Her heart skipped a beat when Detective Danny Mariano and his partner, Audrey Gaines, entered the office.

Since she had taken the job with Dr. Slikowski, Jenna and Danny had worked together many times. They'd become friends. Very good friends. He cared about her, and she about him. And maybe it was more than that. Jenna had let herself fall in love with Danny early in the school year, despite their age difference, and she was confident he felt more than simple fondness for her as well. But Danny had made it clear that he thought it was a bad idea, that the age difference mattered to him, that they were in such conflicting places in their lives, they couldn't be more than good friends.

Jenna had accepted that. She'd had another boyfriend in the meantime. It looked like fate wasn't going to be kind to her where Danny was concerned. So . . . friends.

But, as friends, they had not seen each other very often for the past couple of months. Jenna had thought some distance might make it easier for her to shake off the lingering feelings she had for Danny.

So it was hard for her to explain the little flutter in her chest when Danny smiled at her as he approached the glass partition above her desk. The twinkle in his eye made her smile back in spite of herself. *So much for shaking off those feelings,* she thought. Jenna wondered if she was ever going to be able to be around Danny and not be in love with him, at least a little bit. Maybe she just needed to fall in love with someone else again. Make room for someone else in her heart.

Not that she was going to push that. If there was one thing she learned from her mother's example, it was that she had to define herself based on her own mind, her own heart, and not on having some guy in her life.

"Good afternoon, Detectives," she said, gazing up at Danny. Even if she was trying to move away from her feelings for him, that didn't mean she couldn't appreciate how damned handsome he was.

*Just be cool, Blake,* she cautioned herself. *No need to get all crazy.* She got up and walked around the desk to greet them. Not sure whether to shake hands with Danny or give him a hug, she did neither.

"Hello, Jenna. How've you been?" Danny asked.

Was there another question there? Was he wondering why he hadn't heard from her lately, why they hadn't been out to lunch in a while?

Jenna realized it didn't matter. If Danny had wondered those things, he was smart enough to figure out the answers for himself. He was a detective, after all.

"Doing well, thanks," she said. "Nose to the grindstone, even though finals are over. But I'm guessing you're not here on a social call."

Danny laughed softly, understanding in his eyes. "No. Not this time. Slick around?"

Audrey had not said anything since entering the office. In fact, Jenna thought she looked more than a little irritated. Jenna wondered if the detectives had been arguing about something, or if it was something else.

*They're just here to do their job,* she told herself, *so you just do yours.*

"Dr. Slikowski and Dr. Dyson are downstairs. They've already started the autopsy," Jenna said, amiable enough but professional. "I can take you down there if you'd like."

When Danny glanced at Audrey, there was a moment of tension that Jenna could not ignore. It practically crackled in the air, like summer lightning. A sudden weight lay upon her as she began to fear that there was something they weren't telling her, that the detectives brought with them some terrible news. "What is it?" she asked. "Is something wrong?"

"Someone's dead," Audrey replied snippily. "Or did you mean something more than that?"

Danny actually chuckled and shook his head. "Only the usual crap, Jenna. Oh, and one added wrinkle to our day . . ." He glanced at his partner. "But just to the day, nowhere else."

Audrey shot him a withering glare. "Danny."

Jenna knew that she would never want *anyone* to look at her like that. Not ever.

"Aww . . . she's just a little grumpy," Danny said, but the devilish gleam in his eyes brightened. "It's not the big five-o, but it's close enough."

"Do you mind?" Audrey snapped without a trace of amusement.

"It's her forty-fif—"

"Don't go there, partner," Audrey interrupted, wagging a finger at him.

Danny's smile instantly melted, and he adopted an innocent expression.

"Audrey, I didn't know it was your birthday," Jenna said. "I'm sorry. I would have gotten you a card if I had known."

"Spare me." Audrey sighed, shaking her head grimly. "I can find my way down to the autopsy room. You two can stay here and chitchat if you want. I've got work to do."

With that, she turned on her heel and strode out of the office. At the door, she paused for a moment and looked back to Jenna. "I like what you've done with your hair," she said, sounding almost pleasant for a moment.

"Uhh—thanks," Jenna replied, self-consciously running her fingers through her hair.

Without another word, Audrey squared her shoulders

and left the office. For several seconds they could hear the steadily receding *click-click* of her shoes on the linoleum floor, even through the door.

"I'm guessing there won't be any cake and ice cream," Jenna said, the corners of her mouth turning upward as she glanced at Danny.

"I don't want to die young," he replied. They shared a little laugh, and then he sighed and regarded her closely. "I like it too. Your hair, I mean." One corner of his mouth rose into a nervous half-smile.

Jenna nodded her thanks and was about to lift her shirt to show him her navel piercing when she realized how completely inappropriate it would be. She put the thought out of her mind. *Yeah, that'd be really professional. Just lift your shirt up in the office. College Girls Gone Wild. Where's Snoop Dogg when you need him?*

"So," she finally said, redirecting the conversation back to business. "Slick says you guys found another drowning victim."

"Uh-huh," Danny replied, nodding. For a moment, a dark shadow flitted across his face, dimming the glimmer in his eyes. "In the Somerset public water supply, no less. And it's been tangled up in red tape ever since."

"What do you mean?"

"A maintenance worker found the body a little after eight o'clock yesterday morning, but the mayor's office knew about it an hour or two before we did. That's why it took so long to get the body over here. By the time we had the DOA for you guys, Slick and Dyson were out for the day."

"You're kidding," Jenna said, aghast.

Danny was scowling deeply now. He shook his head and snorted with disgust. "Wish I was. They called the *mayor's* office before they called the police or even checked to see if the poor bastard was still alive." His frustration, his anger, were almost palpable. She could see the muscles in his jaws working as he gritted his teeth. "Assholes."

"Hey," she said, sliding her hands into her pockets to keep herself from reaching out to comfort him. "You'll get your guy. That's what matters."

Danny took a long breath and nodded as he let it out slowly. She could see that he was all worked up over this one, and she could understand. She knew from firsthand experience how easy it was to get carried away, to get dragged into it. Somewhere out there was a killer, a soul-less creature who enjoyed taking the lives of other human beings. Yet on the autopsy table was a man who had family and friends who needed to know how such a thing was possible, how it had happened to their friend, to their brother or father or son. More importantly, they needed to know what was going to be done about it.

Jenna had a history of getting too involved in Dr. Slikowski's cases. Over the past year it had put her in danger too many times. But she was learning her lesson. Danny couldn't maintain a reasonable distance from his job. While she could admire his dedication, she could also see how he let it run his life. But Danny was a cop. That *was* his job. It wasn't Jenna's. The job of the medical examiner's office was to provide the facts, to suggest answers when they presented themselves. It was not to run an investigation. Just like she was trying to keep her emotional distance from Danny, she was trying to do the same with her job.

Neither thing was easy to do. But both were necessary. She had to cultivate a more detached, impersonal, professional demeanor.

"Dyson mentioned that you're gonna be around for the summer," Danny said. "That you had a place over on Walker Street."

Jenna nodded. The sparkle had returned to his eyes. It was obvious he was glad she was going to be around. That made her feel happy and forlorn at the same time. It would have been so much easier if he hated her, or even if he dismissed her as just a kid, a school girl with a silly crush. But he had never done that to her. The son of a bitch had always treated her with respect. She smiled to herself, trying not to laugh at the irony.

"And you're done with finals?"

Jenna nodded.

"How do you think you did this semester?"

"Fine, I think. They weren't as hard as I'd expected." Jenna nodded toward the door. "We'd better get after Audrey. I hope we've given her enough time to fume."

"Gonna need a week or two for this one," Danny said.

He went to the door and held it open for her. Jenna locked it behind them, tapping her pocket to make sure she had her key card so she could get back in. They went down the corridor together, walking side by side. The hell of it was, they *were* friends. She enjoyed his company, whatever the circumstances.

*Just do your job, Blake,* she reminded herself as Danny pushed the button to call the elevator that would take them down to the basement. *Do your job and let all this other stuff go.*

When Jenna and Danny entered the autopsy room, Dr. Slikowski's wheelchair was pulled up as close to the autopsy table as he could get it. She was pleased to see him at work. When they had been at Mass General for the autopsy of the aquarium victim, it had been obvious that Slick was uncomfortable merely directing traffic. Here at SMC, his custom-designed table allowed him to do the job himself without difficulty. Watching him work, Jenna saw that this was his element, this was where he was most at home.

Strange, or at least some people would think so, that a man could be more at home among the dead than the living. But Jenna understood Walter Slikowski. The man had a calling, and she admired that. Her mother had told her that too many people went through life never knowing what their purpose was. Slick had his. He solved the puzzles of death. And in doing so, he provided solace to the people left behind. Yes, Jenna and Slick understood each other very well.

Dyson was hunched over a steel table against the far wall, running a scalpel along a section of the dead man's stomach. The steel instrument made a sort of hissing noise as it sliced across the large dissection tray. Dyson seemed so intent on what he was doing with the dead man's stomach that he barely acknowledged Jenna's and Danny's presence.

Audrey was leaning against the far wall, her arms folded tightly across her chest as she watched the procedure. A deep scowl lined her brow, and she looked like she was still ready to take off someone's—anyone's— head at the slightest provocation. Although she wasn't standing anywhere near the body, she wore blue latex gloves and a protective surgical mask. She seemed to be focused on Slick's progress with even more than her usual intensity.

Slick and Dyson had been working on the body for over an hour, and Jenna couldn't help but wish she had been down here assisting them right from the start. The preliminaries had been completed. The subject's chest cavity had been opened, and the organs had been removed. As he had for the previous autopsy at Mass General, Slick had taken the internal organs out individually instead of as a single block for analysis.

Jenna was all too aware of how important the administrative work upstairs was and that she should get right back to it. She was a pathology assistant, a part-time employee—the low man on the totem pole, as it were. That meant doing what Dyson always called "the grunt work." But she also knew that Dr. Slikowski respected her work and admired her dedication to the job. When she watched the focus, the intensity that he put into his work, she knew that *this* was where she truly belonged. Everything else—even her friends and her schoolwork— paled by comparison. As important as her college work was, ultimately it was just a means to an end.

*This* end.

"The chlorine level of the water in the victim's stomach registers quite high," Dyson said, speaking clearly and somewhat formally so the microphone close to Slick would pick up his voice. Spread out on the table next to the dissection tray was an array of detection test strips for chlorine and other chemicals, and several labeled test tubes filled with water. Squinting, he held one of the strips of paper up against a plastic-covered sheet with an array of colors, ranging from light blue to deep vermilion. "Somewhere between 5.5 and 6 parts per million."

"I need as precise a reading as you can give me, Dr. Dyson," Slick said as he straightened up from the corpse and leaned back in his wheelchair to relieve the pressure on his back. Taking a clean, white towel from the tray beside him, he wiped his forehead. "You have done your research, I presume?"

Dyson glanced up, noticed Jenna, and they shared a smile at their boss's businesslike manner.

"I have," Dyson replied. He cleared his throat slightly, wanting to speak clearly for the microphone. "The public water supply generally runs between .3 and 1.8 parts per million. The variance is largely based upon the distance between the filtration plant and the source of the sample. Even so, at its highest in the filtration tanks, they generally keep it below 2 p.p.m., so it's highly unlikely the water in the victim's body came from the filtration tank."

Slick nodded. "I concur." He glanced over at Jenna

and raised an eyebrow. "Swimming pool water, however, is sometimes as high as 5 parts per million. In a public pool, it might even be as high as 7 or 8."

Jenna said nothing, but her pulse quickened. It was exactly as she had expected. Someone had drowned this guy in a swimming pool and then dumped his corpse at the water treatment plant. She had no idea why. But, she reminded herself, the *why* wasn't her job.

"Do you think this is connected to the Jaffarian case?" Audrey asked. The curtness in her voice surprised Jenna. Audrey might be cranky because it was her birthday, but Jenna never would have expected this woman, a consummate professional, to let that affect her work. And copping an attitude with the medical examiner would definitely affect her work.

"You're positive the victim drowned somewhere else and was merely dumped into the filtration tank?" Audrey prodded.

Slick turned in his wheelchair and looked at her. His eyes narrowed above the top of his surgical mask. Even without seeing his expression, Jenna could tell that he wasn't at all pleased with Audrey's tone of voice. Dr. Slikowski did not like to be pushed, and he never appreciated attitude.

"A more detailed analysis and a comparison of the water in his stomach with that in the treatment plant will determine that. But I would say—yes. This man was drowned in water with a much higher chlorine level than is found in the public water supply."

He turned back to the body, spread open before him,

and inched his wheelchair closer. "The blow to the side of his head wasn't severe enough to be fatal. Because of the water in the lungs and stomach, it's obvious this man died by drowning. But as to determining whether this case and the Jaffarian case are related"—he turned to arch an eyebrow at Audrey—"if I recall correctly, that would be your job, Detective. Mine is to provide you with facts."

There was a moment of tension between them, and then Audrey softened. "Sorry. Bad day."

Slick nodded. He took a deep breath, making the front of his mask form an O across his mouth, then turned his attention back to the corpse. "What I find particularly curious is the residual blood on his forehead. There's just a trace of it, but it must have dried there before he was submerged, or it would have washed off and we wouldn't have found any sign of it at all."

Curious, Jenna could no longer restrain herself, and she took a step forward. As she picked up a surgical mask and gloves and started to put them on, Danny tapped her on the shoulder. "Didn't you tell me not too long ago that you were going to ease up a bit, not get so involved?" He whispered, nodding toward Slick. "The docs seem to have everything under control."

"I just want to see what Dr. Slikowski is talking about," she said, hearing the edge of defensiveness in her voice. "Just curious. And I don't want to contaminate anything."

After adjusting the mask, she came up close to the corpse and stood where she could see better. Staring down at the dead man's face, she watched as Slick indicated the faint marks on the victim's paste-white forehead.

"Do you see this?" Slick said, tracing a line in the air an inch or so above the dead man's puckered skin. "The agitation of the water in the tank has washed most of the blood away, but here, in the wrinkles on his forehead. Tell me. What do you see?"

Jenna squinted and leaned closer to inspect the faint red markings. She turned, grabbed a magnifying glass from the lab bench, and looked even closer, studying the pattern the dried blood had made in the folds of the man's skin.

"It certainly looks like dried blood," she said, and then remembering that they were being recorded for the record, she spoke more clearly. "There appears to be a residual line of dried blood in the center of the victim's forehead, from just below the hairline to the bridge of his nose between his eyes." She paused a moment and studied the mark in silence, then added, "It doesn't appear to be a typical blood splatter pattern, however. It looks more like . . ."

She paused and glanced at Dr. Slikowski, who was watching her closely. He nodded once, silently urging her on.

"I would guess—"

"Don't guess, Jenna," Slick said. "This is science, not a guessing game."

"Well, it looks as though someone has drawn a line of blood straight down the center of his forehead and then—" She focused the magnifying glass on the faint markings, not quite believing what she was seeing. "It appears as though another line was drawn across the first, making a—"

And then, in a flash, it hit her.

She saw what someone—either the victim himself, or possibly his killer—had done. Swallowing with difficulty, she looked over at Slick as she tried to accept the full impact of her observation.

"Yes?" Slick said, the inquisitive gleam in his eyes urging her on.

Without any further hesitation, Jenna said clearly for the record, "It looks as if he's been anointed. Someone has made the sign of the cross on the man's forehead with blood."

Slick exhaled loudly as he rolled his wheelchair back from the autopsy table and pulled down his surgical mask. Jenna saw the smile of satisfaction on his face.

"It's *so* nice to have my observations confirmed." He turned to Danny and Audrey, who were standing by the wall, and said, "And now we have another piece of the puzzle."

"'Positively ghoulish.' Those were her exact words," Jeff said, looking like he felt equally disgusted and apologetic for telling Jenna what Virginia, their roommate, had said to him about her work-study job.

It was late Saturday afternoon, and the setting sun was streaming through the window in spite of the city grime that stained the glass. The living room glowed with a rich, dusty golden light. A warm breeze wafted in through the open window, carrying with it the distant sounds of the city traffic. She and Jeff were sitting on the couch.

Jenna sniffed and shook her head. "And this is coming from someone whose graduate thesis topic is 'Demonic Female Archetypes in Eighteenth-Century Gothic Literature'?"

Jeff looked at her with a lopsided grin and shrugged as though helpless. "The Ice Queen has her own problems, you know," he said, adopting a mock-serious tone. Virginia was at the library, as usual, but he glanced around as though he half-suspected to see her lurking nearby, eavesdropping on their conversation. "For one thing, she lacks that essential human ingredient known as a personality."

Jenna felt a twinge of guilt as she chuckled. But not too much. Not after the dirty-dish incident. "Hey, you know what I was thinking?" she said.

"What's that?"

She hesitated then. The last thing she wanted was for him to get the wrong idea, to think she was flirting with him. But she had already started the conversation and she did like his quirky company, so she went on.

"Maybe I could study with you for that anatomy class you're taking. It'll help me 'cause I'll be taking it next year, and maybe it will help you focus to have someone to study with."

Jeff looked up at her for the first time, but he couldn't hold her gaze for long. He lowered his head and stared at the floor. "You don't have to do that, you know," he said softly. "If I can't make it, you know . . . if I'm gonna flunk out or if I drop out or something, it's my own damned fault."

"I know I don't *have* to do it," Jenna said. "I want to. It'll be good for both of us. If you don't mind, y'know, studying with me."

When he looked at her again, an almost desperate flash of hope lit Jeff's eye for an instant. Then he smiled that lopsided smile of his. "That'd be cool," he said.

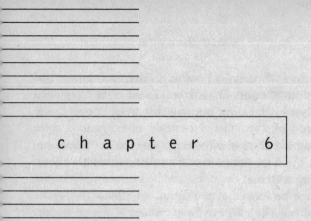

## c h a p t e r 6

Long days had passed since the Somerset P.D. had fished Michael Sullivan's body out of the water treatment plant, and the case was no closer to being solved than it had been that first day. Danny Mariano knew that the Boston cops—Castillo and Yurkich—weren't any closer to solving the murder of Nicholas Jaffarian, the DOA who'd been dumped in the central tank at the New England Aquarium. But it was cold comfort. He was a homicide detective. Unsolved murders always gnawed at the back of his mind.

It was healthy, on the one hand. Good that he could still care so much about the victims. But that was just surface crap. Deep down, it wasn't healthy at all. He held on too tightly, felt the weight of the murders on his conscience. It was even worse in a case like this. The perp had killed more than once. That meant the body count was likely to rise unless they could do something about it in the meantime.

And so far, they had nothing. Forensics on site had turned up nothing. Dr. Slikowski's office had provided some vital details, but nothing that would point in the direction of the killer. Homicide investigations were nothing like how they were portrayed on television. Most TV cops solved every murder within the hour. They glowered at the perp, and he crumbled. Even the media didn't help that perception. The news reported a murder, and they reported the capture of a suspect. But if there was no suspect, if there was no arrest, people tended to forget all about the murder victim.

But the families didn't forget.

And the investigating officers, like Danny and Audrey, didn't forget either.

Most crimes that went unsolved for more than seventy-two hours remained unsolved. That was a simple fact. In homicide investigations, it seemed to him that it was even more solidly true. There were overdoses and accidents. There were suicides. Gang killings. All of those were simple enough. Domestic violence accounted for the majority of the work he and Audrey did. It was a sad bit of reality, but most murders were committed not by some faceless, mysterious stranger, but by someone the victim already knew, maybe even loved at one time. Boyfriends and girlfriends. Husbands and wives. Co-workers and neighbors.

Any murder case was heavy with the sorrow of death. But domestic violence cases and workplace killings presented no challenge. The real work came when there was an actual mystery, when he and Audrey had to put the pieces together themselves. But they were only human. There were limits to how much they could accomplish. And without more clues, without more evidence, whoever had murdered Michael Sullivan and Nicholas Jaffarian was going to get away with it at least until they killed again.

It was a sunny Wednesday morning in the middle of June. The weather girl on the morning news had pinned the temperature at seventy-seven degrees in the city of Boston, and rising. It was going to be in the mid-eighties today, but thankfully it was early enough in the summer—hell, was it even summer yet? Danny could never remember if the first day was the twenty-first, twenty-second, or twenty-third. Whichever it was, he was happy with the warm weather as long as it wasn't humid. Late June was perfect that way. But late July and most of August in the greater Boston area could be a sweltering hell.

He sat at his desk in the squad room shared by Somerset's homicide detectives. The lieutenant had already sent the night shift guys home, though Audrey hadn't shown up yet. But it had been a quiet night, and thus far a quiet morning, so no worries there.

Other investigations had interrupted the Sullivan case, but Danny kept coming back to it even when he and Audrey weren't focused on it. On a quiet morning like this, with a warm breeze sweeping in through the windows and ruffling the papers on his desk and splashes of sunlight stretching across the room, Danny could really focus.

He sat in front of his computer, several windows open on the screen. One was the autopsy report on Michael Sullivan. Another window had photographs of the crime scene as well as photographs given to them by the Boston P.D. from the aquarium, showing Jaffarian's body suspended in the massive fish tank. The two police departments were cooperating on the case. Danny had worked with Jace Castillo before. Neither of them was the sort to let ego get in the way of solving a case. And from what he could tell of Castillo's partner, Terri Yurkich was pretty determined as well. She was a serious woman, though he'd seen her smile at Castillo once in a while. He didn't know if Yurkich had ever been pretty, but the life of a homicide cop had taken that away if she had. The weight of the job was in her eyes. The same thing Danny saw when he looked at himself in the mirror.

Boston or Somerset, it didn't matter. They were on the job, and in this together. All four of the detectives wanted to solve the case without outside help. But if they could confirm the connection—or if there was another murder—they might have to call in the State Police. Eventually, if it appeared that the perp had crossed state lines, it might even involve the FBI. For now, though, it was just two bizarre cases, and four homicide detectives who weren't at all happy about the way things were going.

"We've missed something, I just know it," Danny whispered to himself, shaking his head and letting his gaze crisscross the screen.

They had done the requisite background checks, interviewed the family and co-workers of the victims, but there were no leads. No leads, and no apparent connection between the two men. Not that he had expected to find any. Jaffarian was a computer software salesman from Newton. Sullivan was a dockworker from Dorchester. It was possible the killer had chosen his victims at random, but usually there was a pattern. Some kind of connection.

And at least so far, he didn't see a single thread connecting Jaffarian to Sullivan.

"Good morning, partner."

Danny turned to see Audrey stride into the squad room. She was wearing sunglasses set back on top of her head, a cream-colored blouse, and a copper-colored skirt. Audrey dressed well—she always looked stylish—but skirts were unusual for her. No more unusual, however, than the broad smile on her face and the lightness of her tone.

"Hey," he said, smiling doubtfully. "You're awfully chipper this morning."

"Yes. I am," she agreed, nodding. She set her purse down and propped herself against her desk, crossing her legs at the ankles. "So, what've we got on the docket for today?"

"Nothing. It's quiet. I'm looking at unsolveds."

"Meaning the Baptist."

Danny frowned. He didn't like the name, but Audrey and Jace Castillo had both taken to using it. Yurkich was a quiet one, but Danny had the idea she didn't like it any more than he did. Slick and Jenna had found traces of a bloody cross drawn on the second victim's forehead. It could mean nothing at all, but they were reading religious significance into it, calling the killer The Baptist. But Sullivan was Catholic, and Jaffarian was Armenian Orthodox. If there was a religious element, it was solely in the killer's mind, and Danny wasn't going to waste time going down that route unless they had something a little more concrete to go on.

"Yeah," he agreed, glancing at his computer screen. Then he frowned. "But you're not dodging me that easily. I'm a detective, Miss Gaines. You're not a stranger to mood swings, but something tells me you've got a reason to be so giddy this morning."

Audrey raised an eyebrow and tried for her trademark withering glance. She couldn't wipe the smile off of her face, however, and so it was hardly as devastating as she might have hoped.

"First of all, I have never been *giddy*. Not even in junior high school. Second, the next mood swing you see will be my foot swinging toward your produce section."

"Ouch!" Danny said, crossing his legs with a grin.

But then Audrey paused and glanced out the window. She sighed and moved around her desk to settle into her chair and turn on her computer. "Since you asked, though," she said without looking up, "I'm in a good mood because I went to dinner last night with Henry Bolling."

Danny grinned. "You had a date? Audrey Gaines went

out on a date? Did you hold hands? Make shy eyes? Did you get a good night kiss?"

He expected her usual response to his teasing, some brutal retort coupled with the old-fashioned glare o' death. Instead, Audrey gave him a sassy smile. "D. All of the above."

"My, my, my." Danny shook his head, comparing this Audrey with the cranky birthday Audrey of three weeks ago. "Will wonders never cease? Maybe turning forty-five was the best thing that ever happened to you."

Her smile faded. "Don't push your luck."

"There you are. That's the partner I know and fear. You had me worried, there, for a minute."

"Say what you like," she replied, her smile returning. "No way anything's going to tarnish my morning."

"So, Hank Bolling. Firefighter. He's a good-looking guy. Muscleman, if I recall."

"Oh, yes. The man is fine, fine, *super*fine."

Once again, Danny laughed, shaking his head and sighing in amusement. Of all the developments that came his way in the course of a day, this was one he never would have expected. Audrey had dated several men in the time they'd been partners, but he had never seen her so obviously taken with a guy. He silently wished her the best, hoping her firefighter treated her well, but he kept those thoughts to himself, not wanting to "tarnish" her morning.

After Audrey got herself some coffee, they settled down to work. She checked her messages and returned a phone call to the daughter of a hit-and-run victim who'd been killed the week before. Danny returned to the Sullivan case. To the Baptist. The good feelings Audrey had brought into the squad room suffused him, and though his frustration lingered, he felt more hopeful now. What he needed was a fresh perspective.

He pulled out the hard-copy paper files on Michael Sullivan and started perusing them again. Nothing grabbed him. His eyes began to glaze, he had read these pages so many times. He riffled through several other pages, interviews with family members. Darcy Sullivan, the victim's wife, was a petite brunette who must have been attractive once upon a time. Time had not been kind to her. She was roughly his own age, but Danny thought she looked a decade older at least. He chalked it up to a hard life and her relationship with her husband. The man had been a drinker, often out of work, and he never passed by a bar brawl without throwing a punch or two.

Darcy had insisted that her husband see a therapist, but that had lasted only four sessions before Michael Sullivan quit. They had learned all of this interviewing his wife. Although spouses are often considered the first, most likely, suspect, neither he nor Audrey had seriously considered the woman as her husband's killer. There was no connection to Jaffarian, and no—

"Hold on," Danny muttered to himself. He flipped a couple of pages. Nodded to himself. Then he went to the computer and clicked open the file on Nicholas Jaffarian. "Son of a bitch."

Audrey got up from her chair and came over to his desk. "What? You've got something?"

"Try this on for size. Darcy Sullivan works as an administrative assistant at a law firm in Cambridge. When she wanted her husband to see a therapist, she got a recommendation from one of the paralegals there for a Dr. Virgil Cosgrove. Guess who else was a patient of Dr. Cosgrove?"

Audrey raised an eyebrow. "Nicholas Jaffarian."

"Oh, yeah."

Dr. Cosgrove's Cambridge office was three blocks from Harvard University, on Ellery Street, a side street that ran beside a park lined with trees. Danny sat in a chair nearest the window in Cosgrove's office and tried not to bite his tongue while Audrey questioned the man. Cosgrove was in his early fifties, maybe six feet tall and at least forty pounds overweight. He had round, rimless eyeglasses that were too big for his face, curly hair, and a mustache, both of which were dyed a reddish brown. Danny had never understood men who dye their hair, but then, he didn't have a single gray hair yet, so maybe time would change his mind.

Though he didn't think so.

"Doctor, I'm afraid you're not being very helpful," Audrey said, trying to be as pleasant as she was able.

When they did what police call a "Mutt and Jeff" routine, Danny was usually the one who tried to charm people during questioning. Audrey played the role of hard-ass particularly well. Today, she was handling the tension a lot better than he was. Danny was grateful to Hank Bolling for that.

They had called Jace Castillo before coming over, but he and his partner, Detective Yurkich, were out on another case. Danny would update them later. Not that there was going to be much to tell, judging by the way things were going at the moment.

Cosgrove smiled and spread his hands wide like a magician proving he had nothing up his sleeve. His leather chair creaked as he leaned back in it. "I'm sorry, Detective. I can confirm that both of the men you're talking about have been my patients at one time or another. I don't remember Michael Sullivan very well, but Nick Jaffarian has been my patient for many years. I was very sorry to hear the news when he was killed. I hope you catch the person responsible."

"But," Audrey said, "you're not going to help us catch that person."

The doctor blinked his eyes several times and then removed his glasses. He began to clean them with the end of his striped tie. "I'm sorry, Detective, that you view it as noncooperation. That's not my intention. I promise you that if I saw any connection between the two men that would help you, I would reveal that to you. I'm not a particularly stubborn man. Not with something like this."

"The difference, Doctor," Danny said, tearing his gaze from the peaceful image of the park and glaring at the man, "is that we're homicide investigators, and you're not. This is what we do. Why not let us decide what would help us and whether there's a connection? Because right now, Doctor? Right now, *you're* the connection. That makes you our only suspect."

Cosgrove only sighed tiredly and rubbed his eyes before replacing his glasses. "Detective . . . Marciano, is it? I've already explained where I was when both men were killed. Please, I have patients to see. I wish I could help you, but you're asking me to break the confidentiality agreement I have with all of my patients."

Audrey leaned forward in her chair, and now Cosgrove seemed to react to her presence in a way he had not before. Even in a good mood, Audrey could be intimidating.

"Dr. Cosgrove, privacy in America is not what it used to be. Your confidentiality agreement with your patients dies along with them. You know that. We can compel you to cooperate."

Any trace of a smile was gone from Cosgrove's face. He adjusted his glasses on the bridge of his nose and rose from the chair, striding toward the door. This was their clue that the meeting was over.

"If you can compel me, Detective, then that's what you'll have to do. My legal obligation of confidentiality may have ended with the deaths of these men, but my moral obligation remains. If you are not willing to accept my assurance that there's nothing in their files that will help you, then you are, of course, welcome to get in touch with my attorney."

He opened the door and held it for them. Audrey hesitated only a moment, and then she rose. Danny waited a moment longer, took a deep breath, and stood up. He supported individual privacy as much as anyone. Especially in recent years, it had been a commodity that was growing more and more scarce. But this sort of crap really pissed him off.

As he followed Audrey out the door, he shot Dr. Cosgrove a harsh look. "We'll be in touch, I can assure you."

Down on the sidewalk, the warm summer breeze rustled the trees in the park across the street. Danny tried to shake off his annoyance but found he could not. "What'd you make of that?" he asked.

Audrey did not even glance at him as she marched toward their car. "I'll tell you this much. The son of a bitch tarnished my shiny, happy morning."

*I hope she's having a good time, but I've gotta confess, I hope she's not having too good a time.*

Jenna lay on the bed in her room at Virginia Rosborough's apartment and stared at the screen of her laptop. Suddenly the Instant Message conversation she was having with Hunter had turned private, and she glanced at her partially open door. Not that anyone was going to come in and read over her shoulder, but she didn't feel like this was her place at all. It was as though she were visiting friends or, more accurately, relatives she didn't really like.

It was the last day of June. Jenna had become accustomed to her summer sublet. But that did not mean she was comfortable there. Jeff was all right, but Virginia . . . *brrrrr.* Calling her "the Ice Queen" didn't even come close. The girl spent every waking moment at the library, and yet even when she wasn't around, the apartment had a seriously uninviting quality. It was a nice place, but Virginia's coldness had tainted it.

Her I.M. screen beeped.

*Jenna? Where'd you go?*

It was Hunter. They had been Instant Messaging a lot in the last few weeks. His time back home in Louisiana had begun darkly. How else could it have begun when he was returning for the first summer he had ever spent at home without his older sister, Melody? The two had fought the way siblings do, but they had been close. Hunter had filled the void in his life with school, with his friends, and especially with Yoshiko. But now he was sleeping in his old bedroom, next to the empty room where Melody had once played her music too loud.

And yet, Jenna had been pleasantly surprised by the news arriving on her computer screen from down south. Hunter's mother was an alcoholic, but she had started going to meetings and had not had a drink since April. Several of his high school friends had dragged him white-water rafting. All in all, he was doing pretty well. But then, there was the issue of Yoshiko.

*I'm here. Sorry, just lost track of my brain for a second,* she typed.

*Happens to the best of us,* Hunter replied.

Jenna stared at the screen, trying to decide how to reply to his comments about Yoshiko having too good a time at home in Hawaii.

*Too good a time?* she asked. *In what way?*

*Don't know. It's just that I almost never see her online, and it takes a couple of days for her to reply to e-mail. Trouble in paradise? Maybe. Maybe not. I just wish it felt like she missed me as much as I miss her. And now I'm being a total girl.*

Jenna laughed. *Nothing wrong with being a girl*, she wrote. *Trust me. I'm one. And for the record, I've noticed the same thing. But she's probably just busy. You were just home for spring break. Yoshiko hasn't been back since Christmas. Her family is pretty close. I'm sure they've got her running around. Have you mentioned to her how you feel?*

*No. And don't you mention it either. I know how you are about solving problems.*

*I'll be good*, she typed. *But you should say something. Get some peace of mind. And if you do, make sure to give her crap from me. I'd like to hear from her more too.*

*Will do. GTG, though. Going into New Orleans with my mother to meet some of her friends. Just what I wanted to do today!* :)

*Ah, you'll have fun. Com'on. It's New Orleans. CU lata.*

*Later*, Hunter typed.

The icon representing him in her I.M. window showed that he had logged off.

For a moment, Jenna just lay there on the bed staring at the screen. She debated e-mailing Yoshiko and asking her what was going on, but she was afraid it would come off as an accusation. If she had a chance to bring it up in some subtle way, of course she would. Otherwise, it would have to wait seven weeks, until Yoshiko returned to Somerset. Still, she felt bad for Hunter. And she was a bit hurt for herself as well. She had been working four days a week since classes had ended, hanging out with her father and Shayna, going over the wedding plans, trying to convince her future stepmother—and how weird was *that* to consider—that she had enough flowers for the ceremony. But even with all that, Jenna always had time for her friends, especially Yoshiko.

With a sigh, she shut down the laptop, closed it, and got up from the bed. She stretched, hearing bones popping in her back, and went to the half-open door of her room. The living room was empty, the apartment quiet, and she went to the kitchen to get something to drink.

Jeff was seated at the table, leaning back in a chair and reading a book.

Jenna jumped a little when she saw him, a tiny sound escaping her lips.

"What?" Jeff asked, giving her a rare smile as he glanced up from the book. It looked like a hard science-fiction novel by a writer named Neal Stephenson, the sort of thing Jenna would never read.

"Nothing," she said, laughing nervously. "Just thought nobody was home. I got spooked when I saw you. It happens to me a lot."

She didn't mention to him that she had been attacked during her first semester and beaten up. Any time she thought she was alone—at home, in the office, wherever—and found she wasn't, it took her a moment to adjust.

"Sorry," Jeff said, a heartfelt expression on his face.

"No, no. It's me. I'm a goofball." She went to the refrigerator and found, to her dismay, that there wasn't any Coke, so she poured herself a glass of orange juice instead.

"Enjoying your day off?" Jeff asked.

Jenna did a little flourish with her hands, showing off her ensemble of gray cotton shorts and oversize Somerset T-shirt. She had not even bothered to take a shower yet today. "Don't I look relaxed?"

"Oh, very."

"How was your anatomy class this morning?"

Jeff closed the book, holding his page with a finger. "Not bad, actually. Thanks to you." She started to demur, but he wouldn't let her get a word in. "Seriously, Jenna. Studying with you is really helping."

"I'm glad. And though it requires studying when I'm not supposed to have to study, oddly enough, I'm enjoying it. If pathology is really what I want to do, I'm going to need to know all that stuff, anyway."

"I'd rather work with patients who have a pulse," Jeff said, looking a little bemused.

"Nah. Sometimes they die on you. Then there's all that paperwork, not to mention guilt. The M.E. can't ever lose a patient. Which is a bonus."

They both laughed, and Jenna leaned against the sink, sipping her juice. He was a bit nerdy and eccentric, completely not her type, but he was sweet and a good listener. She'd found herself telling him her life story, including her star-crossed love life with Damon and Danny. It was really nice to be able to talk about it with someone, but a surprise, too. As quiet as he was, Jenna doubted she ever would have even noticed Jeff if they hadn't ended up living together.

Which made her wonder if Yoshiko might actually have met someone over the summer, and if Hunter really did have something to worry about when they all got back to school.

The glare of the autopsy room lights glinted off the steel table and made the exposed organs of the victim gleam. His name was Kirk Mayr, twenty-two years old, from Roxbury. Dyson was off for the day, and Jenna was assisting. Slick had told her the story of Mayr's death before he began the autopsy.

The guy was a bicycle messenger. He had darted through the wrong intersection at the wrong time and had been struck by a woman driving a Cadillac. He hit her windshield with enough force to crack it and went up and over the car, even as she slammed on the brakes. Now Kirk Mayr was on Dr. Slikowski's table, more exposed than he had ever been before, or ever would be again. The truth was, he was never going to be *anything* again.

It was always worse for Jenna when it was someone young. Someone close to her own age.

Slick was as thorough as always. It didn't matter that there were witnesses, that there was no real mystery about how Kirk Mayr had died. Anytime anyone died violently, an autopsy was called for. It didn't have to be murder or suicide. A drowning or a car accident merited the same close scrutiny. That was simply the way things were done, and Slick wasn't going to give any less attention to the people whose deaths posed no great mystery.

The M.E. had opened the chest and removed the organs in a single block before separating them. One by one he had given them to Jenna so she could weigh them. Slick had taken a sample of vitreous fluid from Mayr's left eye, which Jenna found curious. It was a test Slick did sometimes and skipped at other times, and she had never quite figured out how he made that decision. When they were done with the organs, they would be put back inside the cadaver, and Slick would sew Kirk Mayr's chest shut. In the final step of the autopsy, the top of Mayr's skull would be removed and his brain examined.

Or, at least, that was what was supposed to happen.

"Jenna?"

She glanced up from the dissection tray to find Slick looking at her over the top of his mask. "Yes?"

"Care for a challenge?"

Curious, she smiled. "Always."

He sat up a bit straighter in his wheelchair. Jenna loved it when he got like this, embracing the mentor-student relationship they had developed. Walter Slikowski saw in Jenna someone a bit like himself—well, not quite as uptight, maybe, but otherwise—and he enjoyed testing her mind.

"You know I don't like to make any comments until the autopsy is complete and all the results are in."

"I can hear a 'but' coming."

Slick nodded. "This young man was not killed by the car that struck him. The answer to this is simple, once you see it, but I want you to tell me what I'm going to write on my report under 'cause of death.'"

"All right," she said, putting down her scalpel and

going to the autopsy table to look down at the body. She glanced back at the dissection tray but saw nothing out of the ordinary in the kidney she had been examining.

"Talk it out," Slick suggested.

Jenna shot him a sidelong glance, then held one finger of her bloodstained glove up in front of the surgical mask that covered her lips to hush him. She was not going to give him the satisfaction of talking it out, explaining the process. Not if he was going to give her easy ones. She didn't have the answer yet, but he had said himself that it was simple. And if the car had not killed Kirk Mayr, a handful of things immediately presented themselves to her.

She looked at the dead man's eyes, at the burst blood vessels there, a result of the trauma. But there was a yellow, unhealthy glaze to them as well, common to some of the junkies and overdose victims they'd had on this table. That explained why he had taken the vitreous sample, at least.

The organs had all been removed, so she only gave a cursory glance inside the hollowed chest cavity. Nothing looked out of the ordinary there, and Slick had said it would be obvious. There were no bullet wounds, that was for certain, so it wasn't some drive-by shooting. Cops could make mistakes, but they probably weren't going to miss something like a bullet hole.

Most of the organs had been sampled and weighed already. She had set them out on trays, and now she went over to the dead man's heart. If she examined it closely enough, she might be able to tell if he'd died of a heart attack, but she kept coming back to Slick saying it was simple, "once you see it."

The dead man's stomach was on a tray. She had not studied it, but had just weighed it and taken a sample as protocol demanded. Now she went back to it and slid her fingers into the incision Slick had made. She wanted to glance over at him to see if he would give her any indication that she was on the right track. A stomach's contents were always helpful in determining the time of a person's death, but sometimes they helped with the cause as well.

She opened up Kirk Mayr's stomach.

It was filled with dozens of little crystalline balls that looked like rock candy. Some of them were almost entirely digested, but others were only partially dissolved. Jenna winced and turned her eyes away. With a shudder she removed her hands from the stomach and turned toward Slick. "Accidental overdose. That's your cause of death."

"Precisely," the M.E. replied, nodding proudly. "But why accidental?"

"He couldn't have been biking around Boston with that much crack in his belly. He's either a dealer or a supplier. The car hit him. The cops were coming. The ambulance was coming. He had to get rid of the crack, and somehow he managed to eat it all without anyone realizing what he was up to."

Slick had been sitting forward, but now he relaxed into his chair and quietly applauded. "Well done. Very well done."

Jenna beamed.

"I'm nearly through. It's well past lunchtime. Why don't you head back up to the office? I'll be along in a while."

She hesitated, but he insisted, so she stripped off her gloves, removed her mask and jacket, washed up, and told him to call upstairs if he needed anything. Once upon a time, she never would have been able to even think about eating lunch so soon after an autopsy. But like the burning, stinging smell of formaldehyde from the row of sample jars in Slick's autopsy room, she had gotten used to it.

Even as she ate the chicken salad sandwich she had brought from the apartment, Jenna felt a swell of pride. Yes, it *had* been simple. One look in the stomach, and the pieces had fallen into place. But it still had required some logic and a basic understanding of pathology. And Slick had been pleased.

Still thinking about Kirk Mayr's foolhardy death, she spread the day's *Boston Herald* out on her desk. *July 12*. She bought it on her walk to campus in the mornings because its tabloid size made it easier than the *Globe* to read at work. As she ate, she skimmed through the newspaper for stories of interest.

Her attention was seized by a headline at the top of page seven: "BODY WASHES UP ON REVERE BEACH." Jenna frowned, knitting her eyebrows as she quickly scanned the news item. Her sandwich was all but forgotten in her hand. The article revealed that yesterday, an early morning jogger had discovered the fully clothed body of an unidentified male on the beach. *Fully clothed,* Jenna thought, so he hadn't drowned while swimming.

As she read on, she saw that an anonymous source with the Revere Police Department had confirmed her instinct, noting that the man was not likely to have been swimming or to have fallen overboard from a boat because of the clothes he was wearing. Not too many people went boating wearing a sports jacket and tie. The condition of his body indicated that the victim had not been in the water for more than a few hours before being discovered on the sand.

The investigation was ongoing. Anyone with information regarding the man's drowning or his identity was urged to contact the authorities.

Jenna stared at the newspaper.

Though the drowning murders of Nicholas Jaffarian and Michael Sullivan had lingered in the back of her mind, she had kept them there. It was not her job to investigate murders. She worked for the M.E. Sometimes Slick became involved and aided the police in investigations, but only when he had a theory or when he was asked for his help. There were already homicide detectives from two cities working these cases. Now the Revere drowning made it three, and the State Police would probably be brought in if anyone discovered a solid connection.

And why was she so sure there was?

There was nothing in the article about chlorine in the man's stomach . . . nothing about the man being dumped on the beach after being drowned elsewhere.

But that bit about how he hadn't been in the water very long . . . that small and apparently insignificant detail got to her. She was not certain this most recent drowning was related to the others, but in her heart she believed it was. As much as she had been trying to keep her distance from her work, from the lives of the people whose empty husks came across the autopsy table every day, she could not ignore this one. Just in case none of the others saw the story or made the connection, she would bring it up to Dr. Slikowski.

Just in case.

# c h a p t e r 7

"Too many choices . . . too many choices."

A John Mayer CD was playing in the background, but Jenna was barely aware of the music, and the lyrics were certainly lost to her. Her mind was otherwise occupied. She muttered to herself as she scanned through the fall course listings on the Somerset University Web site. It was the middle of July by now, and she had long ago pre-registered for her fall classes, but after coming home from work, she couldn't help but take another look at the range of courses being offered.

*Stop second-guessing yourself.* But that wasn't as easy as her Jiminy Cricket conscience made it sound. With the exception of the economics courses, everything looked so interesting to her that she wished there was a way she could take even more classes. But she was already carrying a full load of six classes, and taking gross anatomy and developmental biology in the same semester would be like some kind of academic death wish. Add those to her work-study job with Dr. Slikowski and she would be lucky to have a couple of hours a week to try living *some* kind of life.

Even so, she continued to peruse the Web site. The course description for Women in America to 1900 made it sound pretty interesting. And it was taught by Professor Aili Heikkinen, who was new on the campus this year but had already earned a rep as one of the most dynamic teachers at Somerset.

Jenna thoughtfully curled a strand of hair around one finger. It might be worth adding Women in America and dropping something else. She could save music theory for the spring semester, or even next year. *Too many choices,* she thought. It was almost impossible to make up her mind.

Focused as she was on the computer screen, Jenna still jumped every time Virginia made a noise in the kitchen. Her roommate had given her permission to use the desktop computer because the DSL hookup was so much quicker than the dial-up service Jenna used with her laptop. Despite this courtesy, she couldn't help but feel as though she was intruding on Virginia's space by just being in the apartment.

Jenna clicked on the highlighted course description and scanned the list of books she'd be reading if she took the class. After another few seconds, she gave a little sigh and chuckled softly to herself. "Ah, what the hell," she said. "You're only young once, right?"

"Are you talking to me?" Virginia called from the

kitchen. She had arrived home earlier than usual from the library and was cooking supper for herself. She hadn't even asked if Jenna would like to join her. Jenna found herself wishing that her roommate would move into the library permanently, or at least make a little effort to not act like she viewed Jenna's presence as an intrusion. After all, she was paying rent too.

"Ah—no. No," Jenna replied. "Just talking to myself."

Whatever Virginia was cooking, it sure smelled good. The spicy aroma filled the apartment, and Jenna's stomach growled. But she made it a point not to hang around, especially whenever Virginia was in the kitchen. Sighing softly, she closed the window on the computer and shifted the cursor over to the Windows Start box, preparing to shut it down. Virginia might have appeared generous when she allowed her to use her computer, but Jenna suspected—like everything else with Virginia—that it was all an act. At least she would be out of there soon. It might seem like forever while she was living it, but it wouldn't be that long until all of her friends would come back to school, and she and Yoshiko would be living in Whitney House.

"Do you need to use the computer?" Jenna asked. Her finger was poised on the mouse button, ready to shut it down.

"No. Thank you," Virginia said, officious as ever.

Jenna clicked on Shut Down. Just when the screen winked off, the telephone rang. Before Jenna could move to answer it, Virginia picked up the kitchen extension.

"Hello," Virginia said, her tone even more aloof than

usual. There was a short pause, and then she said, "Yes, she is. Just a moment, please." Then she called out, "Jenna, it's for you."

Jenna got up from the desk and walked briskly into the kitchen, wondering who would be calling her. Virginia didn't even bother to make eye contact as she extended her arm and handed the phone to Jenna. A flicker of a smile passed across Jenna's face. As uncomfortable as Virginia could make her feel, there were times when her behavior was so devoid of any mark of kindness or courtesy that Jenna could only find it amusing. She started down the hallway to her bedroom and raised the phone to her ear, assuming it was Slick or Dyson, calling to ask her to come in to the office. "Hello?"

"I was hoping I'd catch you at home. I was afraid you'd still be at work." Yoshiko's voice was tinny and a bit distant, but Jenna felt a surge of joy just hearing her roommate's—her *real* roommate's—voice.

"Yoshiko! Oh, my God! Where are you? You're still in Hawaii, aren't you?"

"Of course I'm in Hawaii," she said, and Jenna could almost hear her smile. "Where did you think I would be?"

"No, I—of course you're still back home," Jenna said. She swung her bedroom door closed so Virginia wouldn't overhear her conversation, and sat down cross-legged on the edge of her bed. "So tell me. What's happening? Are you having the *best* time? It's so great to hear your voice again."

"You too," Yoshiko said.

Yet Jenna sensed a strange detachment that didn't seem like it was just the long-distance connection. She remembered Hunter's suspicions from their I.M. chat, and she shifted uneasily on her bed. Outside the window, the late afternoon sunlight was dull with humidity. "Hey. Is everything all right?" Jenna asked. The words were out of her mouth before she could stop them.

"Yeah. Yeah, of course. Why do you ask?"

"Oh. No reason," Jenna replied, cringing inwardly. "It's just that I—"

She cut herself off, but realized that it was already too late. Yoshiko knew her well enough to guess that Jenna was holding something back.

"You what—?" Yoshiko said, prodding.

Jenna wished she'd taken some time to think everything through before saying anything. She was angry at herself. But she had already said too much. The only way out of this conversation was the truth.

The silence between them went on for far too long.

"It's nothing serious," Jenna said at last. "It's just that . . . look, I was talking to Hunter on I.M. and—"

"I know," Yoshiko interrupted her. After a quiet moment, she sighed audibly and repeated the words. "I know." Just from the defeated tone in her voice, Jenna knew something really *was* wrong. "Well . . . are you going to tell me about it?" Jenna asked. "Or should I use my extraordinary psychic powers?"

Her attempt to lighten the mood was rewarded with a soft chuckle on the other end of the line. "There's really not that much to tell," Yoshiko said. "It's just that I—"

Yoshiko paused as though she did not know how to continue. In the eternity of that hesitation, Jenna could not help but imagine the worst. "You hooked up with someone else," Jenna said, hating the sound of the words.

"No! It isn't . . . it's not like . . ." Yoshiko swore. "Okay, let me start that again. Do you remember me telling you about Tony Maleko?"

"I don't . . . wait, yeah. High school Tony? Crush-boy? You liked him, but he was oblivious."

"Totally. We were friends, but he didn't even seem to notice I was a girl. I had the crush of all crushes, especially senior year. Anyway, he's been home for the summer, too, and we've been hanging out a lot. And I mean a *lot*."

"Define 'hanging out,'" Jenna said. She began to gnaw on her lower lip.

"I've changed a lot since high school, you know," Yoshiko said, her voice lowering almost to a whisper. "Not like I'm some wild child now, but I'm more me than I ever was before. I feel like I was sleeping most of my life, and it took going to college to wake me up. And Tony, well . . . I guess he notices that."

There was another even longer pause, but Jenna said nothing, waiting for Yoshiko to unravel her feelings at her own speed. Even as she held her tongue, though, the tension winding up inside her made her want to scream. All she could think about was how much it would hurt

Hunter if Yoshiko broke up with him for some other guy. It was selfish even to think about, but if Yoshiko broke up with Hunter, it would change *everything*.

"I'm not . . . I mean, nothing's happened. I haven't cheated on Hunter or anything. I'd never do that," Yoshiko said, though whether she was trying to convince Jenna or herself was not entirely clear. "The thing is, I'd be lying if I said I wasn't tempted. And it's killing me."

Jenna let out a long breath and shook her head. "Look, Yoshiko, I'm not going to tell you what to do or what not to do. You've got to follow your heart, no matter how hard it is to do that. But whatever it is you feel, you know you owe Hunter the truth."

"I know. I do. But how can I tell him what I feel when I haven't figured it out myself? I love Hunter. At least, I think I do. But this new me, this just-woken-up girl who's trying to figure out life? Can she . . . I mean, can I do that while all my focus is on a commitment to one person? How do I know Hunter's who I'm supposed to be with?"

"Do you want an answer to that, or was it a rhetorical question?"

Yoshiko laughed, but when she replied, her voice was dead serious. "No. Answer."

"I'm not sure I believe there's a 'supposed-to-be' person. I think there's just what you feel, and how hard you work at feeling more of it. You *have* changed," Jenna said, and before Yoshiko could interrupt her again, she went on. "And that's a good thing. Look, I don't blame you for wanting to hook up with Tony. Hawaii's a long way from Massachusetts. A long way from Hunter. And to have crush-boy notice you after all this time— well . . ."

"Seriously," Yoshiko said. "I mean, there are times I wish I hadn't even come home for the summer, and then there are times when I wish I'd never left the Islands."

A terrible thought went through Jenna's mind. "You're not thinking about not coming back, are you?"

"No, of course not. I'm just really confused. Somerset is where I finally grew up. But now that I have . . . I guess it took getting some distance from there, being back home, for me to even start figuring out what it all means."

"Yeah? Well, when you do figure it out, let me know, will you? 'Cause you're not the only one with questions," Jenna said, falling back onto her bed. She stared at the ceiling. "Look, back to the point of all this. A girl's gotta do what a girl's gotta do. Otherwise, you'll end up regretting it."

Even as she said this, Jenna couldn't ignore the mental picture of Danny that arose in her mind. She had the distinct impression she was talking out loud to herself about *her* feelings for *Danny*, not Yoshiko's feelings for Hunter.

"Of course, exactly *what* you've gotta do is the real question," Jenna said, forcing a joking tone into her voice that she didn't really feel. "But no one can give you advice in that department. They can only give you opinions. That and four bucks'll get you a cappuccino at Starbucks . . . maybe. But I mean it. Follow your heart no matter what."

"Thanks, Jenna," Yoshiko said softly. "I think I really needed to hear that." And for the first time in the conversation, Jenna heard the warmth and friendliness in her roommate's voice that she'd been waiting to hear. She felt relieved, too, because she had suddenly become fearful that, over the summer, the three of them—she and Yoshiko and Hunter—might all change. It was nice to know that the bond of friendship between her and Yoshiko hadn't weakened with distance.

"I really miss you," Jenna said, shooting a glance at her closed bedroom door. She couldn't stop thinking that Virginia was listening to everything she was saying. Lowering her voice to a whisper, she added, "You have no *idea* how much I appreciate you as a roommate after living here with the Ice Queen."

They both giggled at that.

"Hey," Jenna said, "we should probably go. I don't want to run your phone bill up to the moon. What time is it there?"

"Noon, and you wouldn't believe how beautiful the weather is."

"I wish I could be there," Jenna said. "I'd like to see you, but I'm glad we talked. And I won't say a word about *any* of this to Hunter. As long as you promise you'll be straight with him when you figure things out."

"I do. I promise. And hey, I'll be seeing you in a— what—five weeks, right? Not even!" Yoshiko said brightly. "I love you and I really miss you."

"You too," Jenna said. "Bye."

Yoshiko said her final good-bye, and Jenna slowly

lowered the phone from her ear and switched it off. She lay on her bed and turned her face to gaze out her window, but only for a minute or two. Sucking in her breath, she decided it was about time she took her own advice. Without thinking it through, she clicked the telephone back on and quickly dialed the number for Danny's apartment. Her heart was lodged in her throat as she waited for him to pick up.

"I can't believe it!" Jenna said, her eyes widening with surprise. "You *seriously* have never seen *Citizen Kane*?"

Danny Mariano glanced down at the sidewalk and shook his head.

"But it's a classic. It's *the* classic. And *you're* the old guy here."

Danny raised his hands as though helpless. "I just never had a chance to see it. I don't have a lot of free time to catch many movies. I'm pretty busy with the whole 'protecting and serving' thing."

"Yeah, but come on. *Citizen Kane* came out in nineteen forty-one. You've had decades to see it!"

"Hey!" Danny grinned and gave her a light punch on the shoulder. "How old do you think I am, anyway?"

Jenna knew she shouldn't tease him about his age, shouldn't make the extra effort to keep reminding him how much older he was. But it was like an itch at the back of her brain that she just had to scratch. The years that separated them in age separated them in other ways as well. It frustrated her to be forced to accept that such a small detail could have such sway over their relationship.

*Relationship,* she thought with a trace of sadness. *Whatever the hell* that *means.*

Throughout the evening, as they strolled around Harvard Square, Jenna kept fighting the impulse to hold Danny's hand. The warm summer night had brought out just about everyone who hadn't gone away to Cape Cod or the New Hampshire mountains for the weekend. The eclectic citizens of Cambridge moved in a ballroom dance rhythm along sidewalks and through shops and restaurants, crossing the streets in mobs whether the light was red or green. There were neo-goths, neo-punks, frat boys, and skate rats, and herds of students and once-students who didn't fall into any easy categorization. But what Jenna noticed most was that there were so many couples. It was a perfect night for lovers.

But she and Danny weren't lovers. They were just friends.

*Just friends.*

Nights like tonight, those could be the two cruelest words in the English language.

They strolled through the Square, window shopping and watching the street musicians who performed on every corner. Acoustic guitars, accordions, flutes, trombones, and even a steel drum band filled the night with conflicting rhythms that magically blended with the noise of the traffic and the sounds of people talking and laughing, creating an almost carnival atmosphere.

As they wended their way along the crowded sidewalk, Jenna couldn't help but steal furtive glances at Danny whenever he wasn't looking at her. His smooth, dark olive complexion glowed with the multicolored city lights, and his eyes glistened whenever he smiled. She was so happy just to be with him.

"How 'bout some coffee, maybe an iced cappuccino before the movie?" Danny asked as they approached Cup o' Joe, a sidewalk café just around the corner from the Harvard Coop. They still had an hour or so to kill before the late showing of a digitally remastered version of *Citizen Kane*. A few feet away, a street magician was doing sleight-of-hand tricks for a small crowd.

Jenna wasn't really in the mood for coffee, either iced or hot. She was wired enough as it was, trying to figure out where she had gotten the nerve to call Danny and ask him to go out with her tonight, and what to do with him now that they were here. The truth was, she had not really expected him to say yes. She had been expecting that he'd be working late, like always.

"Maybe a smoothie or something," Jenna said. "A caffeinated Jenna is bad for everyone." She maneuvered her way between the white cast-iron tables and chairs, finally choosing one as far away from the sidewalk as possible so they could have a little bit of privacy.

Once they were settled and had ordered their drinks, she eased back in her chair, trying to relax. She kept telling herself that she should simply enjoy this for what it was—two good friends hanging out on a gorgeous summer night before catching a movie—but there were things that needed to be dealt with first.

She took a sip of her Raspberry Frostie and cleared her throat.

"So, I have to ask you something," she said. The frozen chill of her drink lodged in her chest and seemed to make her heart stop beating for a second or two.

"Yeah?" Danny said, frowning slightly as he looked at her. "What's on your mind?"

Jenna's mouth went suddenly dry, and she took another sip of her drink. She glanced downward, but then raised her eyes once more to meet Danny's gaze. "Aren't you, like, a detective or something?" she said, smiling weakly. Then she took a deep breath. "You've been kind of avoiding me, Danny. I just need to know if it's because you're afraid of what you feel, or because you're afraid of what *I* feel."

Danny leaned farther back in his chair. One hand came up to his face, and he absently ran his fingers over his stubbly chin. The sounds of the city seemed to fade away in the background as she looked into his eyes.

He quickly broke the stare, turning his head to look at the crowd. "I haven't been avoiding you, Jenna. Tonight . . . it just worked out, is all. Work has been—"

"Kind of quiet, actually," she interrupted, forcing him to focus on her. "Don't bullshit me, Danny. I'm not a cop, but I read the papers. I see the bodies that come across Slick's table. You've had your fair share, but the last few months haven't been nearly as bad as earlier in the year. Yeah, you've got these drownings, but how many times can you re-interview potential witnesses? I know you get depressed when you've got an unsolved case, but some of us actually realize that murder investigations aren't usually solved as quickly in real life as they are on TV. So, talk to me."

Danny frowned. "It's not just bodies, Jenna, and you know that. I don't know if it's the budget cuts and all or attitudes or what, but the whole department seems to be stretched really thin lately. And yeah, okay, The Baptist case is really grating on me. It's not my first unsolved, but most of them are bodies found on the side of the road somewhere. These killings are the same perp, and he's gone out of his way to make them attention-getters. Scumbags like that come in two varieties. The ones who are such glory hounds that they trip themselves up and get caught quickly, and the ones who are smarter than we are. It's been a couple of months since Jaffarian was dumped in the fish tank, Jenna. Bad enough I have no answer when someone in his family calls to ask if we've made any progress. But on top of that, I'm starting to think the bastard is smarter than me."

With a nod, Jenna reached out and placed a comforting hand on his arm. "That's a sucky feeling, isn't it?" She could not resist a little mischief. "But you must be used to it, from hanging around with me."

Danny laughed in spite of himself. Then all the humor left him and he studied her carefully. "Look, obviously you don't want to talk shop tonight, and neither do I. So let's get back to what you were not saying to me a minute ago."

Jenna gnawed her lip a moment, staring at him. "All right. Maybe I'm imagining it. But even if you haven't been avoiding me, I guess the truth is that I *have* been avoiding you."

For a moment, Danny was silent as he studied her, his eyes narrowed. Then he sat forward and put his hands on the table, and for a moment she thought he might reach for hers, but he didn't.

"Are you going to tell me why?"

Uncomfortable, Jenna shifted in her seat. She shot him a hard look that she hoped he understood. With just her eyes she tried to tell him how frustrated she was that he was making her do this. She could not believe for an instant that he didn't have at least a clue what she was talking about. At length she sighed. He was going to make her do it the hard way.

"It's like with my work," she said softly, almost to herself. "You know how I've been so afraid of getting too involved, so I've been trying to ease up. Take a few steps back and get some perspective. It's the same thing with . . . you know how strongly I feel about you."

"Of course I do," Danny said, lowering his voice until she could barely hear him above the city sounds. "And I think you know how I feel. But it's not as if that's news. This is . . . some things are . . ."

He stared at her. Then he shook his head with a small, self-deprecating laugh, and muttered, "Shit."

Danny reached across the table and covered her hands with his. Jenna stiffened, and he quickly pulled his hands away. Where he had touched her hands, her skin tingled.

"I'm a whirling ball of confusion, huh?" she said. She

fixed her gaze firmly on his again. "Here's what I've been thinking. It's crazy of me to close myself off like I've been doing. And it's cowardly. If I can't sort my own feelings out and deal with them right up front, then building a wall to hide behind isn't the answer either. And I don't want to hide what I'm feeling anymore."

"That's never a good thing," Danny said.

He started to smile at her, but then his expression dropped and he got that same intense, serious look he got whenever he was stewing about a case.

"You know what?" he said as he leaned back and folded his arms across his chest. "You're right. We only pretended to resolve this, just to avoid what we're feeling right now. We've been dancing around this issue for way too long, so let's get it out in the open. Put the cards on the table—right now—where we both can see them."

Jenna felt paralyzed. This was what she had wanted, but she had not expected it of Danny.

"All right, look." He shifted his chair closer to her but didn't reach out to touch her again. "Truth? I want to sleep with you. I'm pretty sure you feel the same. I love you as my friend, but I'm a little bit in love with you too. Maybe more than a little. And I know the feeling's mutual. We've touched on that. So there they are—all the cards on the table. Is that too blunt for you?"

Absolutely stunned, Jenna shook her head slowly from side to side. "No, it . . . uhh . . . works for me, too."

Danny nodded. "Okay. We've both said it. But the thing we have talked about is . . ." And here he softened, searching her eyes as if seeking to protect her from his own words. "It's not going to happen. It can't happen. Not now, anyway, and maybe not ever. The question is, can we stop avoiding each other now, stop avoiding this thing that's between us? I mean, can we just accept what we feel, not try to make it go away but just accept it, and still deal with each other?"

For a long moment, Jenna only stared at him, her heart aching. Then she uttered a small, conspiratorial laugh.

"What's funny?" Danny demanded.

"So, you *were* avoiding me. Big fat liar."

He shrugged, trying not to smile. "Yeah . . . well . . . maybe a little."

There was a long pause in the conversation as they sized each other up. Finally, Jenna nodded.

"If we can stop pretending that we don't feel this way, that we're not supposed to feel this way, that there's some magic wand we can wave to make us, like, sitcom friends, I think I can live with that. I think that was what I was running from. This idea that I was supposed to act like knowing it wasn't going to happen should make me not have these feelings anymore."

When Jenna took another long sip from her Raspberry Frostie, the taste was spectacular. An amazing sensation of relief flooded through her. The crowd watching the street magician suddenly burst into gales of laughter and applause, and Jenna had the weird feeling that their reaction was for her and Danny, not for the entertainer. She smiled so wide, her cheeks started to ache. She felt almost giddy and had to fight back an urge to laugh out loud.

"We can do this?" Danny said.

"Yes. Absolutely," Jenna replied. She grinned. "So, you want to sleep with me, huh? Dirty old man."

This time Danny laughed out loud, shaking his head.

Jenna stood up from the table and reached for his hand. "Come on." All the uneasiness between them had evaporated. As they clasped hands, she pulled him away from the table, leaving their unfinished drinks behind. "Let's see what else is happening in this town."

Danny dropped a few bills on the table and was smiling like a kid as they walked side by side out onto the sidewalk. For the next hour or so, they wandered around Harvard Square, stopping occasionally to drop handfuls of spare change into the upturned hats or opened instrument cases of the musicians. They laughed and talked about all sorts of mundane things. It wasn't until they were standing in line at the movie theater that Jenna brought up something that was even close to work-related. "So you must have heard about the body that washed up in Revere."

"Sure," Danny said. "We got the report."

For the first time that evening—for the first time in a long time—Jenna felt totally comfortable just chatting with him about work and how their jobs intersected. It was one of many things that she enjoyed having in common with him.

"Slick was wondering if it might be related to the murder you and Audrey are investigating. He said something about looking into it."

The ticket line was longer than they had expected.

Apparently a lot of people hadn't seen *Citizen Kane* or wanted to see it in this new, modified format. The line was moving slowly, and Jenna felt suddenly self-conscious talking about something like this in public. It was business, after all, and they were out to have fun tonight. They were going to have to learn how to put—and keep—things in their places. Danny paid for their tickets, refusing the bill Jenna offered him to pay for hers.

"How 'bout I spring for the popcorn and drinks, then?" she said.

Danny considered for a moment, then shook his head. "At these prices? It's a major investment."

"Maybe that's why you don't go to the movies very often." Jenna laughed and touched his arm, but only for a moment.

"No. Usually it's because I don't have someone to go with."

"Well, you do tonight, and I can't watch a movie without an extra-large tub of popcorn in my lap. Come on."

She dragged him over to the concession stand, and once they had their arms loaded with treats, they started down the hallway to the door of the screening room.

"I'll check in with Slick first thing in the morning," Danny said, not missing a beat of their previous conversation.

They entered the darkened theater and looked around for two empty seats. Jenna preferred to sit ten to twelve rows from the screen, but all of those seats were already taken, so they had to be satisfied with something off to one side, almost all the way to the back. They got settled, but Jenna still felt odd, somehow, that they weren't holding hands.

*I can handle it, though,* she told herself as she replayed their conversation back at Cup o' Joe. She felt good about it.

Better than good.

Early the next morning, Jenna showed up for work at the hospital carrying a cardboard tray with three cups of Dunkin' Donuts coffee and a dozen assorted Munchkins. She didn't want to make a practice of providing coffee and doughnuts for Slick and Dyson, but she was feeling really good after hanging out with Danny last night. She had enjoyed spending time with him. It would have been fun even if all they did was walk around Harvard Square, go to the movie, and then hang out for a while talking afterward. But it had been better than that because—finally—they had confronted their feelings for each other without skirting around the issue or pretending they could make those feelings go away by denying them. Even though she wished things were different, she felt a huge weight lifted off her.

They couldn't be together. It was easier to deal with

that fact when she knew she could at least talk to Danny openly about it.

*"Not now, anyway,"* Danny had said.

She smiled as she thought of that phrase. In the spirit of their new openness, one of these days she was going to press him to elaborate on exactly what he'd meant by *that*.

But not now.

Not now, when she felt closer to him than ever. There were other guys she was close to, sure: Dyson. Hunter. Even Slick, though he was old enough to be fatherly and so that sort of didn't count. But with Danny, their deep, honest interest in each other added an intimacy that she had never really shared with anyone. Sure, she and Damon had been together, but she had never felt as free to be herself with him as she did with Danny.

It was all good.

They could hang out. They could *really* be friends now. And that was what she had always hoped. Losing him completely over their unresolved feelings would have crushed her. Now, though . . . Danny had enjoyed *Citizen Kane* more than she'd thought he would. They'd had a great time. Jenna was glad to see that he was open to new—or, in this case, old—things.

The movie had let out just after midnight, but in spite of the late hour, they had gone to Jillian's, a small, out-of-the-way café on Brattle Street, for coffee and dessert. Blueberry cheesecake was one of Jenna's many guilty pleasures. She hadn't gotten back to the apartment until two o'clock in the morning. Concerned that she might disturb Virginia, she had tiptoed down to her room after washing up, but apparently her roommate was a sound sleeper.

Jenna, however, felt wired from her night out and hadn't been able to fall asleep until some time after three. That meant she was functioning on less than four hours of sleep, but . . . so far, so good.

Dr. Slikowski was reviewing a file at his desk when Jenna bounced into the room, whistling some tune she could not have named. He glanced up at her over the rim of his glasses and smiled a greeting as she set the tray of doughnuts and coffee on her desk.

"'Morning," she called out merrily.

"You're awfully chipper this morning," Slick observed, placing the file on his desk and smoothing it with the heel of his hand. "I thought you didn't like it when the humidity got this high."

Jenna only smiled and brought him his coffee. "One sugar and whole milk, right?"

"Precisely," Slick said, taking the coffee cup from her. "But I know I don't pay you enough to spring for coffee and doughnuts."

"They're Munchkins," Jenna said mischievously. "I couldn't afford whole doughnuts on what you pay me. But I figured I could spoil you and Dyson just once."

"Well, it's appreciated. Thank you." His eye shifted to the paperwork in front of him as he wedged the plastic lid off the cup. Steam rose from his coffee, fogging the lenses of his glasses as he brought it up to his mouth.

"Looks like you'll have to drink the other two cups

yourself. Though I wonder how much caffeine you've already had today."

Jenna frowned, puzzled.

"Dr. Dyson has the day off. He and Doug are heading up to Cape Ann for a day of sailing with some friends, remember? That's why I asked you to come in early."

"Ohh, yeah. Right," Jenna said, snapping her fingers and nodding. She eyed the tray with the two remaining coffees and shrugged. "All the more for me, I guess."

"Actually, you may need it today." The back of Slick's wheelchair squeaked as he leaned into it, slid his glasses from his face, closed his eyes, and massaged the bridge of his nose. After a moment, he sighed, straightened up, and took a tentative sip of coffee. "We're going to be quite busy this morning."

Jenna shot him a questioning look as she raised the tab on the coffee lid. Holding the Styrofoam cup with both hands, she took a noisy sip, wincing from the heat.

"That man whose body washed up on the beach in Revere," Slick continued. "The one you read about in the newspaper the other day. I'd like you to accompany me to Mass General." He stretched his arm out and glanced at his watch. "They're expecting us in half an hour. I was just waiting for you to arrive before I left."

"Haven't they already done the autopsy?" Jenna asked. "Or are they holding off on it until you get there?"

"The autopsy has been completed. I was just reading the preliminary report. But I asked them not to release the body to the funeral home until I have a look at it." Slick took another gulp of coffee. "Are you going to share those doughnuts, or are they all for you?"

Jenna smiled, flipped open the box of Munchkins, and walked to Slick's desk, holding it out to him. His face lit up like a kid's as he studied the contents for a moment and then withdrew two glazed Munchkins. He popped one into his mouth, tipping his head back to savor the taste before washing it down with more coffee.

"I've already spoken with Detective Mariano about this," Slick said.

"He mentioned last night that he was going to call you."

Slick raised his eyebrows and looked at her, but he let the question that was in his eyes pass without comment.

"Who did the autopsy at Mass General?" Jenna asked.

"Dr. Hallett. Dr. Vieira is on vacation again all this week and next."

Jenna rolled her eyes heavenward. "Jeez. Must be nice." She bit a chocolate Munchkin in half and chewed thoughtfully. She guarded herself against saying anything negative about Dr. Hallett. She didn't want to come across as being petty or unprofessional. It didn't mean the man was incompetent just because she didn't care for his personality. And he had been very patient when he'd shown her the procedure for testing for trace chemicals in a subject's stomach.

Which reminded her . . .

"Was there any chlorine in the man's stomach like in the other cases?" It was just a hunch, but from the moment she had read about the strange circumstances of the body found on the beach, she had suspected that this incident was related to the other two murders. It *had* to be. She was surprised when Slick shook his head no.

"That isn't covered in the preliminary report, but Detective Mariano told me that his contact with the Boston police said there wasn't," Slick replied. "I've asked to have a look for myself. I had them fax it over and was just reviewing it." He gestured toward the paper on his desk.

"So why are you checking it out? You don't trust Dr. Hallett's report?"

Slick's expression turned stern. "Dr. Hallett is an excellent pathologist. He trained with the best."

"You mean you," Jenna said with a smile.

The medical examiner showed no sign that he had meant to amuse her. But Jenna was wise to him by now. Slick had a sense of humor, even though he rarely allowed anyone to discover that secret.

"Before I reach any conclusions, I *would* like to have a look at the body," he told her. "Not even the most complete report can substitute for actual hands-on investigation. The victim is Charles Flood, works as a loan office for a bank downtown. Forty-seven years of age. He lived on Beacon Street."

Jenna was trying to make Flood's drowning fit with the other two in her head. "Did any of the detectives mention a connection between this case and the other two?"

Slick took another sip of coffee and regarded Jenna with a long, steady gaze that made her feel a little nervous.

"I don't need to remind you that this is a police matter. Our part of the investigation is limited to the autopsy table. As the M.E., I advise and inform. That's all. This case has two police departments at work on it already, and if there is a connection, that will make three counting Revere. Our job at this point is simply to determine how and when Mr. Flood was killed."

"So it *was* homicide," Jenna said. "They know that much."

Slick popped a second glazed Munchkin into his mouth and washed it down with a final gulp of coffee. He nodded. "Oh, it was clearly murder."

"How did they determine that? What were the findings?" Jenna asked. She had to restrain herself from coming around behind Slick's desk and looking at the report.

Without another word, Slick tossed the coffee cup into the wastebasket. He pushed his wheelchair away from his desk and started to leave the office. Jenna held the door open for him and then walked along beside him down the hallway toward the back door.

"How do they know this guy was murdered?" Jenna asked again once they stepped outside into the parking lot.

The humid air lay heavily upon them as they walked the short distance to the van Dr. Slikowksi had had customized to allow him to drive. It was parked in the handicapped area close to the door. When he was about ten feet from the van, he pressed the button on his remote keyless entry to unlock the doors. The horn beeped once, and the lights flashed.

"You'll find out soon enough," Slick said, with just a hint of a smile.

When Jenna followed Dr. Slikowski into the autopsy room at Mass General, the homicide detectives from the Boston P.D. were already there waiting. Jace Castillo broke off a conversation with Dr. Hallett and nodded a friendly greeting, but his partner, Terri Yurkich, was standing off to one side. She looked a bit uncomfortable as she glanced at Charles Flood's pale, bloated body on the table. The man's chest was spread open, exposing the empty cavity.

"Isn't that lovely?" Detective Yurkich said, wrinkling her nose.

*You're in the wrong profession if you're squeamish about seeing dead people,* Jenna thought, but she reminded herself that it had taken her a while to get used to dealing with human corpses. Maybe Yurkich had not been a detective for all that long. Uniformed officers didn't usually end up at autopsies.

Still, even for Jenna, this particular corpse was difficult to look at. The stomach and chest had been stretched from bloating, and even the extremities were swollen after being immersed in the ocean. Gashes and bruises covered the body, probably from banging against the rocks and shells after washing up.

They exchanged greetings with the detectives, and then Slick was all business. He rolled his wheelchair as close to the table as he could get it.

"We can dispense with the preliminaries," he said,

speaking clearly for the voice recorder. He glanced at Jenna. "We're working under a bit of a time constraint. The visiting hours at the funeral home are this afternoon and evening, so we have to finish up with everything by noon so they can come and pick him up."

Jenna was still uncertain what Slick's motives were here. The pathologists at Mass General were more than competent. They had already photographed and detailed the external wounds and marks on the victim's body, and all of the internal organs had been removed, weighed, dissected, and put aside for analysis later. The man's stomach and lungs were lying in separate dissection pans on a lab bench against the far wall.

Confined as he was to his wheelchair, Slick could not get a full view of the body. Since their last trip here, Dr. Hallett had arranged mirrors in place above the autopsy table—just the sort of thing a dentist might use, but in this case, set up for Dr. Slikowski. Yet even that was hardly ideal. He indicated for Jenna to get close to the body and have a look.

"Tell me what you see," Slick said.

Jenna saw immediately what he had hinted at back at the office: There were two thin, deep cuts on the man's forehead, marking the pale skin directly between the man's eyes.

"It looks like he was cut with a knife or razor." Jenna leaned closer to inspect the wounds. "They're certainly not deep enough to have killed him."

Traces of blood had dried into dark brown lines that had scabbed over the superficial slices. Jenna turned to

Slick, who was watching her with an expectant look. She thought for a moment and then made another observation, this one for the record.

"The incisions are in the same location and are approximately the same size as the residual blood marks we found on Michael Sullivan's forehead."

"I'd expected something like this," Slick noted. "So even though there was no indication of chlorine in the victim's stomach and chest cavity, I'm suspicious that there may be a connection between this and the Sullivan case after all."

"Are you sure about that? The body wasn't in the ocean too long, but we're still talking hours," Castillo reminded them. "He's all banged up from the surf and rocks or whatever. It looks like some fish or crabs might have even nibbled on him. He could've been dragged along the bottom by the tide." He paused and shrugged. "Just playing devil's advocate."

"Are we sure it was murder? Absolutely," Slick said.

Jenna thought he sounded a bit snappy, and she almost cracked a joke that the next time she bought coffee, he was getting decaf, but she let it drop. This was a serious matter. "No. These cuts were deliberately made," she said. "The symmetry is too perfect."

"So what does this suggest to you?" Slick asked.

Jenna paused, her gaze fastened on the wound, its edges faded white from being submerged in the water. She considered for a moment, and then said, "If at first you don't succeed . . ."

"Try, try again," Slick finished for her, nodding in approval.

"The first time the killer did it," Jenna said, "the blood washed away. So this time, he wanted to make sure his message was clear. He cut the cross into the victim's forehead."

"That is my analysis," Slick said. "While we're here, we might as well run another test for chlorine in the stomach." Slick glanced from Jenna to the detectives. "Chlorine is very unstable and breaks down rather quickly. Even if there isn't any detectable quantity in the water found in the victim's stomach or chest cavity, trace amounts maybe have been absorbed by the stomach lining."

Feeling the expectant stares of everyone in the lab boring into her, Jenna took a deep breath and walked as confidently as she could over to the lab bench where the dissection pan that contained the dead man's stomach rested. The organ had already been cut open, and slices had been removed for later analysis. Picking up a scalpel and forceps, she leaned close and probed the tissue before cutting into the stomach lining. A thin liquid ran down the tip of her scalpel. She knew she could just be imagining it, but the tissue looked a bit lighter than she thought it should.

*Almost as if it's been bleached,* she thought, but she cautioned herself not to jump to any conclusions before she had evidence.

"Do you have a—"

Before she could finish her question, her eyes started to water, and she sneezed. Startled for a moment, she glanced back at Slick, who was watching her carefully.

"I need a test strip to check for chlorine," she finished, but her sneeze had already been enough to convince her. Lowering her surgical mask, she leaned close to the dead man's stomach and sniffed. The faint smell of chlorine immediately stung her nose, and she turned her head to one side and sneezed again.

"Here you go," Dr. Hallett said as he stepped toward her and handed her a plastic bottle of chlorine test strips.

Jenna's hands were shaking slightly as she unscrewed the cap and shook a strip of light blue paper into her palm. The room was hushed with expectation, and even though she was painfully aware that everyone was watching her, she focused on her work. Using the tip of her scalpel blade, she made a few small slices in the stomach lining and then pressed the tissue until a clear liquid flowed. Then she pressed the test strip against the stomach lining and stared at her wristwatch as she counted to ten.

Even before she pulled the test strip away, Jenna knew what the result would be. But she also knew that she had to have her suspicion confirmed scientifically or else it wouldn't do anyone any good—especially the victim. The rush of exhilaration she felt was undeniable as she straightened up, raised the test strip to the light, and saw that it had changed very slightly from light blue to light pink.

"The color change is barely detectable," she said, "but there does appear to be a small trace of chlorine in the stomach fluid." She made sure she spoke clearly for the tape recorder, but she was smiling as she turned to Slick, who nodded to her. It was strange, speaking so stiffly, so formally, but when the recorder was on, she wanted to sound professional.

Slick then turned and looked at the two detectives, who were standing off to one side, watching the proceedings. Castillo was grim while his partner, Yurkich, looked a shade or two paler than usual.

"It may be coincidental," Slick said. "We'll have to run some more exacting tests to determine if seawater can give us a similar result. But I think we have two things, now, that connect this man's death with the other two cases you and the detectives from Somerset are investigating. It might behoove us all to meet at my office later today so we can discuss the matter. We should have some more lab work done by then, as well. Agreed?"

Castillo nodded gravely, and Jenna felt she could almost read his thoughts. Because she was thinking the same thing . . . something nobody wanted to say out loud, at least not yet.

But if they conclusively determined that Mr. Charles Flood had been drowned in chlorinated fresh water before being dumped into the ocean, then things would grow even more complicated. With a single murder, the killer was usually a friend or relative of the victim. With two killings that were similar, the investigators could search for connections between them, like Jaffarian and Sullivan having both been patients of Dr. Cosgrove.

Once the number rose to three, and with no other solid leads, it became far more likely that there *were* no connections between the victims. That they had been selected at random by someone who simply wanted to draw blood, someone who just wanted to end lives.

Jenna was sure they had all suspected it earlier. Already they had given him a name—The Baptist—as if they had already been certain what they were looking for. Not someone on a revenge kick, or anyone with a money motive. They could no longer pretend this was an ordinary homicide case.

No. There was little doubt now. They were after a serial killer.

And without any real ties between the victims, they were going to have to wait for The Baptist to make a mistake, to give them a clue, before they had any real hope of catching him.

Jenna tried not to wonder how many more people would have to die before that happened.

"Damn it!" Jimmy Balzarini muttered as his car bucked and sputtered. It died with a harsh grinding sound of metal against metal. *"Damn* it!" The engine went dead, and he coasted to a stop, easing the car over to the curb. The headlights were still bright, so he knew it couldn't have anything to do with the battery, but *something* was definitely wrong. He turned the headlights off and waited a few seconds, counting to ten before he turned the key again.

The solenoid clicked a few times, but that was all.

He tried it a few more times, and still nothing happened. Slumping back in the seat, he closed his eyes and was silent for a moment. The only sound was the steady clicking of the hot engine as it started to cool down.

"Great . . . just frigging great," he whispered.

With a grunt, he opened his eyes and stared down the deserted road in front of him. The streetlights cast a powdery blue pall over everything. Shadows clung to the darkened doorways and boarded-over windows of the abandoned brick warehouses that lined both sides of Chelsea Street. The buildings were covered with the colorful graffiti of gang tags and logos. Overhead, etched against the night sky, loomed the dark shape of the Tobin Bridge. It looked like it might come crashing down at any moment. The strobe aviation warning lights at the top of the bridge flashed steadily in the night, but Jimmy couldn't tell if there was much or any traffic on the expressway.

Jimmy was here—underneath the bridge, by a row of abandoned warehouses near the dock—to do something he shouldn't be doing. *Wouldn't* be doing if he didn't need the money so badly. But he did need it, and if he could turn this deal, he'd be set for a while. It was as simple as that.

He patted both jacket pockets, feeling for his cell phone, and then realized he didn't have it with him. He remembered that Kim had asked to use it earlier in the evening, just before he went out. She must not have put it back in his jacket pocket.

"How many times do I have to . . ."

Jimmy's voice faded away as the glow of headlights appeared in his rearview mirror.

*It's the cops,* was his first thought, but he told himself not to worry. He didn't have any drugs in the car, so even if they stopped and talked to him, even if they searched him, the most incriminating thing they'd find was the roll of hundred-dollar bills in his jeans pocket. It might seem a little suspicious, him being alone in such a dangerous part of town so late at night, with two thousand dollars in cash, but there wasn't any law against having money in your pocket.

Jimmy squirmed down into the car seat and waited for the flashing blue lights to come on. He was already mentally rehearsing his excuse for being down by the docks at two o'clock in the morning. *Sorry, Officer. I was just visiting a friend who lives near Bunker Hill Community College, and I must have taken a wrong turn. Can you tell me how to get back onto the expressway?*

The car closed the distance, its headlights looming in the rearview. Then another thought occurred to Jimmy: *What if it isn't the cops? What if it's gangbangers?*

After making sure the windows were up and the car doors were locked, Jimmy shrank even further down into the seat, holding his breath and watching as the car crept up behind him. He clenched his fists until they throbbed, wishing he had a can of Mace with him, or maybe even a gun. It was stupid to come down here after dark without *some* kind of protection, but with his prior arrests, he was in enough trouble with the law as it was. Carrying an unlicensed handgun would have guaranteed him time inside.

Jimmy wasn't sure whether to turn, watch the car as

it passed, and try to look dangerous himself, or to pretend that he was asleep—maybe even dead—behind the wheel. Maybe the driver was just as nervous as he was about being in this neighborhood. Narrowing his eyes to slits and tilting his head slightly to one side, he leaned his forehead against the driver's window and watched as the car passed.

He saw right away that there was one person in the car—just the driver, no passengers. Not a cop car, not even an unmarked, and—thankfully—not gangbangers. Jimmy straightened up in the seat. This could be his salvation if he could get that guy to stop and help him. Maybe all he needed was a jump-start. He pressed down hard on the horn, letting out a single, long blast that echoed from the warehouses, but the car sped up a little as it pulled away. The brake lights flickered once as it rounded the corner and then disappeared behind one of the warehouses.

"*Damn* it!" Jimmy shouted, pounding the steering wheel so hard, it made his hand ache.

*What do I do now, get out and walk, or sit here and wait for daylight?*

Neither option seemed very promising, but he wasn't much of a mechanic. He could get out and check under the hood, take a look at the engine, but he doubted he'd be able to figure out what was wrong. A cop passing by was starting to sound like a good thing. At least then he could get a tow to the nearest service station, where a mechanic could figure out what was wrong with the car in the morning.

A sheen of sweat dampened Jimmy's upper lip, and his stomach was fluttering as he gazed up and down the street. There was no sign of life anywhere. When he unlocked the door and swung it open, the only sound was the distant hiss of traffic on the bridge above him.

*This is* never *going to happen again,* he vowed as he reached down and pulled the hood release. He got out and moved quickly around to the front of the car and bent to raise the hood, propping it open with the metal support bar. Jimmy leaned over the engine and looked all around, trying to see if there was anything obvious. The nearest streetlight was behind the car, so the opened hood cast a swatch of shadow that made it impossible to see anything. The engine was still warm, and the smell of hot oil and grease filled his nose, making him cough. Faint wisps of blue smoke drifted up into the night. He jumped when he heard a sound behind him, and he banged his head against the opened hood as he straightened up and turned around quickly to see if he was in any danger.

The street was deserted. Not even a stray dog, rummaging through the trash cans. The heavy, humid night air clung to him like a wet woolen sweater, making it almost impossible to take a deep enough breath. He scanned the street, looking for any signs of danger.

After several moments, he heaved a sigh and turned back to his car, leaning over the engine. His hand brushed against something hot, and he hissed in pain as he jerked back and shook it. He started fiddling with the wires and connections, but he knew he was kidding himself. He didn't have a goddamned clue what he was doing. There was no way he was going to get his car started, but what else could he do?

He was reaching to unscrew the top of the air filter to see if something might be blocking it when he heard a faint scuffing sound behind him. This time when he turned around, his elbow knocked the metal rod that held the car hood up. It dropped on him like an anvil, the edge catching the back of his neck. A spray of white stars shot across his vision as the side of his face slammed into the radiator. Dazed, he slowly reached up to raise the hood when the scuffing noise came again.

Louder.

And this time he knew what it was: shoes, scraping on pavement.

Someone was coming up behind him.

"You need any help there, Jimmy?"

Struggling to clear his mind, Jimmy wasn't sure if he had actually heard the voice or simply imagined it. Did they really say his name? With his head cocked to one side, he could see legs and feet, but that was it.

Jimmy groaned as a hand gripped the edge of the hood and pushed it up. He was starting to straighten up and was just about to offer his thanks when the hood slammed down on him again. The blunt point of the hood latch caught him on the left temple, just beside his eye. Pain thumped inside his head like cannon shot. His knees buckled, and his legs gave out on him. When he collapsed forward onto the still-hot engine, he barely noticed the hot metal that seared his face. A high-pitched ringing filled his ears, and a gush of something warm and sticky started running down his cheek. It sizzled and crackled as it splattered across the hot engine head.

Jimmy felt himself drifting . . . spiraling down into darkness. The hood went up again with a creak of springs, then slammed down a third time, but by now the pain was distant, almost like it was happening to someone else. He clung to a single thread of consciousness and could barely hear, much less understand, the voice that whispered in his ear.

"I'm here to baptize you, Jimmy," the low voice said, "in the blood and in the water."

# chapter 9

"I'm sorry. Dr. Cosgrove can't see you now. If you'd like to come back this afternoon . . ."

The receptionist glanced down at her schedule book, completely unmoved by the presence of two homicide detectives in the office. Danny stood with Jace Castillo, staring down at the woman. He didn't know about Jace, but Danny was more than a little disappointed that she did not find him imposing enough to at least be nervous. Then again, it was clear she didn't think she had any reason to be nervous.

The Somerset and Boston Police Departments were working more closely together now, mainly because everyone knew they were teetering on the edge of federal involvement, and the two cities would rather join forces than lose the case altogether to the State Investigative Unit. In the spirit of cooperation, Audrey was working with Yurkich, doing a little brain work, while Danny and Jace visited the Cambridge office of Virgil Cosgrove, who'd been the therapist for the first two victims of The Baptist.

Castillo glanced at him, obviously looking for a cue as to how Danny wanted to proceed. They knew each other but had never worked together before, so each of them was careful to give the other one some basic courtesy. Danny nodded for Castillo to deal with the situation as he saw fit.

"I don't think you understand," Castillo told the receptionist. The woman glanced up at him, frowning. He frowned back. "This is a homicide investigation. You're welcome to announce us. But we're here to speak with Dr. Cosgrove."

With that, he turned and went toward the door that led into the therapist's well-appointed office.

Danny smiled at the receptionist. "You have a nice day."

She was completely baffled by that. So much so that though she opened her mouth to protest, it was clear she had no idea what to say.

Castillo opened the door and strode in. Danny followed behind him but stood just inside the office, holding the door open. Dr. Cosgrove was sitting in one of the chairs next to his coffee table. In another was a strident-looking woman in her forties, her dyed-black hair tied back in a severe braid. Danny would have expected a patient to be upset, to feel vulnerable and exposed if her therapy session was interrupted. This woman just looked pissed.

"What do you think you're doing?" Dr. Cosgrove demanded.

"Excuse me!" the patient snapped. "You're intruding upon time I've paid for. You don't belong here."

But Castillo already had his badge out. For formality's sake, Danny flashed his as well. "Dr. Cosgrove, I'm Detective Castillo, Boston P.D. You already know Detective Mariano from Somerset."

Danny smiled at the patient. He was full of smiles today. "Ma'am, you might want to wait outside for a few minutes."

"Like hell I will!" She glared at him.

So much for smiling.

"Yes," Dr. Cosgrove said, his face reddening. "I'm more than familiar with Detective Mariano. He and his partner have been the bane of my existence this summer. Not to mention my bank account. The trouble they've caused has cost me considerable amounts of money in legal fees."

"My heart bleeds." Castillo sighed, rolling his eyes. "It wouldn't be a problem if you would simply cooperate."

"I've turned over the files on Jaffa—" His gaze went to the woman who sat across from him. His expression softened. "Alice, maybe it would be best for you to go to the waiting room for just a few minutes. I don't think these detectives are going to go away. And I promise you won't lose a minute. I have lunch scheduled after your session, and we'll just use some of that time so that you're not cut short."

The stern woman crossed her arms and glared at him. "Why are the police in your office, Dr. Cosgrove?"

The therapist sighed and ran a hand across his chubby cheek and then through his curly, red-dyed hair. "Clearly, because they lack the imagination to solve their current case and want to make my life miserable. They're inquiring about a previous client of mine. I have made it clear to them that the information they want is privileged."

She stood, watching him warily. After a moment she went to the door, where she paused and surveyed the three men in the room, her gaze landing on Cosgrove. "It had better stay that way. What we talk about in this room is supposed to stay in this room."

"Absolutely," Cosgrove promised.

But as Alice shut the door behind her, she didn't look convinced.

Cosgrove was speechless. He stared after his departed patient, his face growing even more scarlet. Castillo pretended not to notice. Danny liked the other detective's style. "You were saying, Doctor?"

"I was saying," Cosgrove went on, still glaring, "that my attorney has provided you with files on both Jaffarian and Sullivan, and—"

"Your attorney gave us files thinner than Kleenex," Danny interrupted. He'd spent all that time trying to be upbeat, but all his smiles were forgotten now. He had lost patience for Cosgrove even before they had arrived. "Yes, you've got alibis. Fine. But we've told you before, this isn't just about you as a suspect. It's about connecting the victims. You gave us nothing more than a name, address, and a generic write-up on the reasons each were seeing a therapist. But none of your notes—

nothing we can use to try to connect them."

"All true," Dr. Cosgrove said. He fidgeted a bit in his chair. Enough that Danny was beginning to think they should have leaned harder on the therapist a lot earlier. He sure seemed like he was hiding something. "But I've given you all I'm willing to. Those people, dead or alive, have rights."

Castillo slid into one of the chairs and crossed his legs. It was his turn to smile, but there was no humor in his expression. "So do the people who are still alive, Doctor. Already there's been another death. You might have prevented that if you hadn't spent all this time spinning our wheels. Doesn't that bother you at all?"

"Of course it does!" Cosgrove shouted, getting to his feet. He turned his back on them and began to pace a bit. A bead of sweat ran down the back of his neck. Eventually, he stopped and focused on them again. "Of course it does," he repeated. "But I'm not going to surrender my principals. There is no connection between these two men, I tell you. There isn't."

"Have you had any other patients recently who stopped showing up for appointments?" Danny asked.

Cosgrove appeared to consider the question, but then he shook his head. "No. I'm telling you, you're wasting your time here."

"You're right about that," Danny said. Castillo glanced up at him, and he nodded.

"Look, we've been over this time and again. You've cost me a lot of money, but I'll keep paying my attorney as long as I need to." Dr. Cosgrove swallowed, and now his face went from flushed to far too pale. "I'm not going to change my mind. I'll fight you until the Supreme Court forces the issue. I'll keep delaying. I'll drag it out as long as necessary. And if that means that after all of it I end up in jail, then I'll have to live with it."

Castillo stood up, looking like he was about to applaud. "Okay," he finally said. "Okay, Doc. If you insist."

"Wait! What are you doing?" Cosgrove cried, horrified.

Danny was surprised to discover that his smile had returned. "Arresting you for obstruction of justice."

Audrey Gaines smiled thinly as she hung up the phone at her desk. She shook her head, liking her partner's style. Her dismay at the coming of her birthday was long gone, at least until next year. Actually, things had been going fairly well of late. One dinner with Hank Bolling had turned into several, and they'd been seeing each other regularly.

Her mood had improved dramatically. She had even found herself whistling happily once or twice. But she tried to downplay it as much as possible. As a woman, not to mention a woman of color, it had been a long, uphill climb to make detective. She had earned the respect of men who were reluctant to give it. Not all of them were like that, but there were still such dinosaurs in the city. Audrey wanted to make sure the newfound lightness in her heart did not dull her edge.

"Was that your partner?"

Audrey glanced up. Detective Terri Yurkich sat at

Danny's desk, hunched over his keyboard. She had been focused on the computer with a fervent determination that Audrey envied.

"Yep." Audrey smiled.

"Did he and Jace come up with anything?"

"Not really. But they're not coming in empty-handed. They arrested Cosgrove."

Yurkich laughed. "On what charge?"

"Obstruction."

"Seriously? That's never going to stand up. Doesn't matter if it's your boss or mine, either one will have the guy kicked in an hour. Two max."

Audrey shrugged. "I think they just want to sweat him. Even if there isn't a connection, we'd all be a lot happier if we could stop thinking that we're missing something because Cosgrove won't cooperate."

"That's for sure."

"Any luck on our mission?" Audrey asked. "And when I say 'our mission,' I'm clear on the fact that you're doing all the work."

The Boston detective smiled. "I don't mind. Computers and I get along just fine."

That was an understatement. Yurkich had some serious computer skills and was following up a line of inquiry they'd developed using nothing more than the Internet. Audrey marveled at that. She had no use for computers, herself. Sure, she had e-mail and bought books and CDs from Amazon from time to time, but beyond that, she was clueless. Yurkich was good, though. Once upon a time, the search she was doing would have taken hours on the phone, waiting around in public records offices, and probably even some time on the street, checking out facilities in person.

Audrey stood and went around to stand behind the other woman. She bent over to peruse the spreadsheet on the screen. There was a list of various YMCA and YWCA locations in the Greater Boston area.

"Do you really think you're going to be able to narrow it down?" Audrey asked.

Yurkich glanced over her shoulder, pursing her lips thoughtfully. "I think the question is, are we going to be able to narrow it down *enough*. We've all agreed that the perp's using a swimming pool. If it's a personal pool at a private home, we don't stand a chance. But if not—"

"Maybe we'll get lucky," Audrey said.

It was a stretch. Yurkich was understating. The Baptist clearly wasn't killing people at a public pool during ordinary hours of operation. At private spas and swim clubs, that kind of thing, there was always going to be a handful of people—managers and maintenance staff, for example—who had access after hours. But even if they limited the area they were looking in, there were well over a hundred pools to check out.

"This isn't going to get us anywhere, is it?" she asked.

Yurkich used the mouse to click on the Print button, and the printer began to hum, churning out the list on her screen.

"Until we come up with something more, it's all we've got."

Audrey didn't have anything to say to that. Yurkich was right. But she didn't have to like it.

Jenna had spent the day behind her desk dealing with paperwork, answering the phone, and transcribing some of the tapes from Dr. Slikowski's most recent autopsies. There were days when she didn't mind this kind of work. After all, it was precisely what she had been hired for in the first place. But there were also days when she felt chained to her desk and bored to tears. Once upon a time she would have been horrified at the idea of assisting at an autopsy, but she had developed a passion for the job. What she struggled with was the idea that to do this job that intrigued her so much, people had to die.

These were the kinds of dark thoughts that were on her mind as she arrived back at her summer sublet. The morning had started out bright and clear, but over the course of the day the sky had darkened, thickening with gray clouds. Now rain seemed imminent. Jenna was relieved when she got inside without the heavens opening up and drenching her.

She went up to the second floor, looking forward to relaxing a bit, listening for Virginia. It was always more pleasant for her when her roommate wasn't around. *Only a few more weeks,* she told herself as she reached the top of the stairs and went into the apartment.

Virginia was sitting in a chair in the living room, very clearly waiting for her. The TV wasn't on. Jeff wasn't around. There was no book in Virginia's hand, no sense that she had been doing anything other than sitting there, waiting.

"Hey," Jenna said, forcing a smile. "How's it going?"

"Jenna, I need to speak with you," Virginia replied stiffly. Her tone was as icy as ever. "Why don't you sit down?"

Most of the time, Jenna was the kind of person who would make the best of any situation. At least, she thought this of herself. She tried to get along. But hearing those words come out of Virginia's mouth, and in that tone, sent a shudder of annoyance through her. More than annoyance. Jenna was angry and, frankly, sick of her roommate's superior attitude.

Crossing her arms, she chose to stand. "What can I do for you, Virginia?"

The grad student was clearly surprised by her attitude. Virginia raised an eyebrow. "Well, to begin with, you can stop leaving glasses and dirty dishes around. You can put things into the dishwasher instead of leaving them in the sink. More importantly, you can stop using my toothpaste and get your own."

"Your toothpaste?" Jenna stared at the older girl in utter astonishment. From time to time, when she was in a rush, she might leave a glass in the sink, planning to deal with it later. And she could recall precisely one time, the previous week, when she had left an open bag of cookies in the living room. As for toothpaste . . .

"I hadn't realized you were so protective of your toothpaste," she said, careful not to use the words that she really would have liked to use. "I confess. I'm a toothpaste thief. It isn't the sort of thing I thought of as stealing, but if you'd like the quarter for the two times I used your toothpaste, I'd be happy to make restitution."

Virginia's nostrils flared. "And what about the orange juice? You've been drinking my orange juice."

Jenna stared at her. "Are you serious with this stuff? Come on. What the hell is the matter with you?"

"I should be asking you that question, I think."

Dumbstruck, Jenna could only stare. The two glared at each other for a long moment before Jenna sighed and shook her head. "Look, guilty as charged, okay? Not on the juice, though. I never touched your stupid orange juice. You can ask Jeff about that. And you can be sure I'll never go near anything in this place again."

Virginia sniffed haughtily and rose from her chair. She picked up the shoulder bag with her laptop computer and started for the door. As she passed Jenna, she glanced over at her. "August can't go by fast enough," Virginia said softly.

Jenna knew she ought to have a comeback for that, but she just didn't have the energy. Virginia went out the door, leaving Jenna alone in the living room. She waited until she heard the ground-floor door slam shut. Then she groaned and rolled her eyes. "*God,* what a *bitch!*" she roared.

But moments later, her anger had begun to wear off, and she started to feel really bad. Virginia was a bitch, no question about that. But it was awful to have anyone— even someone that horrible—dislike her so intensely. She felt suddenly very lonely and went to see if Jeff was in his room. The door was closed, but it was always closed, and she could just imagine him lurking in there, listening to them battle it out and not wanting to get in the middle of it. Jenna wouldn't have blamed him for that. "Jeff?" she ventured, rapping lightly on his door. After a moment, she knocked again. "Hey. You home?"

Apparently not. She sighed and rested her forehead against the door, and it swung inward with a slow creak. Jenna's face flushed. She didn't want to intrude on Jeff's personal space. She certainly would not want anyone coming into her room when she wasn't around. Reaching to close the door again, she took a step deeper into the room.

And froze.

A frown creased her forehead. On the bureau was a copy of *Lonesome Dove,* by Larry McMurtry. A bookmark stuck out from the top of the book. She felt oddly certain that this was not simply any copy of the book, but *her* copy. It had been in her room. She could just go and look to see if it was still there, if somehow Jeff had picked up a copy for himself and just happened to have the very same *Powerpuff Girls* bookmark.

That didn't seem very likely.

"What the hell?" Jenna muttered.

She hesitated only a moment longer before pushing into the room and picking the book up off the bureau where it lay beside a thick, well-read Bible. Her heart started beating a little faster. As angry as she was with Virginia, she was really hoping this wasn't her book, that Jeff hadn't borrowed it without asking. She didn't want to be pissed off at both of them.

*Then again,* she thought, *maybe I'm overreacting. I don't want to end up being a bitch like Virginia.*

Jenna thought about that for a moment. As she did, she flipped open the book to look at the bookmark, and a photograph fell out from its pages and drifted to the dusty, wooden floor. For a second or two she could only stare at the picture. She felt as though she ought to pick it up, but her brain could not force her body to bend over and reach for it.

It was a picture of her. Grainy. A profile shot, taken on the street somewhere. Or maybe on campus. Very clearly, it had been taken without her knowing. "Oh, no. Oh, shit," she whispered.

Anxious, she started backing toward the door, the book in her hand. Her gaze drifted around the room. To the Bible on the bureau. To the crucifix on the wall. To the small picture of Jesus, exposing his Sacred Heart. Jeff was religious. It had never registered with her before.

*So this guy's—what, obsessed with me? What the hell's he doing with this picture, otherwise?*

Pulse racing, her mouth going dry, she searched his room more thoroughly. She opened the four drawers of his bureau and glanced inside but did not push the clothing aside. Even now, there was a limit to how far she was willing to intrude. The back of her neck was hot, and her breathing came in shallow, dry gulps. She moved on to his bedside table and opened the top drawer.

Where she found her missing hairbrush. And the earrings her mother had given her. And a pair of lace panties she had assumed she had lost at the Laundromat.

"Oh, Jesus . . . oh, Jesus," she whispered, her breath burning in her throat, her body tingling with fear and revulsion. She jumped back, closing the drawer, and her heel caught something that was sticking out from underneath the bed.

Her eyes were drawn to it.

A scrapbook.

Jenna bent down, scarcely able to think as she pulled the scrapbook out. She opened it and flipped to the first page. Holding her breath, she went through page after page of photographs and newspaper clippings.

*All about her.*

The cases she had been involved in since going to work for Dr. Slikowski. The times she had almost been killed. The horrible crimes whose investigations she had been a part of.

Her heart was beating so loudly it deafened her. She backed out of the room, her mind a white blank. As soon as she hit the living room, she bolted for the telephone and dialed Danny's cell phone number. It rang half a dozen times, and it was like an eternity to her. When it switched over to his voice mail, she hung up. What would she say in a message?

Quickly, she dialed Dyson's home number. It rang once. Twice.

On the third ring, she heard the downstairs door open. Virginia was at the library by now, so it couldn't be her. It could only be Jeff. *Damn it!* If she'd thought for a second he'd be coming home at any moment, she would have run from the apartment. Even now, she knew she should hang up and get into her room, block the door, call from her cell.

"Hello?"

Dyson had answered the phone. He was her lifeline. No way would she hang up now, even to call him back. "Oh, thank God you're home," she whispered.

"Jenna?"

"Listen to me. I found some . . . some really weird stuff in my roommate's room. He's . . . I think he's a stalker or something."

She could hear the stairs creak under Jeff's weight as he trudged up to the second floor. Dyson was talking, trying to find out more, but Jenna could barely make sense of what he was saying.

"I can't talk right now. He just got home. Call Danny. Come over here. Please, hurry."

The door opened behind her. Dyson was still calling out to her, but Jenna hung up the phone.

When she turned, Jeff was standing just inside the living room. Even as she looked at him, she saw his eyes shift toward the door to his bedroom. The *open* door. He knew she had been inside.

"I don't know, Bobby."

With a smirk and more than a bit of swagger, Bobby Goslin stood at the rim of the Keates Hill Quarry. His girlfriend, Heather Ames, was doing her best to convince him not to jump. And the way she looked at him, her eyes so wide and sweet, he had a hard time arguing

CHRISTOPHER GOLDEN AND RICK HAUTALA

with her. Girl looked damn fine in a bikini too.

"Come on, Bobby! What're you doing just standing there?"

He stiffened, a little of the swagger going out of him. Bobby had heard stories about the quarry ever since he had moved to Somerset the previous year. He was fifteen, running with some local guys a year or two older, and the last thing he wanted was for them to think he was scared to dive. Heather thought only an idiot would swim in the quarry, never mind jump off the rim. There were girls who made the dive, but there was also a double standard. The ones who didn't jump never got grief from the others.

Guys were different.

Bobby looked over the edge of the cliff. He'd be plummeting past dozens of feet of sheer granite wall before hitting the water. There were so many stories, local legends about the quarry. It was bottomless. It was where the mob dumped bodies. People drove stolen cars off the side. Kids sunk shopping carts and other odd things in there. So when you jumped off, you never knew what might be waiting underwater—some sharp edge of metal to rip your skin right open, or a car jutting up high enough to break a leg.

But Bobby had been here almost an hour, hanging out, and he hadn't seen anyone get hurt.

A whooping shout like a battle cry filled the air. Bobby turned to see his buddy, Ramon, running toward the rim. He had already been in and out of the water several times, and his shaggy hair was wet. He shook it off, and a spray of water hit Bobby as Ramon flew past.

"Come on, Roberto!" Ramon shouted.

Then he launched himself off the cliff and fell, whooping the whole way down, into the spring-fed water that had collected in the quarry over the decades. Bobby laughed, watching him hit the water.

"All right!" he called. "Here I come!"

Heather touched his arm. He turned and was almost caught by those wide, pleading eyes. But Bobby smiled at her and pulled his arm away. "It's too hot to stay up here. I'm going in."

"You jerk," she muttered, all the sweetness going out of her. "You're going to get yourself killed."

Bobby only laughed. He glanced down to make sure Ramon had surfaced and was swimming out of the way. Then he backed away from the rim to give himself room to get up momentum, ran toward the edge, and leaped out into space.

He did not laugh or shout or let loose a wild *whoop*. He held his breath, and it felt as though his heart had stopped. Wind whistled past his ears. A hundred terrible images flashed through his mind, images of things that could happen to him doing something as stupid as this. Heather was right. Heather was—

Then he hit the water, plunging downward with such speed, he was afraid he would hit the bottom. And how far down was the bottom, anyway? It couldn't really be bottomless.

His heartbeat returned, pounding with such triphammer speed, he thought it would burst through his chest. When his face emerged, Bobby pulled toward the surface. He was sucking air into his lungs and couldn't control the grin on his face. "Damn," he whispered. Then he shouted it. *"Damn!"*

It had been the most thrilling moment of his life. He couldn't wait to climb up and do it again.

Still grinning, he swam toward the nearest ledge, a place where he might pull himself out of the water and start the careful climb back up to the top of the cliff. Only when he had reached it, had hauled himself up onto the stone shelf, did he realize that he had chosen the wrong ledge. Over time, kids swimming up here had worn a pretty safe path back up to the top. But he wouldn't be able to reach it from here. He'd have to swim over to the next ledge.

Up on the rim, Heather shouted his name and did a little dance for him, a little cheer. So much for her protests . . . at least until he tried to do it again. He shook his head and went to the edge of that stone shelf, then dropped into the water.

His feet struck something that gave way beneath him. Something was stuck beneath the ledge, just under the water. He had dislodged it. It felt strange to him, soft and squishy. As he swam to one side, a shudder ran through him.

Bobby stared down into the quarry water.

A pale, dead face was staring back at him.

# chapter 10

"Hey, what's up?" Jeff asked.

He had just closed the door, locking it behind him, and stood there gazing at Jenna. His dark eyes looked moist in the dim light, and there was a wildness in them that genuinely frightened her. She had noticed it before, but—until now—had just written it off as part of who he was and the upbringing he'd had. Up until a few minutes ago, she would have sworn she knew Jeff, at least a little bit. Over the summer, they had sat around the apartment, shooting the breeze a few times, and Jenna had reviewed some of the assignments for the anatomy class he was taking with him.

But now . . .

Now she felt threatened by the dull glow in his eyes. Even the way he regarded her, with his head cocked a bit to one side. It was like he couldn't just stand there and look her straight in the eye. Even his awkward posture seemed threatening.

Jenna had no idea what to say or do. She had been in dangerous situations before, but this seemed different. With all of those weird, fetishistic souvenirs he'd stolen from her, Jeff was a powder keg, and the fuse was lit and burning. The problem was, she had no idea how long the fuse was. She was still holding on to her copy of *Lonesome Dove,* and she noticed the way Jeff's focus kept shifting from her to the book and then back to her.

"I was just . . . just getting my book back," she said with a shrug.

Even as she said it, she could see anger rise up within him. Anger and hurt and suspicion. She cringed, waiting for the explosion, but finally Jeff lowered his gaze to the floor. His lower lip was pale and trembling. The skin on his forehead looked almost translucent. She could see the faint tracing of blue veins beneath the skin. One vein on the side of his head, just above his left eye, bulged as it throbbed with his pulse.

"Why were you in my room?" Jeff asked, his voice low and meek, almost as if *he* owed *her* an apology.

"I—uh, I thought you were home, and when I knocked on the door, it sort of opened, and I . . . I just saw my book there."

"And decided to take it back," Jeff said, his voice sounding raw and strangled. The vein on the side of his head was bulging with every pulse.

Jenna's mind was a roaring blank, but before she could reply, the door buzzer sounded, startling her and making her jump. She glanced past Jeff to the door, realizing that he was standing between her and it. If he was going to hurt her, he probably was never going to get a better chance. In that awkward moment, a thought struck her so hard she gasped.

*The religious things: the Bible, the crucifix, the picture of Jesus on the wall.*

*What if it's him? What if Jeff is The Baptist?*

"I—uh, I've been waiting for my friend," Jenna said, all too aware of the strain in her voice. "We have plans for tonight."

Jeff's body seemed to deflate as soon as she said that. With downcast eyes, he stepped to one side. Jenna moved stiffly to the panel by the door and buzzed in whomever it was—Danny or Dyson. Her hand was shaking, and her breath came in cold sips as she undid the chain lock, opened the door, and stepped out into the hallway. The tension made her want to scream, and she wanted to—but didn't dare look back over her shoulder to see what Jeff was doing.

She let out a loud shout when she first heard and then saw both Danny and Dyson coming up the steps, taking them two at a time.

"Are you all right?" Danny snapped. His hand was underneath the flap of his jacket, resting on his service revolver as he looked past Jenna at the opened doorway.

Jenna nodded quickly, then turned and looked behind her.

"Thanks for getting here so fast," she said, pausing to

give each of them a quick hug as they joined her on the landing.

"He still here?" Danny asked, his voice clipped and all business.

Jenna nodded, and with Dyson on one side and Danny on the other, they entered the apartment together to find Jeff seated on the couch. He was leaning forward stiffly, his hands folded together and pressed tightly between his knees. His face paled even more when Danny flipped open his badge and held it up for him to see.

"Detective Mariano, Somerset Police," Danny said. "Mind if we talk a bit?" The tone of his voice made it absolutely clear that there was no alternative. Jeff swallowed, throat bulging, and then he nodded. Danny turned to Jenna. "You want to fill me in on what's going on here?"

Her legs felt stiff and brittle as she walked over to Virginia's chair by the computer and sat down. Dyson walked over and stood close beside her, his hand resting lightly on her shoulder. The pathetic expression on Jeff's face made her feel a sudden wave of pity for him. He looked so alone and vulnerable.

*Can he really be dangerous? Could that awkward, self-deprecating thing all be an act?*

"Well," she began, and then paused to lick her lips before continuing. "I was in his bedroom and I—"

"*Without* my permission," Jeff said, his voice as thin as glass.

"*She's* talking right now," Danny snapped, his voice

sharp with command. Jeff started to say something back, but then dropped his shoulders and hunched forward, apparently resigned to whatever was going to happen next.

"Well, when I looked into his room, I saw that he had a book of mine," Jenna said. "And then, when I walked in to get it, I found all this other stuff. Things that belong to me. Personal stuff, including my . . . including a pair of my underwear. And some things *about* me."

"That's not true," Jeff said, so softly he might have been talking to himself.

"He has newspaper clippings about a few of the cases I worked on this past year. There were even some candid photos taken of me around campus."

Jeff opened his mouth to speak again, but this time the only sound that came out was a low, watery gasp. Danny turned and glared at him until he shut his mouth.

Jenna forced herself to look at the guy she'd been sharing an apartment with. "I thought you were a nice guy when we first met. But this is just too creepy."

Jeff sat squirming on the couch, so distraught that Jenna was afraid he was going to start crying. He looked so pathetic, it almost broke her heart, but then she remembered the fear and the feeling of violation she'd experienced when she realized that, all along, he had been stalking her.

*Stalking?*

There was no other word for it. As benign as Jeff might have seemed at first, he must have had some kind of twist in his personality, because on some level, to some degree, he was obviously obsessed with Jenna.

"You want to show me those things?" Danny asked, turning to Jeff.

Jeff's eyes were glazed over with that faraway stare Jenna had seen many times in the eyes of some of the corpses she and Slick worked on. His lower lip was trembling, and his voice shifted up an octave when he said, "You can't go in there without a search warrant."

Danny nodded. "True. And I can get one in less than an hour, so why don't you cooperate with me before I arrest you and bring you down to the station."

"For borrowing a book without permission?"

"It wasn't just the book," Jenna said, finding a measure of courage. "And that religious stuff . . . what's the deal with that?"

Jeff held her gaze for only a second or two before he had to turn away. The apartment was absolutely silent for several seconds as he stared out the window. Then a look of genuine shock hit his face, and he looked back at Jenna. "Wait a second," he said. "You think I'm him. You think I'm that Baptist guy who's in all the newspapers. Is that it?"

The fear in his voice was palpable, but no one else in the room replied. Jenna certainly didn't want to be the one to say it, and Dyson was silent, his hand still resting reassuringly on her shoulder. Danny was giving Jeff a hard look.

Jeff straightened up and, folding his arms across his chest, shook his head. "No way! No way in hell," he said in a voice that quavered wildly. "I'm no killer."

"What are you, then?" Danny asked, leaning forward threateningly. "A stalker?"

Jeff looked like he was about to laugh at the suggestion, but then his expression clouded. "No way," he said. "I'm not a stalker. Honest to God, I'm not."

"So what's the deal with these pictures and articles about me?" Jenna asked. She could see how scared he was, but she couldn't forget how frightened she had been just a few moments ago.

Jeff sawed his teeth back and forth across his lower lip, his eyes unfocused as he stared down at the floor. Finally, he cleared his throat and said, "I'm a fan."

Jenna snapped back in the chair as if he'd actually slapped her across the face. "A fan?" she echoed, not convinced she had heard him correctly.

Jeff tilted his head and looked at her out of the corner of his eye. Then he nodded. "I'm in premed, so over the school year, I heard a lot about you and what you were doing. Then I started reading about you in the news, and then, last winter, when I saw you for the first time, I . . . I felt a real admiration for what you were doing."

Jenna felt compelled to tell him that she was just doing her job, but she was too freaked out to speak. The idea that someone would be a *fan* of hers—it was just too much to take.

"So you developed a crush on her, is that what you're saying?" Danny said. His expression was flat, absolutely neutral.

"A crush," Jeff said, shaking his head and lowering his gaze to the floor again. He clasped his hands tightly and shook his head as though deeply saddened. "That sounds so high school, doesn't it? But"—he took a deep breath that made him shudder—"yes. Maybe that's what it was. But I know that . . . that guys like me don't get girls like you. So I never said or did anything about it."

"What do you mean, you never did anything about it?" Jenna asked, her anger suddenly flaring. "You followed me around. You took pictures of me without me knowing it. You cut out newspaper articles about me and put them in a scrapbook. You took my goddamned underwear out of my laundry! And if this has been going on since last winter, how the hell did you end up here, subletting this apartment for the summer? Don't tell me that was just coincidence!"

Jeff started to say something, then stopped himself. He looked at her with genuine anguish in his eyes, then bowed his head and shook it. "No," he said faintly. "I was looking for a place to stay because I wasn't going home for the summer. I had Professor Emerson for English comp my freshman year. She mentioned that you might be renting from Virginia, so I . . . I called to be the other roommate for the summer."

"So you *were* stalking me," Jenna said, unable to resist a shiver.

"There are laws against that kind of activity," Danny said in a voice as hard as nails.

"It's not like that, I swear," Jeff said as he looked back and forth between him and Jenna. For a moment, Jenna could almost believe that he was harmless, but she couldn't stop that oily, creeping feeling that ran beneath her skin.

"Look . . . I'm sorry, all right?" Jeff said. "I was just . . . I didn't know what to do. I wanted to meet you. Just to hang out with you. Maybe even—you know, like be your friend. I swear to God I'd never do anything to hurt you. I'm really sorry."

An awkward silence filled the room. Jenna had no idea how to respond to that. A part of her wanted to reach out to Jeff because she knew how lonely and miserable he was. But when she recalled some of their conversations over the summer, it just felt wrong. She didn't like feeling as though he had betrayed her trust or was toying with her, using her for his own ends.

"Well," Danny said, finally breaking the tension in the room, "I think you'd better pack your things and find another place to stay for the night. It's not fair to Jenna to have to live with this situation."

Jeff sat absolutely immobile for a moment, and then he shifted his weight forward, about to stand.

"No," Jenna said sharply. "I'll move out. The other roommate and I aren't exactly getting along, either, so it's best all the way around if I find another place between now and when school starts."

"You don't have to do this, Jenna," Dyson said, speaking for the first time now that the official police business was concluded.

"It's all right. Just give me a few minutes to pack a bag or two."

Danny nodded, but his eyes never shifted away from

CHRISTOPHER GOLDEN AND RICK HAUTALA

Jeff, who sat hunched on the couch. "You can stay at my place," he said.

"Or mine," Dyson piped in.

"We'll figure that out later," Jenna said as she stood up to leave the room. Her heart ached for Jeff as she looked at him, and she was even more infuriated and disgusted with him because he brought that emotion out in her. There was no way she could ever be under the same roof with him again. Already her mind was flashing forward to the days ahead. She would probably have to get a restraining order or something.

"I'm going to ask you to come down to the station and answer a few more questions," Danny said, still glaring at Jeff. "Are you willing to take a polygraph?"

Jeff visibly tensed. He ran his teeth back and forth across his lower lip, turning it bloodless. Then, with a deep sigh, he nodded and said, "I get to have a lawyer, right?"

"You're not being charged with anything, but—yes," Danny said, and for the first time he appeared to respond with a trace of sympathy for the frightened young man. "And if you can't afford one, we can provide one for you."

Jeff looked over at Jenna with a strange, sad longing in his eyes as he got up from the couch. Even standing, he seemed to have shrunken in on himself.

"Okay, then," he said, bowing his head meekly. "Whatever you say."


"Thanks for helping me out like this," Jenna said as she hefted her overnight case up onto the couch and blew a strand of hair from her eyes with an exaggerated puff of breath. The aromas coming from Al Dyson's kitchen were tantalizing. Jenna turned and looked at her friend. "I'm really sorry. I didn't mean to mess up your supper plans."

"Oh, that's okay," Dyson said with a casual wave of the hand as he started for the kitchen. "Doug has it covered."

She snagged Dyson by the arm. "You didn't tell me that Doug's here. I *really* messed up your plans, didn't I?"

"Jenna," Dyson said, looking at her with a scolding expression on his face. "You were scared. You needed help. Do you think I wouldn't be there for you?"

"Yeah, but I—"

"You didn't mess up anything. Doug's always glad to see you."

Jenna followed him into the kitchen where Doug was standing by the stove, stirring a bubbling pot of spaghetti sauce. The smell of garlic was strong enough to make Jenna's eyes water, and the rumbling in her stomach reminded her that she hadn't eaten supper yet.

"There's plenty of everything," Doug said, beaming her a smile. "I haven't even cooked the spaghetti yet, so it's no sweat."

Despite what Dyson had said, Jenna didn't know Doug very well and she felt suddenly awkward, intruding like this. "Seriously?" she said, looking back and forth between them.

Dyson smiled and shook his head as he clapped her on the shoulder. "Seriously. It's no trouble. We want you to stay. What did you think I would do, turn you out in the cold?"

"No, but I could have stayed with Danny," Jenna offered. Even as she said it, though, a sudden flushed heat ran up the back of her neck.

"You think?" Dyson said, arching an eyebrow suggestively.

Jenna laughed softly. "Well, okay . . . that might have been a little awkward."

"Just a little," Dyson said. "Not to mention he has a suspect down at the station right now and is giving him a lie detector test."

Doug was glancing back and forth between them, trying to pick up the thread of their conversation. Jenna smiled at him.

"Sorry, Doug," she said. "It's rude of us to talk shop. And probably pretty boring."

The man frowned. He was handsome and rugged-looking, with rich brown eyes that were wide and kind. Doug crossed his arms and regarded her with those eyes like a stern parent.

"Enough of that. It isn't shop talk when you're in trouble, Jenna. Al cares for you. That means I do too. And besides, I'm always fascinated by this sort of thing. Don't you find that what's boring to others about their own lives is often fascinating to you just because it's different?"

She smiled. "I guess."

He threw his hands up. "Well, there you go. Now. Talk."

When Doug turned his back to her and stirred the sauce, which was just starting to bubble over onto the stove, Jenna felt a sense of relief wash over her. She could not remember how a smile had snuck up on her. Dyson was watching her, and Jenna gestured to Doug and gave him the thumbs-up.

Dyson rolled his eyes, but she could see that he loved it, that he was happy she and Doug got along well.

"Anyway, where were we?" she said. "Oh, right. Polygraph. I don't think Jeff's really a suspect. I mean, not in The Baptist case. Okay, yeah, when I saw all that stuff in his room, I really panicked."

"That's because it's *really* creepy," Dyson said as he took out a large pot. He filled it with cold water at the sink, poured a dollop of olive oil into the water, and then placed it on the stove. Then he reached up into the cupboard and took a package of spaghetti down from the top shelf.

"My advice to you," he said, "is just stay away from him. He may look all innocent and harmless, but—" He shrugged. "You just never know."

"No," Jenna said, nodding her agreement. "You never do."

"We'll go back there tomorrow morning and bring all of your things back here," Dyson said. He went to the refrigerator and got lettuce, spinach greens, cucumbers, sprouts, and tomatoes to make a salad.

"You don't have to—" Jenna started to say, but Dyson cut her off with a harsh look.

"I'm not even going to discuss it with you," he said.

"We'll get you packed up and moved out of there before anything else happens." Turning to Doug, he asked, "Can you give us a hand in the morning?"

Doug scowled and shook his head. "Sorry. No can do. I have to be at work early tomorrow. The regional manager from corporate is coming in."

"Well," Dyson said, "we can probably do it all ourselves." He deposited the salad makings onto the counter. "Why don't I give Slick a call to let him know we'll be a little late."

With that, he left the kitchen and walked down the hall. Wanting to forget about the evening's events, Jenna walked over to the stove and, leaning down over the pot of spaghetti sauce, inhaled deeply. "Think you used enough garlic?" she asked as the almost overpowering aroma filled her nose.

Doug looked at her with one eyebrow arched and said, "You think it needs more?"

Jenna grinned. "No. It smells perfect."

Feeling completely at home with Doug, she walked over to the counter and started working on the salad. Moments later, Dyson came back into the kitchen. "Well—" he said. "Do you want the bad news or the terrible news?"

Jenna panicked, thinking for an instant that something might have happened down at the police station between Danny and Jeff.

"We can't move your things until later in the day," Dyson said. "We've got another one on the table."

"The Baptist?"

Dyson nodded. "Sure sounds like it."

Jenna couldn't miss the trace of resignation in his voice.

"Was there a cross? On the forehead?" she asked.

Again, Dyson nodded. "Oh, yeah. That and—" He cast a quick glance at Doug, then looked at Jenna. "This doesn't really make for the best dinner conversation. How about we deal with it all in the morning? Then, after work, we'll get your things moved."

"Agreed," Jenna said, but even as she felt sadness at the knowledge that The Baptist had taken another victim, she could not deny a tiny burst of anticipation. Another piece of the puzzle had just fallen into place. It was almost enough to make her forget how frightened she had been just a short while ago.

The autopsy was over by ten o'clock, and Jenna and Dyson were doing a final cleanup of the table and equipment while Slick went upstairs to his office. He had called and asked that all four detectives involved with the case—Mariano, Gaines, Castillo, and Yurkich—join him before noon.

Jenna couldn't help but shudder whenever she glanced at the autopsy photos of the victim, a young man from Dorchester, named James Balzarini.

There was no doubt in Jenna's or anyone else's mind that The Baptist had struck again. The most recent victim had not died from the severe trauma to his head, which Slick had identified as repeated blows from a car hood. Like the other victims, Mr. Balzarini had died by drowning in chlorinated water before being sunk in a quarry on the outskirts of town.

Besides another red cross, which had been sliced into his forehead, the police had discovered something else—something much more disturbing. The killer had also carved a single word into the man's chest. Before cutting into the dead man's chest for the autopsy, Jenna had photographed it and indicated its location on the human body diagram of the autopsy chart. She still remembered the chill that had run through her when Slick, dictating his report for the tape recorder, had carefully pronounced the single-syllable word: "Saved."

The letters of the word had been carved with a child-like blockiness, but it was obvious that no child had done this. James Balzarini had been a fairly large, well-muscled young man. It was obvious his killer must have closely matched him in size or else taken him completely by surprise. And the killer had to be strong, just to carry Balzarini's body once he was dead.

"You doing all right?" Dyson asked, his gaze steady and bright above the edge of his surgical mask.

"Sure," Jenna said with a shrug. "Why not? I'm used to this by now."

Dyson shook his head. "No, no," he said. "I mean about moving your things out and all."

Jenna paused and considered for a moment; then she nodded. "When I talked to Danny last night, he told me that Jeff passed the polygraph test with flying colors, so he's definitely not a suspect. Still . . ."

"Yeah . . . still, it's very twisted. If he's going to be

around next semester, you might want to consider getting a restraining order."

"Trust me. The thought's already crossed my mind. But I guess I'd rather not think about that right now."

Jenna hosed down the table, washing the blood and other body fluids down the drain at the foot of the autopsy table. Fifteen minutes later, she and Dyson entered Slick's office to find everyone gathered around, drinking coffee and making small talk.

"All right, then," Slick said once Dyson closed the office door. "We have a lot of information to assimilate and put together, but I think we can begin by agreeing that this *is* a serial killer, and he won't be caught until we figure out a pattern to what he's doing."

"So far we haven't had any luck tracking down leads with the pools," Audrey offered. "There are a lot of public pools in the Boston area, and we simply don't have the head count we need to cover all the private pools in the surrounding suburbs."

"How about the psychiatrist?" Yurkich asked. "That Dr. Cosgrove?"

"He's stonewalling us," Castillo replied. "Even so, he has an alibi for his whereabouts during the time frame of this last incident."

"True," Danny said, "but his alibi is his mother, so we can't discount that she might lie to protect him."

"There is that," Castillo said, nodding. "One interesting thing in this is, it appears as though the killer actually stalked Mr. Balzarini. We found—"

"Whoa. Wait a second," Audrey said, suddenly

straightening up and turning to face Castillo. "What was that name again?"

"James Balzarini," Castillo said. "Why?"

"I know him, if it's the same guy. On the street they just call him Twitch." She turned to Danny and continued. "He's that dealer we busted right after we first partnered up. He was hanging around here in Somerset, dealing off campus to students. Remember? We thought we had him cold, but he wiggled off on a technicality."

"Yeah," Danny said, nodding thoughtfully. "I do remember that."

"He had a rap sheet a mile long, too, but we could never get him on any of it." Audrey sniffed with disgust and shook her head. "I hate to say it, but I'm not exactly heartbroken that Mr. Balzarini won't be down for breakfast, as they say."

"Well, whoever killed him set him up," Castillo said. "They were stalking him."

"How do you know that?" Audrey asked.

"Carbon residue—lots of it in his carburetor. We figure someone put sugar into his gas tank and then followed him, waiting for him to break down."

Audrey sighed and shook her head. "This takes us in a whole new direction. There could be any number of people out to get Balzarini if he burned them in a score or a robbery or whatever. If we start checking his record, it'll take us years to run down all the possible connections."

"What about the other victims?" Jenna asked suddenly. Everyone in the room turned to look at her.

"What do you mean?" Slick asked, leaning back in his wheelchair and steepling his fingers in front of his face.

"Their police records," Jenna repeated. "Has anyone checked to see if they had committed any crimes?"

"Of course we did," Castillo offered, "and we didn't find anything on any of them except Balzarini."

"What if it was something they weren't convicted of?" Jenna asked. "Wouldn't that be removed from their record?"

Danny nodded. "Sure. But it would still come up when we did a search on them. It would just come up that they'd been charged and then the charges were dismissed or continued without a finding. It wouldn't be a 'record,' the way you think of it. But it would still show up."

Jenna felt a bit embarrassed, certain that the detectives would all think it had been a stupid question. It was a reminder to her that no matter how involved she became in the cases that came through the medical examiner's office, she was just a student. Just a girl with a lot to learn. If she wanted to do anything like this for her career, she had three more years of college and then medical school to get through.

She shrugged sheepishly, about to apologize for such a dumb question, when her gaze landed on Audrey Gaines. The other detectives had moved on to other topics, but Audrey looked pensive, frowning as she watched Jenna.

"Wait a second."

Audrey had an air of command about her. She was kind enough, but could be a grimly serious woman.

When she interrupted, everyone in the room turned toward her.

"We're not thinking clearly, here," Audrey said. "Let's go with Jenna's suggestion for a minute. If there's a criminal connection in all of this, Balzarini would be the key. Just because the DOAs don't have records, that doesn't mean they never committed a crime. How many perps get arrested every day and then get kicked without any charges being filed?"

Castillo shook his head. "All right. Let's say there's something to that. Do you have any idea how long it would take to check on something like that? You're talking about getting in touch with every police department in the state—"

"Maybe not just the state," Danny interjected. "You could be talking about crimes committed out of state. And even if you narrow it down to narcotics crimes only, that's still an impossible search to do. It's even more of a needle-in-a-haystack hunt than searching for the swimming pool The Baptist is using."

Jenna smiled. "Well, it was just a thought."

"And a good one," Audrey told her. "Don't stop having them. It just might be a little impractical. But it's definitely something we've got to keep in mind."

"I don't know," Detective Yurkich said. "I mean, have we reached the point where we can afford not to look into the long shots? Maybe we'll get lucky."

Dr. Slikowski had his hands crossed on his lap, but now he reached up and slid his glasses off. "Detective Yurkich—Terri, if I may—is correct. I'm no policeman, but there must be some way to look into this possibility."

Castillo and Audrey exchanged a long look. They were the senior detectives in their respective partnerships. At length, Castillo nodded.

"We could re-interview the known associates of the DOAs, with an eye to finding out if any of them had ever been arrested," Audrey suggested.

"But we can't spend too much time on it," Castillo cautioned. "Even if Jenna's right, and they were connected by criminal activity, there's no reason to think the others ever got caught. And if they never were, then we're just spinning our wheels here."

The meeting began to break up, the detectives talking among themselves as they prepared to depart. Danny was the last of them to leave, and he glanced back at Jenna with a sly smile. "You ever think about getting into detective work?" he asked.

"I'm happy doing what I'm doing," Jenna replied.

Slick regarded them both gravely. "And she's *damned* good at it."

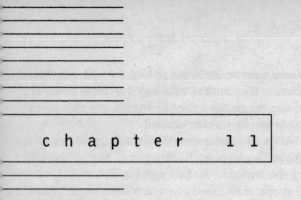

On Saturday morning, two days after Jenna fled her summer sublet to get away from Jeff Tilton, she still had not gone back for the rest of her things. Dyson and Doug—who each had his own apartment but were for all intents and purposes living together—had been wonderfully welcoming to her. Though Jenna had an older half brother, she had not grown up in the same house with him, and so had only the vaguest notion of what it meant to have a big brother. Over the course of the year she had come to see Al Dyson more and more in that role for her. Now, in the space of forty-eight hours, Doug had joined him. It was like having a pair of body-guards. They treated her like their little sister, and she would have been lying if she'd told herself it didn't make her feel somehow special.

On the other hand, much as she loved them, she was already tired of living out of her overnight case. She had brought so little with her from the apartment that she would have to do laundry tonight just to have something clean to wear the next day. But all of them had agreed to retrieve the rest of her things on Sunday, and Danny had phoned Jeff to make sure creepy, sad, stalker-boy would not be around at the time.

Today, there were other things to do. Dyson was not the only one who had found a companion this year. Dr. Slikowski had rekindled an old romance, and his girl-friend, Natalie Kerchak, was determined to make him more sociable. Thus, the heretofore unimaginable: Slick was having a barbecue.

"Remember, Jenna," Dyson said, adopting a mock-stern voice as he and Doug escorted her up the brick-lined path to the front door of Slick's apartment house. "We're here to have a fun afternoon, okay?"

"Sure," Jenna said.

Doug sighed and rolled his eyes. "Al. She's a big girl."

With a grin, Dyson linked arms with Jenna. "I know that. But I also know Jenna Blake. Danny will be here. Audrey Gaines is supposed to be bringing her new beau. Jenna's going to want to talk shop."

Doug now took Jenna's other arm, but he raised one eyebrow and gazed down at her. "Oh, that won't do, dar-lin'. There will be no talk about autopsies. No conversa-tions with dead people in them."

She snickered. "I'll do my best."

"Damn straight," Doug replied.

Over the summer, the restored Victorian in Arlington where Slick rented the first floor had been renovated and repainted. Various bright, contrasting shades of blue and yellow glowed in slanting rays of the afternoon sun. The steady, winding buzz of cicadas filled the air. The well-trimmed lawn glistened emerald green in the spray of the sprinkler that was running under the oak trees that lined the driveway. Because of the high humidity and no wind, the oak leaves looked dusty brown and hung limply.

"Gotta confess," Jenna whispered, "I feel guilty bringing a bag of store-bought salad."

"Don't sweat it," Dyson said. "Everyone knows what you're going through. Your father's going to be here."

"Yeah, well, that's a whole 'nother thing." Jenna frowned and shook her head. "He's pretty annoyed that I didn't call him. But I didn't want him to worry. I think he's ticked that I'm not staying with him and Shayna, but they're trying to plan a wedding. I didn't want to intrude."

Doug squeezed her hand. "He's your father. He's just worried about you. We'll make sure he knows you're being well looked after. And don't worry about your things. I'm sorry I can't help tomorrow, but you and Al can borrow my 4Runner."

Jenna nodded her thanks as they continued up the short flight of brick steps to the front door, which was painted with three different shades of yellow. Off to one side was the ramp that had been built to accommodate Slick's wheelchair. The house faced west, so the setting sun beat warmly on their backs. Jenna was grateful that the barbecue would be in the backyard, out of the sun.

She had no problem with warm, summer days, but she didn't like it when the humidity was this high. Lowering her eyes, she sighed and shook her head. "I just wish it was all over," she said, as much to herself as to the guys.

"Well, try to loosen up a bit and have a little fun," Dyson said as he pressed the doorbell with his forefinger. The solemn *gong* of the doorbell sounded from somewhere inside the house. Moments later, Natalie Kerchak opened the door. She was wearing a plain white T-shirt, khaki shorts, and flip-flops.

"Oh, good. I'm so glad you could make it," she said with a wide smile as she leaned forward and gave each of them a light hug and a kiss on the cheek. Her face hadn't seen much sun that summer, but her red hair was bleached out a bit. It looked like pale copper wires in the sunlight. "Here. Let me put those in the fridge." She took the bag of salad from Jenna and a bottle of wine from Doug, then stepped back to allow them to enter. "Everyone else is already here—even your father and Shayna were on time."

"That's a first," Jenna said.

"They're all out back. Go on. I'll be out in a minute."

Ever curious, Jenna couldn't help but look around the apartment as they walked slowly down the hallway, through the sitting room, to the door that led out onto the back porch. In Slick's study, off to one side, she could see the rows of books that lined the dark oak bookshelves, and the brass ornaments and mirrors that adorned the walls. Throughout the house the furniture looked worn but comfortable. The air inside was cool and, although there was no evidence of dust anywhere, it carried the hint of an indefinable aroma that made Jenna think of her grandmother's old house in Acton. In the family room at the back of the house, the stereo system was set up so the speakers were pointing out the windows. Jenna recognized the song that was playing: "The Sinister Minister," by Bela Fleck and the Flecktones.

"Whoa, you're getting pretty progressive with your taste in jazz," Jenna said to Slick as they approached him. He was seated in his wheelchair, overseeing the grill. He and Doug shook hands amiably. Long shadows rippled across the backyard like a thin wash of ink.

"One must always keep one's mind open to new things," Slick said, adopting a professorial tone of voice. "It's what keeps one young."

Jenna giggled and said, "Well, if that's the case, let me run out to the car. I think I have the new OutKast CD."

"Whoa. No need to be *that* open-minded," Dyson said with a chuckle while Slick looked back and forth between them, his expression silently asking, *Who the heck is OutKast?*

"Jenna!" her father called out, striding toward her with his arms outstretched to hug her. Shayna, a few steps behind him, was smiling widely.

Jenna kissed her father's cheek and hugged him tightly for a few seconds, then broke it off and turned to give Shayna a hug. "Good to see you," Jenna said to Shayna. "You'll have to fill me in on how the wedding plans are going."

"Oh, I will," Shayna said as she took hold of her fiancée's hand and squeezed it excitedly. Then a look of concern rippled across her features. "But first—tell me how you've been. You've had a heck of a week."

Remembering Dyson's admonition not to discuss work, Jenna smiled and shrugged. "I'm all right. The guy's probably harmless. And the case Slick's been working on is a pretty helpful distraction."

Her father grimaced. "If you're using serial murders to take your mind off your potential stalker, Jenna, I can't say I'm overly comforted."

Shayna elbowed him. "Frank."

He smiled at Jenna. "I'm not supposed to talk about such things today."

Jenna laughed, grateful for the warm feelings that surged up in her, and hugged her father. "Me either! Okay, small talk only. Back to the important stuff. The wedding!"

But when she looked past her father and Shayna and saw Danny standing next to Audrey, who was here with her firefighter boyfriend, Henry Bolling, she wondered how long she could leave her work and The Baptist case behind. In the end, she was rather proud that she maintained social small talk for as long as she did—about ten minutes. Long before Slick had placed the prime cuts of steak, the old-fashioned Polish sausage, and the boned chicken breasts onto the grill, she broke away from a conversation with Natalie and Shayna about her selection of flowers for the wedding, and wandered over to Danny. "So, are we having fun yet?" Jenna asked with a sly smile.

"Oh, yeah," Danny said with a nod. His hand clutched a bottle of Shipyard Ale that was beaded with moisture. "I'm not a big fan of these kinds of social thingies." He cocked one side of his mouth into a tight smile.

"Rather be out on the streets, arresting the bad guys, huh?" Jenna said playfully.

"You bet—either that or strolling around Harvard Square with a friend."

Jenna smiled and raised an eyebrow. Then she laughed softly. "Me too."

"Sometimes I forget how important it is to have down-time like this," Danny said. Get some distance from the job, so it doesn't become my whole life." He shrugged. "So, can I get you something to drink? Soda? Wine?"

"I'm under age, remember?"

"I don't think anyone will bust you," Danny said.

"All right, then. A glass of white wine would be nice," she said, and she walked with him over to the table where an array of drinks and appetizers were spread out. She cast a quick glance in her father's direction, but he seemed either not to notice or care that she was having a drink.

Once she was taken care of, Danny grabbed another bottle of Shipyard from the ice chest and popped the top. Then the two of them wandered back over to the stockade fence, about as far away from the others as they could get without actually looking antisocial.

"So," Jenna said, after taking a tiny sip of wine, "have you found out anything more about the other victims?"

Danny snickered and shook his head. "So much for downtime. That didn't take you long."

Jenna shrugged. "Hey. I'm not dwelling on it or anything. I'm just curious. Making small talk, you know? Like, 'How was your day at work?'"

Danny took a long pull from his beer bottle, swallowed, and stared over at the rest of the partyers. A thin plume of blue smoke was rising from the gas grill, and Natalie was scurrying back and forth between the kitchen and the table where they were preparing the food. Danny appeared to be ignoring her, but then he cleared his throat and said softly, "Yeah . . . we found out some stuff."

Jenna's interest instantly sparked. The sounds of casual conversation and laughter melted away as she looked at Danny and waited for him to continue.

"The third guy who was found—the one who washed up in Revere—"

"Charles Flood," Jenna said, and Danny nodded.

"He was a loan officer at a bank in downtown Boston." Danny lowered his voice as though he didn't want anyone to overhear him. "A couple of years ago, he was also called to testify in a drug case in Boston. There was some suspicion he might be laundering drug money through his bank and taking a kickback, but they never caught him on it."

"Why's that?" Jenna asked.

"Because the man they were investigating—a guy name Manuel Rodriguez who was supposedly connected to a Colombia cartel—ended up dead. He was shot on the courthouse steps, so—" Danny shrugged and then took another sip of beer.

"So, Flood was never prosecuted," Jenna finished for him.

Turning to look directly at her, Danny nodded.

"Do you think there's a connection?" Jenna asked. "This is the kind of thing you were looking for, right? I mean, between Flood and Balzarini? If there are drugs involved—"

"If there are drugs and a Colombian cartel involved," Danny said, "and we establish a connection of any kind, the FBI will step in, and we'll lose our case."

"Do you think that's what it is?" Jenna asked, squinting inquisitively as she looked at Danny. The sun had almost set, and in the gathering twilight, his complexion looked darker than usual. Shayna and Dyson were moving around, lighting tiki lamps that ringed the yard.

"Colombian drug cartels?" Danny said. He took a deep breath and held it as he tilted his head back and looked up at the darkening sky. His eyes seemed to be focused on some far distant point. Then he exhaled and said, "I don't think so. Not really."

"Why's that?" Jenna asked. "If this guy Jimmy Balzarini was dealing, he might have gotten hooked up with the wrong people and owed them money."

Biting his lower lip, Danny shook his head. "No. It just doesn't fit," he said softly. "These killings don't have the earmarks of a gang killing spree. They're too elaborate. One thing that does concern me, though, is that if some element of organized crime is involved, we'll never identify the pool the victims were drowned in. There are just too many private pools in the surrounding area, so following that angle will be a dead end."

"So what does that leave you with?"

Again, Danny shrugged before taking a long swallow of beer. "More interviews with known associates of the deceased. And the religious angle, I guess," he said. "I mean, if you think about it, whoever's doing these killings is being very thorough. Carving crosses on the victims' foreheads and then drowning them in one location before disposing of the bodies elsewhere takes a lot of planning."

"They're also taking a pretty big chance of getting caught, moving their victims around like that," Jenna said. The party was all but forgotten, and her mind was racing as she tried to put the pieces of the puzzle together.

"Hey, you guys! Food's on!" Jenna's father called out, catching Jenna's and Danny's attention and waving them over.

"Well, I suppose we ought to be social," Danny said as he pushed himself away from the fence.

Jenna smiled and nodded. "Yeah. I suppose so," she said, and then she chuckled. "I promised Dyson I wouldn't spend the whole time talking about the case, and look at us."

"Yeah . . . just look at us," Danny said, shaking his head as they walked together over to the table where an impressive quantity of food was spread out. Just once, briefly, their shoulders touched, but Jenna pretended not to notice.

The sun was up, lighting Dyson's living room with a hazy orange glow. Jenna had spent another restless night in Dyson's guest room. Already the day was hot, and she could tell it was going to be another scorcher. For a long while before she got up, she just lay there listening to the songs of morning birds that came through the opened window. Groaning, she glanced at her wristwatch and saw that it was almost nine o'clock.

It had been a while since she had stayed in bed this late, but as much as she would have enjoyed being lazy, she wanted to get her things out of Virginia Rosborough's apartment. Danny had arranged for Jeff to be out that morning, and she wanted to get in and out quickly to avoid any chance of having to see him again. Still, even after she got everything over to Dyson's place, she knew she was going to feel dislocated until the fall semester started, and she and Yoshiko were living in Whitney House.

There was no indication that Dyson was awake, and Jenna wondered if he made a habit of sleeping in or if he was just being quiet, trying to let her sleep. She considered getting up and making a pot of coffee. Maybe she should cook some eggs, bacon, and toast for both of them, but she realized that, as close as she felt to Dyson, she didn't really know all that much about his personal habits. Maybe he didn't even like bacon and eggs.

She sighed as she peeled off the single sheet that had covered her during the night. It was limp and damp with sweat. She dropped her feet to the floor and sighed again as she ran her hands over her face and thought about what she should do next.

Maybe a shower so she'd be ready to leave as soon as Dyson was up. They had a lot of work ahead of them. Maybe they'd pick up breakfast at some fast-food place on their way to the apartment.

She cast her gaze around the room until it came to rest on her laptop. It was pretty early in the morning, but maybe someone would be online. After all the tension of the last few days, it would be nice to chat with a friend or two and remind herself that, in some people's worlds, things were still absolutely normal.

*But not for the people who have met The Baptist,* she thought. In spite of the heat, a shiver tickled up the back of her neck.

Moving quietly so she wouldn't disturb Dyson, she plugged in her laptop, hooked it up to the phone line, and turned the machine on. After it ran through its startup, she was online, checking her Buddy List to see if anyone else had nothing better to do.

As she was scanning through her list, her computer *binged* and the message *Good morning, sunshine* appeared. Jenna smiled when she saw that it was from Hunter.

*Hey. What's up?* she typed.

*Not much here,* Hunter typed in reply. *Just killing time. I'm heading to the airport in an hour or so. Really hot down here.*

*I can imagine,* Jenna typed. *Hot here 2. Why you going to the airport?*

*Gonna pick up Yoshiko,* Hunter replied after a few seconds.

Jenna sat and stared at the message for a while, trying to let it sink in. She didn't quite believe what she was looking at.

*Yoshiko?* she typed.

*Uh-huh. She's flying to N.O. from Hawaii via Cali today. This is a good thing!* He punctuated his message with a large smiley face.

*Yes, it's a good thing,* Jenna typed. *So what—? She decided to come back to the mainland a little early?*

*Her fam is going to ship most of her things directly to school. Says she missed me too much.*

*I can't imagine that!*

*Gonna show her the sights of New Orleans before we both head back to school in a couple of weeks.*

*Excellent!!!*

Jenna looked up when she heard the scuffing sound of bare feet in the hall. Dyson was standing in the doorway, wearing a lightweight bathrobe. His hair was mussed, and he had a foggy, faraway look in his eyes. He made a motion with his hand like he was drinking something and mouthed the word "Coffee?"

Jenna nodded eagerly as her computer *binged*. She looked back at the message Hunter had typed.

Only it wasn't from Hunter.

She didn't recognize the screen name, FisherofMen, and the message—*Is this Jenna B.?*—made her throat suddenly go dry. Her hands froze halfway to the keyboard, and her vision blurred as she stared at the message. Her pulse thudded softly as it raced in her ears. "Al . . . ?" she called out, her voice high and tight.

Her computer made another *bing* sound, and another message appeared in the window, with the FisherofMen address, simultaneously with Hunter's message.

*You still there?* Hunter asked, but Jenna couldn't bring herself to type a reply as she stared at the other message. "Al!" she shouted. "Come here! Quick!"

Within seconds, Dyson was beside her. She pointed at her computer, and he leaned forward to scan the message on the screen.

*You shouldn't interfere with the Lord's work, Miss Blake,* the message said.

"I think it's him," Jenna said. Her throat was so dry, it distorted her voice. "I think it's the killer."

"You don't—"

Before Dyson could finish, another message appeared on the screen.

*Do you need to be SAVED, Jenna?*

"Is there any way you can trace where that's coming from?" Dyson asked.

Biting her lower lip, Jenna shook her head no.

"Do you think this might be your freaky roommate, back at the apartment?" Dyson asked.

All Jenna could do was shake her head slowly from side to side as she stared at the word "SAVED." It could be Jeff. He would have had access to her computer while she'd been living at Virginia's. Could easily have found out her screen name. She jumped and let out a tiny squeal when the computer *binged* again, and yet another message appeared.

*YOU are a SINNER . . . you WILL be SAVED . . . and very SOON!*

And then the window closed.

"He signed off," Jenna said, looking up at Dyson. Under different circumstances, she might have thought he looked sort of funny, standing there barefoot in his thin bathrobe, but now all she could see was the depth of concern in his eyes.

"Can you save those messages?" he asked.

Jenna nodded, but her hands were shaking so badly, she kept hitting the wrong keys as she cut and pasted the files to her document folder. A mental image of her own face with a red cross sliced between her eyes rose up in her mind, sending waves of chills through her.

"We've got to call Danny and tell him about this," she said, fighting to control the tremor in her voice. "And maybe he'll . . . I mean, no offense to you, my favorite bodyguard, but I'd feel a lot better if he was with us when we went and got my stuff."

"Yeah. Me too," Dyson said. He cast a glance over his shoulder toward the kitchen. "The coffee's brewing, so if you want to hop into the shower first . . ."

Jenna nodded numbly as she put her laptop to one side. She wasn't sure if she should turn it off or not. She didn't think there was any way the police could trace the Instant Message, but she wasn't sure. Her legs were shaking as she stood up slowly, turned, and looked Dyson straight in the eye.

"Hey," Dyson said, giving her a reassuring smile.

"Whoever it is, they're probably just messing with you, you know? Just trying to scare you."

Jenna looked back at him, but she wasn't convinced in the least. She knew she wasn't going to feel safe until she saw Danny.

"Hello? Virginia?"

Jenna leaned her head into the apartment and looked around, but everything seemed to be quiet and undisturbed. The living room windows were closed, and the shades were down, so the room still held some of the coolness from the night. Dust swirled like golden powder in the narrow rays of sunlight that shot between the venetian blinds.

"She must have gone to the library already," Jenna said, feeling a measure of relief. She looked over her shoulder at Danny, who was standing so close behind her she could feel the warmth of his breath on the back of her neck. He rested a hand on the butt of his service weapon, but it remained holstered. Jenna found the thought of the gun both comforting and terrifying. Dyson, leaning against the railing, stood a few feet behind them while Audrey waited down on the sidewalk so she could keep an eye on Doug's SUV.

"If I were your Ms. Rosborough, I probably wouldn't want to spend much time in the apartment with Jeff Tilton either," Danny observed, his gaze darting about, searching every corner for a sign of something menacing. After the Instant Message she'd gotten earlier— which had to be from someone who either knew or had managed to learn her I.M. screen name—Danny was not about to take chances.

"Let's just get your things and get the hell out of here," Dyson said as he stepped into the living room.

As they went into her bedroom, she couldn't help but think how quickly her feelings about living here for the summer had changed. She had moved in with such high hopes only to have them dashed because one of her roommates was a total bitch and the other was a total creep.

Jenna was grateful that she had saved all the boxes she'd used to move in with, and the three of them set to work. It wasn't long before all of them were dripping with sweat, but within half an hour, they had everything boxed up and ready to go. They filed back and forth, tromping up and down the stairs until the bedroom was exactly the way Jenna had found it. Doug's SUV sagged on its springs as she and Dyson closed the back gate and then got into the vehicle. Dyson started up the vehicle, but before he drove away, Jenna grabbed him by the arm.

"Wait a second," she said as she unbuckled her seat belt and got out. "I left some things in the bathroom. And I forgot to leave the key behind."

Danny and Audrey were waiting across the street in their idling car. When Jenna got out of the SUV, Danny rolled his window down and shot her a questioning look.

"I left my blow-dryer and a couple of other things in the bathroom," she called out. "I'll just be a sec."

Without a word, Danny slipped his car into Park and got out. He loosened his revolver in its holster as he crossed the street.

"I really don't think I'll need help carrying a blow-dryer," Jenna said with a laugh, but Danny followed her back up to the apartment.

*One last time,* Jenna thought, feeling a trace of sadness as she and Danny walked up the flight of stairs to the second-floor landing. Sweat was dripping down the sides of her face and making her T-shirt stick to her skin. Her heart was pounding heavily, as she opened the door and stepped inside. The utter silence in the apartment seemed almost surreal. The place looked so drab and empty, now. Danny waited in the stairwell as she went to the bathroom and opened the door.

For a second or two, Jenna just stood there, unable to believe what she was looking at. Her throat closed off with a *click*, and she was vaguely aware that she was making a strangled sound as she staggered back out into the hallway. Danny heard her and came running, his revolver in his hand.

Jenna backed up until she banged into the wall opposite the bathroom door and just stood there, pointing at Virginia's naked body, which was lying in an awkward sprawl inside the half-filled bathtub. The water had turned pink from her blood and had sloshed over the sides, leaving splotches on the white bathmat. One of Virginia's hands was draped over the side of the tub. The fingertips were laced with streaks of darker red. Her eyes were wide open and staring at the ceiling. Gashed across her forehead was an open wound in the shape of a cross. It was still raw and crusted with blood.

# chapter 12

"It's okay," Dyson said softly, holding Jenna just a little tighter. They sat together on the sidewalk across the street from the apartment where police officers were stretching yellow crime scene tape across the stairs, tying it off on the railings. The day was hot, and the humidity pressed down on them.

*The water was pink,* Jenna thought. For some reason, that image stuck with her, frightening her as much as the presence of the corpse itself.

*The water was pink with Virginia's blood!*

Yet every time Jenna closed her eyes and she saw the image of the pale, naked flesh of the dead girl in the bathtub, in her mind's eye, instead of Virginia's face, she saw her own.

She kept her eyes open even as she shook her head and whispered nonsense to herself—or maybe to God—and wiped away her tears.

LAST BREATH

"Hush, now. It's okay."

An odd tremor went through her, and a tiny smile flickered across her features. It felt morbid to smile, even for an instant, but hearing Dyson say the word "hush"— something she thought only grandmothers used—gave her a moment's respite from the frightening images that filled her mind and the thoughts that were weighing on her.

"I know. I'm a wreck," she said, her face pressed against his shoulder. "I don't know why I'm crying for her. I mean . . . it's awful to say it, but I really didn't like her. I may have even hated her. She was *awful* to me, and probably to just about everyone else in her life."

"Maybe that's why you're crying," Dyson said, dropping one arm so that he sat there on the curb beside her with one arm draped over her shoulders. "You hated her. You've got to feel a little guilty about that now. No matter how much of a witch she was."

Jenna let that sink in, then nodded. "Yeah . . . I guess. Partly that, at least. And maybe because"— she turned and stared into Dyson's eyes— "because I know it was supposed to be me. Or, even if she didn't die in my place, she died *because* of me. Virginia would still be alive if she . . . if she hadn't rented me that room this summer."

Dyson took a long breath but made no reply.

*What can he say?* Jenna thought. *It was only the truth.*

Her gaze had shifted back and forth between the pavement in front of her and the apartment house across the street. Now she looked up to see Audrey Gaines striding purposefully across the street toward her. Then, behind Audrey, Jenna saw the crime scene unit emerge from the door of the apartment house with a black body bag. She dropped her gaze to the pavement once more, trying not to picture Virginia Rosborough stuffed into that bag.

Trying not to picture *herself* in that bag.

"You okay?"

Audrey's shadow fell across her, and Jenna looked up to see the concern on her face. "Not exactly," she confessed. "But give me a minute and I will be."

She was surprised to find that this was the truth. Her tears were gone. The images in her head might linger for a while, maybe a long while, but she had been around death so much this year—it was her job, after all—that she was sure she would be all right soon enough.

"I'm guessing this means I won't be able to take my things back to Dyson's today?"

Audrey shook her head. "Sorry. You can take some clean clothes—we'll just keep track of whatever goes with you—but you're going to have to wait for the crime scene unit to finish up in there. Everything else we'll have to hold on to until the department decides it isn't a crime scene anymore. Could be tomorrow, but it's more likely to be several days at least."

"Wonderful." Jenna sighed. "You know, I kept promising myself I was going to keep my distance from this stuff."

"You have," Dyson assured her. "It's just . . . somehow . . . you drew the killer's attention."

"Yeah," Audrey said, "well, if it was your other roommate, Jeff Tilton, we know he had you in focus."

Jenna frowned. "You really think it's him? I mean, it's no surprise he's not around. Danny made it clear he wasn't supposed to be here when I came back to get my stuff."

Audrey shrugged. "I don't know. He passed the polygraph, but that's not impossible for sociopaths. He's obsessed with you, and he's fairly religious. He's got to be our first candidate." She paused for a moment and regarded both of them sternly. "You realize, of course, that we're speaking professionally here? Dr. Dyson?"

"Of course I do, Detective," Dyson replied, as if affronted by the remark.

"All right. Danny will be out in a few minutes. I'm sure he'll want to talk to you, so stick around a while longer."

"I'm not going anywhere without some clean clothes," Jenna replied.

Audrey nodded and began to turn back toward the apartment. The heel of her boot clicked on the pavement, and she paused.

"You know, Jenna, this isn't the first time you've drawn this sort of attention. That's no reflection on you, or if it is, it's a positive one. It means you're effective at what you do. You annoy the perps. But if you were thinking before that you want to put some distance between yourself and your work . . . I guess I wanted to tell you I'm not sure that's possible. The only way to keep your distance from a homicide investigation is not to be involved with it at all."

"You mean quit?" Jenna asked, frowning.

Audrey shrugged. "It's an option."

Jenna felt their eyes on her. Dyson had stiffened at the word "quit." He turned and watched her carefully. Audrey waited patiently for her response.

Biting her lower lip, Jenna shook her head slowly. "No," she replied. "It's not an option. I'm not hiding. Not from this guy . . . not from anyone else. People have *died* around me. I lost one of my best friends last fall, Detect—Audrey. To a killer. I've learned a lot, and one of the things I've learned is that sometimes, if I'm lucky, and I work hard at it, I can help." She took a deep breath and held it a moment before letting it out. "So to *hell* with hiding. You're a cop. I'd expect you to understand. Someone does something like this, I'm in it for the duration."

For a long moment, Audrey gazed at her. Then the detective gave her a barely perceptible nod, turned, and headed back toward the crime scene.

Dyson kissed the top of her head. Jenna glanced up at him and saw the pride in his eyes, and she loved him for it. Her world might have grown very complicated lately, and sometimes dangerous, but *God* she was lucky to have friends like this in her life!

"Do you remember what she was like the first time we met her?"

The question took Danny by surprise. He and Audrey had stopped off at Redbone's for a beer after they'd done the paperwork on the discovery of Virginia

Rosborough's body. Technically, they were off duty, but though they had not discussed it, he was sure Audrey had no more intention of quitting for the night than he did. The rest of the Somerset P.D. was out looking for Jeff Tilton. Cops from Boston, Revere, and Cambridge were in on the search as well. An APB had gone out to the surrounding towns. They'd pick him up soon.

He and Audrey had been going over the Rosborough crime scene. There had been no sign of forced entry, which pointed to Tilton. But there were other ways to get into an old apartment like that and leave no sign. And there was no way of knowing who else might have a key. The DOA's other two roommates, for starters— the ones who were gone for the summer and letting Rosborough sublet to Tilton and Jenna.

They'd been talking about murder. About the crime scene. So Audrey's question had come out of the blue. Somewhat, at least.

"Who? You mean Jenna?"

Audrey sipped her beer and nodded.

"Sure," Danny said, casting his mind back to the previous September. "It's sort of strange, isn't it? To think of all that's happened in a year. She seemed like such a kid then."

"But she doesn't anymore, does she?" Audrey asked, leaning forward a little.

For a moment Danny thought she was teasing him about the attraction he might feel for Jenna. But when he saw the faraway, almost melancholy expression on his partner's face, he realized that was not the case. "No.

No, she doesn't. But she's got the same . . . passion, I guess. The same passion that a good cop has to have. Or a good doctor. Or anyone involved in solving other people's problems. She's a fighter."

Audrey focused on him, and Danny thought he saw a trace of sadness in her eyes. "I feel sorry for her," his partner finally said.

"What? Why?"

"Don't get me wrong. I admire the girl. Used to be I didn't want her getting in the way. Now, I'm glad to have her around. To have her on the team. She's a kid, but she's proven herself, as far as I'm concerned." She shot him a hard look. "Don't you dare tell her I said so. I don't want you ruining my image."

He smiled. "Wouldn't dream of it."

"It just seems to me that, in the process of gaining this passion you're talking about," Audrey went on, "she's lost something else. Something none of us ever get back."

"She's grown up, you mean?"

Audrey nodded. "For better or worse."

Just then, Danny's cell phone rang. He slipped it out of his front pocket and glanced at it. The incoming number belonged to Kim, a woman he had dated for a while. He would have liked to know why she was calling, to catch up with her a little. It had been some time since they had spoken, and though he knew there was nothing between them—that was a dead end—he still thought fondly of her.

"Who is it?" Audrey asked, her voice tight.

"Not work," Danny replied, as he turned off the phone's ringer and slipped it back into his pocket. He took a long sip of his beer and then set the mug on the bar. His fingers traced lines in the frosty condensation on the glass.

"You don't think he's the guy, do you?"

"Tilton?" Danny considered for a moment, then shook his head without looking at her. "He's a stalker. But I don't make him for it. I think we're going to pick him up, and he's going to be totally baffled because I was the one who told him not to be home."

"So, what now? We go back to the swimming pool search? 'Cause that shit is tedious, and I don't think it's getting us anywhere. I think it's more likely the drug connection. We've already got two dead guys who were getting away with something—"

Danny looked up sharply.

"What?" Audrey asked.

"That's what The Baptist is all about, right? Cleansing sins? We've known that all along, but we were running on the idea the perp's just a general psycho." He paused a moment, thinking, then said, "But what if there's more to it? What if all the victims—except Rosborough, right? —but what if all of the victims were sinners? What if they'd all done bad things, and gotten away with them?"

Audrey seemed to like the sound of that. "Okay," she said. "But walk me through this. How does The Baptist know? I mean, we know Flood and Balzarini were dirty. But what about the others?"

Danny rolled that one around in his mind. "It keeps

coming back to the psychiatrist. I mean, he would know—right?"

"He's not the guy. We know he's not the guy."

"Do we?" Danny asked.

She stared at him, and he gave a grudging shrug. "Okay. We know he's not the guy. But the other two victims were his clients, and if they were dirty and feeling guilty about it, who would they tell?"

"Their shrink," Audrey replied, already rising up off of her bar stool. She tossed a ten on the bar. "Guess we're back on duty."

Danny smiled humorlessly. "What a surprise."

Jenna loved the little guest room at Dyson's house. The bed was antique cherry wood, one of those that seemed almost too high off the floor. The lamps, too, were antique, their bulbs set inside hand-painted blown glass that was meant to look like hurricane lamps. The wood floor was remarkably dust-free, and though there were two throw rugs in the room, she kept her socks on. The wood was cold.

That night, however, her appreciation for her surroundings was nearly subconscious. Yes, she was comfortable there; but after the events of the day, there was only one way she could get the image of Virginia's soaking corpse out of her head. She sat cross-legged at the fragile little desk in that room and stared at her computer screen.

The Baptist was still out there, and he had his eye on her. Jenna wasn't going to just wait for the police to ride to the rescue. The drug angle that Danny and Audrey had been sniffing around didn't really work for her. It seemed incomplete, somehow, like doing a crossword puzzle and coming up with the answer for a clue only to realize that your answer didn't have enough letters to fit.

While she stared at the screen, her hands worked almost involuntarily on a Rubik's Cube. Jenna loved riddles, brain teasers, puzzles of all kinds. Most of hers were still packed away for the summer, home at her mother's house in Natick. Dyson had given her this one as a gift. It was from junior high school, he said, and he had known that she would get more use out of it now than he would.

She had smiled, then, her heart warmed, grateful that her hands had something to do. Now, though, her fingers worked the Cube, trying to lock the colors into uniform rows, only glancing down every other twist. There was no smile on her face. "I'm missing something," she whispered to herself.

There were several windows open on her computer, minimized so she could view all three at once. The first was a list of YMCA swimming pools in the Greater Boston area. She knew that Audrey and Castillo's partner had been doing this research already. They'd likely be insulted to know that she was second-guessing their work, but she wasn't about to tell them.

The second screen had a list of permits the City of Boston had issued in the last dozen years or so to build in-ground swimming pools. It wasn't much, all things considered. The records dating back further were inaccessible, and there was nothing that said it had to be an in-ground pool. But it was the best she could do. Not that it mattered. She didn't think it was a private pool, anyway. Unless it was someone wealthy enough to have an indoor pool, there were too many chances a neighbor would see something.

No. Jenna felt certain it was a public pool. And that meant someone with access to the pool after hours. An employee.

The third screen was a list of health clubs in Boston and the surrounding towns.

The religious elements of the case had distracted everyone.

*The Baptist.*

The name alone was enough to set anyone off in a particular direction. But both Balzarini and Flood had been criminals. Jenna had been turning this fact over and over in her head all day, the same way her fingers were working the Rubik's Cube, and a couple of blocks had locked into place. She had thought that maybe all four of the victims could be connected to one another through criminal activities, possibly something drug related.

But maybe it was even simpler than that. Maybe their crimes weren't related at all. Maybe the only connection was that they had all committed crimes. Or . . . *sins.*

Balzarini and Flood weren't in jail. Maybe someone had thought they *should* have been. The Baptist thing might be a smokescreen. Even if it wasn't—even if the killer was a religious nut—it might still be about punishment. The Baptist could be a vigilante.

Another block clicked into place.

The whole point of what The Baptist was doing was punishment. So what was the killer punishing the first two victims for? Something. They had done something wrong. She felt sure of it. Something that wasn't on public record; otherwise, Danny and Audrey would have found it right away. But The Baptist knew.

So who had access to that sort of information? The psychiatrist, certainly, but from everything Danny had said, Jenna was sure it wasn't him.

Who else, then? Who might know about crimes people had committed but had not been caught at, or convicted for? A judge, a lawyer, a reporter, a cop?

That line of thinking had dovetailed neatly back into her search for swimming pools. Lots of lawyers belong to health clubs. She would have to try to get the Somerset P.D. to check membership records at those clubs. But it wasn't just lawyers.

Jenna paused, a frown creasing her forehead as she stared at the three windows open on her screen. Her hands moved unconsciously, twisting a row of blocks into place. She sat up straighter and then set the Rubik's Cube aside. Her gaze drifted to it for an instant, and she saw that it was nearly complete. On the blue side there were two white squares. The puzzle was nearly solved.

She wished the puzzle on her computer screen would come together as easily. But she sensed that she was close. Her mind was gnawing at the edges of something.

Not just lawyers. Cops did a lot of moonlighting, from traffic control around roadwork sites to pulling security duty at high school dances, private functions, and places like YMCAs and swim clubs.

"No key," Jenna whispered, shaking her head. Her hand snaked out to pick up the Rubik's Cube again. She had thought she was on to something, but no such luck. Cops on security detail weren't likely to have their own keys to such places. Some of them might, but there was no reason to assume they did. It was another avenue to explore, nothing more.

"Damn."

She focused a moment on the Cube, turning it over to look at it from different angles. With three twists, she was left with only one white square on the blue side, and one blue on the white. Another few twists, and she'd have it solved.

An idea was niggling at the back of her head. Jenna closed her eyes, trying to let it in. Security guards at the Y or some club didn't have a key because they didn't have the run of the place. It wasn't their turf. But there were a handful of swimming pools that *were* their turf.

"Oh," she whispered to herself, her eyes widening. She put aside the Rubik's Cube again and began to type.

The State Department of Conservation and Recreation had an Urban Division. Jenna opened a fourth window and searched for their site. With two clicks of the mouse, she had a list of those public pools. They were broken up into four districts—Charles, Mystic, Harbor, and Neponset—and though a couple of the pools were too far away to be likely, there were more than a dozen that would have been conveniently located for The Baptist. She had no idea what the security situation was at any of these places, but the police had to have access to them: either as security, at opening or closing, or even just for their own recreation. It certainly wouldn't have been difficult for a cop to get a key.

It was just another avenue to investigate. She had no evidence that suggested this was more significant to investigate. And yet she felt it was. Her instincts were often accurate, and she felt that this lead might be important. At least important enough that she didn't want to wait until tomorrow to suggest to Danny that they might take a closer look at the DCR pools.

Jenna went across to the nightstand and grabbed her cell phone. She dialed Danny's mobile number and listened to the happy, trilling ring. A twinge of disappointment went through her when his voice mail picked up.

"Danny, it's Jenna," she said after the beep. "I've been doing some thinking, and—yeah, a little research. Couldn't help myself. Look, what if it's been a vigilante thing? Worth considering, right? If it is, you might want to look into lawyers and cops who have health club memberships. But really, what I'm thinking is DCR swimming pools. Who has keys to those? Do cops? Don't be mad at me for suggesting it. But if it is a vigilante thing, and not just religious . . . anyway, call me back. Doesn't matter what time. I won't be getting much sleep tonight. Not after . . . earlier."

She said good-bye and hung up. Then she stared at

the glow of her cell phone and decided maybe Danny was a little busy. If he had a lot of messages, he might not listen to them right away. But a text message, *that* he'd glance at for sure.

Quickly she keyed in a message. *Hey. Could be vigilante? Lawyer? Cop? Did u guys check DRC pools? Call me. J.*

She sent the message and then simply stood there a long moment. Her comment about not being able to sleep tonight had been the truth. She did not want to disturb Dyson, but she didn't want to go to bed, either. She wondered if any of her friends were on I.M. If not, maybe she would call Hunter and see if Yoshiko had arrived in New Orleans in one piece.

Anything to avoid closing her eyes and seeing Virginia Rosborough's naked body in that tub of blood-tinted water.

As she walked back to the desk, her eyes fell upon the Rubik's Cube again. One white square stared back at her from the blue side like an accusing eye.

*Thump!*

Out in the front room, something had just slammed hard against the door. It came a second time, and Jenna understood. Someone was trying to get in. She swore under her breath, terror firing through her. The Baptist had warned her on Instant Message, but then he'd killed Virginia, and Jenna had thought that was either supposed to be her, or that it was a message for her. She hadn't even considered that the killer might be able to find her here.

With the third thump there was a loud crack and a

splintering of wood, and then the sound of the door crashing open.

It had all happened in a moment, and she was frozen, rooted to the spot. Then she heard footfalls and a shout.

*Dyson!* she thought. *Oh shit, Al!*

His voice boomed outside the closed guest room door. "What the hell do you think you're—"

Then his words were cut off, punctuated by a cry of pain, short and sharp, and another thump. This was softer, different. It was the sound of Al Dyson hitting the floor.

Jenna bit her lip, pulse racing, face burning with the rush of blood and adrenaline. She rushed to the tiny desk, clicked off the lamp beside her computer, then closed the laptop to extinguish its glow. Her gaze darted to the window above the desk. It was open, a lazy summer breeze drifting in.

She did not want to make too much noise, but she knew that was a foolish urge. He was here, in the house. Dyson was down, possibly dead or dying. He would find her. Time was more important than stealth.

Swiftly, she released the latches that kept the screen in place, then gave it a shove. It popped out and fell soundlessly to the grass below.

Jenna climbed up onto the desk in the darkness of the room. The only illumination came from the streetlights, moon, and stars outside. The door crashed open behind her. She risked one glance behind her as she scrambled over the desk and grabbed hold of the window frame, but she caught only a glimpse of the killer's silhouette.

Then she lunged through the open window.

Fingers caught her hair, and she cried out as pain seared her scalp. She kicked backward, tried to turn around to fight, but those fingers in her hair gathered a tighter grip, tugged her backward, and then thrust her forward again.

Jenna had a fraction of a second to flinch before her head slammed into the window frame. Once. Twice.

Then darkness slid open below her and claimed her.

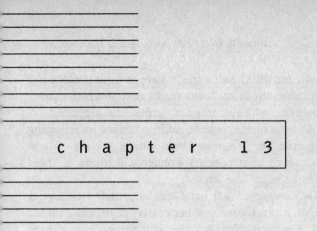

# chapter 13

"Do you have any idea the impact this would have on my practice if any of my patients found out I'd violated doctor-patient confidentiality?"

Dr. Cosgrove was obviously trying hard to maintain his poise, but Danny could see how nervous he was about this late-night visit from the pair of detectives. The psychiatrist's office was still cool to the point of frigid because the air conditioner had been running all day, but a sheen of sweat glistened on the doctor's upper lip. His face looked unnaturally pale in the yellow glare of the desk lamp.

"We can appreciate that, Dr. Cosgrove," Audrey said mildly. She was standing next to Danny in front of Cosgrove's large, mahogany desk, her arms folded across her chest.

Danny scratched the side of his face and frowned as though seriously concerned. "I'm not convinced you've considered the impact it might have on your practice if it ever came out in the news media that you had a direct connection with two murder victims," he suggested.

Without missing a beat, Audrey jumped in, following up before Dr. Cosgrove could muster a reply. "Might make all of your patients wonder which one of them might be next," she offered.

Dr. Cosgrove's left hand was nervously twiddling a pile of multicolored, rubber-coated paper clips on his desk. He stared blankly down at them, his eyes glistening with that peculiar frightened look Danny had seen most often in caged animals at the zoo. "You wouldn't do that. It's slander."

Danny crossed his arms. "No, actually, it's just fact. We've kept your name out of it so far, Doc. In exchange, all you've done is jerk us around. That's going to change now, one way or another."

"There's nothing to debate here," Dr. Cosgrove said, a nervous quaver modulating his voice. "I have to protect the confidentiality of my clients."

Danny took a single step closer to the desk and, leaning forward, splayed his hands on the desk's smooth surface to support him. This close, the glow from Cosgrove's desk lamp was warm on his face.

"Enough of that shit. You know you're not required to protect the confidentiality of a patient who has died. The city's lawyers are fighting it out with your lawyers. But we've got precedent on our side. It's only a matter of time."

"And while you've been stonewalling us," Audrey

said, right on cue, "someone else was murdered in Somerset last night."

Dr. Cosgrove's hand jerked, and he knocked several paper clips onto the floor.

"You're hiding something," Danny said. "Maybe you really don't think it's important. But if there's any similarity between Jaffarian and Michael Sullivan, we need to know. Now."

Both of the detectives eased off a little, moving back in unison as if they'd rehearsed the move a hundred times. But Danny knew—and he knew that Audrey knew—that Cosgrove was close to breaking. Knowing when to press and when to pull back was all part of the skill, the beauty, and the art of interrogating someone that made it almost a ballet.

Dr. Cosgrove didn't say anything as he shifted in his chair. Then he cleared his throat and rapidly blinked his eyes. His hand was shaking when he reached up and wiped the sweat from his upper lip on the back of his knuckles. His eyes darted back and forth between Danny and Audrey. When he finally opened his mouth to speak, his throat made a funny clicking sound, and he looked away as though suddenly embarrassed.

"Please, Dr. Cosgrove," Danny said, sensing that it was time now to plead instead of threaten. "We need your help with this."

"I'm not convinced anything I have to say would be of value to your investigation," Dr. Cosgrove said.

"Let us decide that," Audrey said, and once again she stared harshly at him.

Dr. Cosgrove withered beneath her cool, steady gaze. After a moment, he took a deep breath, held it for a moment, and then said softly, "Well . . . you see . . . Mr. Jaffarian is, or was . . . a pedophile."

His voice was so low, Danny wasn't sure he'd heard him correctly—or that he wanted to hear him—but as the psychiatrist's words sank in, his body tensed. He and Audrey exchanged glances.

"He was arrested four years ago . . . in Boston," Dr. Cosgrove continued. "The D.A. never filed charges because it turned out that the accuser—a twelve-year-old girl—wouldn't testify in court. Her parents were afraid of the trauma she'd experience if they let her take the stand."

Dr. Cosgrove sat back in his chair and sighed heavily as though suddenly relieved of a great burden. When he looked up at Danny and Audrey again, he was unable to maintain eye contact for long. He shifted his gaze down to his left hand, which was still fiddling with the paper clips remaining on his desk.

Danny glanced at Audrey again. He knew instantly by her expression that she didn't want to interrupt Dr. Cosgrove, now that he'd started to open up. The rest would come.

"He came to me for therapy," Dr. Cosgrove said. "Out of fear, I suppose, as much as guilt. He saw this as a warning that he had to stop what he was doing, and I believe he genuinely wanted to change. I know he struggled with it."

"I'm sure he did," Audrey said tonelessly, but Danny heard the sarcasm and disgust dripping from every word.

"What about Sullivan? Do you know of any kind of connection between Jaffarian and Sullivan?"

The sudden shift in topic seemed to take Dr. Cosgrove aback. He raised his head and looked at her. His eyelids fluttered as he leaned back in his chair and studied the ceiling for several seconds. All the while, he was shaking his head slowly from side to side. "No . . . no. There's none that I'm aware of, anyway," he said distantly. "Michael Sullivan came to see me as a result of a court order."

"For what?" Danny asked.

Dr. Cosgrove sighed as though resigned to spill everything. "He had a serious drinking problem and, as a result, was physically abusing his wife. He and his wife were separated, but he wanted visitation with the children. The court demanded he enter anger-management therapy before they would consider his request."

Danny frowned and glanced at Audrey. He could see that she was thinking the same thing he was. There was no drug connection either to Jaffarian or to Sullivan, but each of them did have a criminal past that would not have shown up on a traditional rap sheet search.

But there was a more distinct connection as well. "So the Boston P.D. was involved in both cases."

Dr. Cosgrove didn't look like he quite understood the connection as he nodded slowly. Before Audrey could say anything more, Danny reached out his hand and shook Dr. Cosgrove's. "I want to thank you for your time. You've been very helpful. I hope we can follow up if we have any more questions."

Still looking confused and utterly defeated, Dr. Cosgrove stood up slowly behind his desk and nodded. He started to walk around the desk toward the door, but Danny waved him off. "We can find our way out," he said.

Danny and Audrey left the psychiatrist there as they walked out the door and down the stairs. When they stepped outside into the parking lot, the heavy humidity of the night was like a wall. Danny squirmed from the dampness that clung to his skin beneath his shirt.

"So, why did we rush off?" Audrey said, glaring at him. "I had a few more questions for him. If the kids were abused, we might have connected the two victims."

"And what about the other two?" Danny asked. "No, listen, I think the only connection is that they were all lowlife scumbags who got away with it. Both of them—Sullivan and Jaffarian—had committed crimes, and both of them walked." As he said this, Danny reached into his pocket for his cell phone to see if there were any messages while they'd been talking to Dr. Cosgrove. "And then we have Balzarini and Flood. Both of them got a pass on crimes *they'd* committed."

"You think that's the connection, that none of them were ever convicted?"

Danny shrugged as he switched on his cell phone.

"Hmm," he said. "I've got a text message." He pressed a few keys and watched as Jenna's message to him scrolled across the illuminated screen.

*Hey. Could be vigilante? Lawyer? Cop? Did u guys check DRC pools? Call me. J.*

"Anything important?" Audrey asked as they walked over to their car, which was parked on the street in front of the office.

Danny shook his head. "Not sure," he said as he quickly pressed a few buttons and listened to Jenna's voice message. As he listened, a cold, crawling feeling slithered up the back of his neck. "I want to check in with Jenna," Danny said. "Seems like she's one step ahead of us. And it sounds like she might be on to something."

He hurriedly dialed Jenna's number with his thumb, then held the phone to his ear as he waited for the connection. While he listened to the phone ring at the other end, he said to Audrey, "Jenna thinks it might be a lawyer or cop on a vigilante kick. I don't know why, but we both know she wouldn't suggest something like that without a solid theory. She also thinks we should check any rec. departments with swimming pools that cops might have access to."

"If there's a wrong cop in the mix, that's not a bad idea," Audrey said as she unlocked the driver's door and slid in behind the steering wheel.

"Damn. No answer."

Danny got in on the passenger's side, and Audrey started the car. He thought for a moment, then touched Audrey on the arm to stop her before she pulled out onto the street. "All the victims walked on crimes they committed in Boston," he said. "You think we can trust Castillo?"

"Sure," Audrey replied. "We've worked with him before. You know he's on the up-and-up."

"I guess," Danny said, but even as he was saying it, he was keying in the phone number for the Boston homicide division. He asked the dispatcher if Castillo was in and was told that he'd punched out over an hour ago.

"This is Detective Mariano, Somerset P.D. I need to reach him right away."

"Understood, Detective. You can try him at home, but he might not be there yet. Detective Castillo was heading over to the DRC pool on Soldier's Field Road."

Danny's throat felt dry. "And he left about an hour ago?"

"Yeah," the dispatcher replied. "Maybe less. Half an hour? But the pool closes at nine o'clock, so he's probably on his way home by now."

"Thanks for your help," Danny said as he cut the connection. With a little wag of his finger, he indicated that he wanted Audrey to start driving. Before she took off, though, she looked at him.

"Where to?" she asked.

"The DRC pool out on Soldier's Field Road." Even as he said it, fingers of ice traced lines along his spine.

Jenna was drifting in a dark dream that embraced her with a bone-deep chill. Her body felt curiously buoyed, almost like she was flying or drifting in the wind like a dandelion puff. Strands of her hair clung to her forehead in damp, tightening curls, and dull pain throbbed like tiny hammer blows on the side of her head. The closer she came to consciousness, the worse the pain got until she finally managed to open her eyes. She realized she was floating in water. Her left arm was stretched out above her head so much it hurt. When she tried to pull it down, something sharp bit into her wrist. She opened her mouth to take a breath, and the strong smell of chlorine filled her nose and throat, making her sneeze once . . . twice. The sound echoed oddly in the surrounding darkness.

Jenna knew that her eyes were open, but everywhere she looked there was only darkness. She tried to take another breath, and water sloshed into her mouth. She couldn't stop herself from sneezing again.

*Where am I? . . . What's going on?*

Her eyes began to adjust, and she saw that there was a dim, golden glow in the darkness, just enough to create a gloom in the shadows. She shifted her feet around, trying to get a sense of what she was standing on, but she couldn't tell for sure if she was in a pool or a lake or a quarry.

*No,* she thought groggily, disoriented. *It has to be a pool because of the chlorine, but where?*

The inside of her nose was stinging so badly she knew she was going to sneeze again. The pain in her head billowed like a slow-burning flame.

Her eyes adjusted further, and she saw that she was, indeed, in a swimming pool. Underwater lights provided what little illumination there was. "Hello?" she called out, her voice strangled and raw. "Is anyone here?"

Afraid of going under, she paddled with her right hand, floundering as she splashed about in the water, still trying to orient herself and afraid of overreacting. Her shoulder felt like there was a burning coal lodged against the bone as it was being pulled slowly from its socket. Water splashed into her eyes, blurring her vision, but gradually she was able to make out the dimensions of the large pool, and found that she was in the shallow end, her left hand handcuffed to the metal railing on the steps.

*Handcuffed?* she thought, forcing back a jolt of panic that threatened to sweep through her. *How did I get here, and why am I handcuffed?*

Now that she had shaken off most of her disorientation, it was a simple thing to stay out of the water. It was awkward, certainly, but the water was only three and a half feet deep.

But just as she thought of how simple it ought to be, she began to stand up straight. The manacle on her wrist held her, and the jolt threw her off balance. For a moment she had to scramble and splash to stay on her feet and not go under. Panic seized her again.

It took great effort, but she forced herself to calm down. Once she was sure that her footing was secure, she sat on the steps and listened to the faint sloshing of the water against the sides of the pool. It didn't seem as though anyone was nearby, but Jenna could imagine all too easily that someone was lurking in the shadows, watching her and listening to her and enjoying her panic and pain.

All of her jostling had set the water in motion. Most of the surface of the pool was in shadows, save for those places where the underwater lights shone up from beneath. Jenna scanned the pool as best she could in the gloom, but the one place she had not thought to look was in the dark corners on either side of her.

She jumped and let out a startled grunt when something bumped softly against her side. It wasn't much. Just a brushing touch, but a spike of fear slammed through her, and she almost went under as she turned around to see what it was. The restraint of the handcuffs made it difficult for her to move, but the thing that had bumped into her drifted to one side, and with a jolt of horror she saw a dark, motionless shape floating in the water close beside her.

A body.

Cold and dead, floating in the shadows.

A scream started to build up inside her, but she held it in check as she strained to see the body. It was obvious the person was dead. She could see that whoever it was, they were floating facedown with their arms and legs splayed out wide.

With fear and tension winding up inside her, Jenna reached out with her free hand and touched the cold, slick body. Even in the darkness there was something familiar about the shape. She sneezed again, hard enough to make bright points of light shoot like a spray of comets across her vision. Then, trying hard to control her rising fear, she grabbed the corpse by the shoulder. Bracing both feet flat on the bottom of the pool, she rolled the body over so she could see the dead person's face.

It was Jeff Tilton. Apparently he was not the killer after all. Jeff had met The Baptist, and his faith had not been enough to save him. His eyes were wide open and staring blankly at her with a dull, dead gleam.

The scream that had been building up inside of Jenna finally found its way out.

Audrey doused the headlights as she turned the car into the parking lot of the DRC building. Through the tall, metal fence they could see the flickering lights of traffic on Soldier's Field Road. The parking lot was deserted except for one car, which Danny immediately recognized as the department car Castillo and his partner Yurkich drove. He glanced at Audrey, her features underlit by the green dashboard lights. "Coincidence?" he asked.

Audrey shrugged as she coasted to a stop beside the car and killed the ignition. "Boston P.D. uses the pools a lot. Why wouldn't they come out here, especially since it's been so damned hot lately?"

"Because it's after-hours," Danny said.

"They must have keys," Audrey said.

After checking his service revolver, Danny opened the passenger's door and started to get out.

"No cowboy stuff, all right?" Audrey said, catching him by the arm.

"Look who's talking," Danny snapped back, but as he stood up and inhaled the humid night air, he could feel tension winding up inside him. He had a bad feeling about this, and it was getting worse.

They went up the walkway to the front door, but when Danny pulled on the handle, he wasn't surprised to find that it was locked. "Wait right here," he said softly, and then he dashed back to the car, opened the trunk, took something out, and ran back to where she waited.

Audrey cocked an eyebrow at him when she saw the small crowbar in his hand, an item car thieves call a "Slim Jim." Kneeling down by the door, Danny slipped the tip of the crowbar into the door frame just above the latch and quickly jerked it back. There was a faint snap. They cringed as they waited to hear an alarm sound, but the building remained absolutely silent. When he tried the door again, it opened easily.

"Such talent," Audrey whispered, smiling as Danny held the door for her to enter first.

With their weapons drawn, they started moving down the dimly lit corridor, following the signs that led to the indoor pool. The smell of chlorine was getting stronger with each turn. Just as they were rounding a corner, an ear-piercing scream split the air. Danny tensed and was about to run the rest of the way, but Audrey snagged him by the arm and held him back.

*"Oh, my God! No! No!"*

The voice, high and shrill, reverberated in the cavernous darkness.

"That's Jenna," Danny whispered harshly as the screams rose higher. "Go back to the car and call for backup. I'm going to find her."

Without waiting for Audrey to reply, he broke free of her grip and started down the corridor at a brisk trot, running as silently as he could. He drew to an abrupt halt when he rounded another corner and saw a dark figure silhouetted against the dim light of an opened doorway that led into the pool area.

"Hold it right there," Danny said, his voice low and controlled as he raised his revolver and aimed at the figure.

The person in the doorway visibly stiffened and then, very slowly, turned to face him.

It was Jace Castillo, and he had his gun drawn.

"Drop your weapon and put your hands on the wall. Now!" Danny commanded as he cautiously approached the Boston detective.

Very slowly, Castillo lowered his revolver so it was pointed at the floor, but he didn't drop it.

Danny's body was charged with adrenaline as he approached the detective, but when he was about ten feet from him, he saw Castillo's face break into a grim smile. "It's not me, man," he said in a harsh whisper. "We're here for the same reason."

Keeping his revolver aimed straight at Castillo's chest, Danny took a few steps closer to him.

"Looks like we made the same connection at the same time," Castillo said. "That it had to be an insider— a cop who was doing this."

"How do you know that?" Danny asked, still mistrustful.

"I've suspected it for days. Just been trying to put it all together, figure out who was behind it. Earlier this week I was bitching about the case back at the station, and this patrolman, Hitchcock, overheard me and mentioned that he was one of the arresting officers when they took

Jaffarian in. He filled me in on the case and mentioned how he and his partner were pissed off when that scumbag walked. And so"—Castillo shrugged—"I put two and two together." He paused a moment and took a deep breath. "We're on the same side here, Mariano. Honest."

Another scream—louder, now—echoed through the hallway. Danny's gaze jumped to the doorway, and he knew, with Jenna's life at stake, he had to trust this man.

# chapter 14

The echoes of her screams lingered in the dark, like the ripples of motion her struggling against the handcuff had caused in the pool. The only illumination in the room—coming from the small lights under the water—was just enough to throw shuddering shadows of those ripples onto the ceiling. The water lapped quietly at the sides of the pool, the only sound in that vast room, save for her own labored breathing.

*Stupid,* Jenna thought, her pulse racing, thumping inside her head. *There's nobody alive to hear you, except maybe The Baptist. The killer.*

The pool was deserted. It had been foolish to scream, to shout for help, but the soft bump of Jeff's corpse against her, floating in the water, had put her over the edge for a minute. Jenna had not gotten a look at her attacker's face, but it was long past the point where an identification would help her. She would be dead soon.

Unless she did something about it.

*Get your shit together, Blake,* she thought. *Just get it together. You've been in over your head before.* A tiny smirk twitched her mouth, but it was bitter. Morbid humor.

She had to keep her head if she wanted even a chance at surviving this night. Steadying her breath, she methodically surveyed her surroundings. There were five doors. One was a double-wide main entrance, both doors propped open, and one an emergency exit. There were two locker rooms, one men's and one women's. The fifth door might have been an office of some kind, but she could not be certain in the gloomy near-dark. Jenna knew that The Baptist might come through any of those doors, but she could not help focusing her attention on the main entrance.

The doors were open.

If the killer was anywhere in the building . . . well, she hadn't exactly been quiet.

Cursing herself in silence, she turned her attention to her left wrist, where the steel cuff had scraped her skin raw. The other cuff was attached to the steel railing on the stairs, and she stood in the pool and tried to get a look at the base of the railing, where it was anchored to the bottom. Jenna had read books where people in handcuffs had broken their own thumbs to get out of handcuffs, or broken their own skin with the edges of the manacles and used their blood as a lubricant to slip free. For just a moment these things seemed ridiculous to her.

Then she remembered the corpse of Jeff Tilton floating

behind her. *Guess he wasn't The Baptist after all,* she thought, verging on hysteria. *Just an ordinary stalker.*

Jeff was dead. And a lot of other people were as well. On second thought, broken thumbs or bloody wrists did not seem much of a sacrifice. But she wasn't ready yet to try something that drastic.

She stood in the water and stared at the railing. Her clothes were completely sodden, and their weight pulled at her. Jenna wrapped her hands around the railing, handcuffs clinking against the metal. She set her feet, bent her knees, and was about to pull when she realized how idiotic that was. No way was she going to be able to just tug the thing up, ripping the bolts out of the concrete bottom of the pool.

But there was another way.

Moving around to one side of the railing, her range limited by the cuffs, she crouched down and then threw herself against the upright front post of the railing. In her mind she imagined the shriek of metal as it gave way. Instead, it stood fast, and her shoulder hurt where she had struck it. Her breath came quickly again, and she shot a quick glance to the main entrance.

*You're going to die, Jenna.*

She gave a tiny gasp as the realization struck her. Then she shook her head, slowly, and slid the handcuffs up a couple of steps so that she was mostly out of the pool. The water couldn't impede her momentum that way. And if in her heart she knew that would make little difference, her mind would not allow such thoughts.

Jenna slammed her hip into the railing. The hollow

steel thrummed with the impact, but barely moved. She started throwing herself into it, again and again, and as she did so she felt the panic rising in her. Her eyes burned with unshed tears, and her breathing came ragged in her throat and she no longer cared about the noise she was making.

And her wrist began to bleed from the chafing of the cuff.

She froze, staring at the blood. Then she tested it, pulling at her hand to see if the lubricant would make a difference. It seemed impossible to her, but Jenna was determined to try. She wriggled her hand to get it wedged tightly inside the cuff, bloody skin sliding against steel.

Teeth gritted, she pulled.

And she screamed as the cut on her wrist tore wider.

"Oh, my God," she whispered, black motes dancing in her eyes. She swayed, worried she might faint.

She sat on the steps for a few seconds and stared at the blood seeping along her arm, dripping into the pool, and the truth sank in. She couldn't do it. She was too afraid of the pain to even try again, even to consider doing that to herself. She was going to die because she was afraid. "No," she grunted, lifting herself into a crouched position.

With all the strength left in her, she threw her body against the railing once more.

And it creaked.

Jenna gasped and looked up at the top of the railing, where the post that was anchored to the concrete at the top of the stairs had bent slightly. One of the bolts had come up a fraction of an inch, and there was a crack in the cement.

A cold detachment came over her. Jenna moved up to the top of the stairs, still in a crouch, held down by the cuffs. She set her jaw and threw herself against the post. Metal shrieked. The crack widened, and the bolt came up half an inch. In the back of her mind she knew that the noise of her previous scream and of her actions now might draw the killer's attention, but she did not care. This was her one chance. Her one and only chance.

Once again she prepared to throw her weight against the post, unconcerned with the bruises or with the blood on her wrist. There was a hint of freedom here. Of survival.

Then she heard the sound of water lapping against the sides of the pool. The sound had been her constant companion in the water, and when she climbed out she had barely noticed its absence. Now, though, as it began again, she realized that it had stopped for a time. The shadows had stopped rippling on the ceiling.

Now those shuddering, striated shadows had returned.

But Jenna was not disturbing the water.

She held her breath as she turned to scan the pool. Jeff's corpse still floated there, partially submerged, arms and legs dangling beneath him in the water. But now for the first time she saw that there was another body. In the almost darkness, with only the dim glow from the underwater lights, and with her own panic, she had not noticed it before. It floated.

And then it twitched.

Jenna let out a little shout.

The body went under, its legs kicked, arms pulled toward her beneath the surface, swimming her way.

"No," Jenna said. "No, no, no, no, no!"

She threw her weight against the post, and the bolt that had been pulling loose tore out entirely. Some of the concrete turned to powder. Again and again she rammed her body into the metal railing and it bent over, one of the other bolts pulling up as well.

Then she stopped and stared at it, breathing hard, hip and shoulder aching from using them to batter the thing. And she realized that she would have to go around to the other side of the railing, to strike it from that side, to get it to pull loose entirely.

And she was out of time.

"An 'A' for effort, Jenna."

A chill went through her and she shivered, water dripping from her clothes. A deep, abiding sadness took root inside her, for she knew that it was too late. Slowly, she turned to face The Baptist.

Detective Terri Yurkich was waist-deep in the water, dressed in sodden street clothes. Her face was expressionless . . . or almost so. In truth, there was a kind of peacefulness about her that made Jenna flinch and move as far back as her handcuffed wrist would allow. A tiny whimper escaped her lips. She wanted to say something clever, something about how she had figured out about the pool, and that it was a vigilante thing, and it might be a cop . . . she wanted to say she had suspected

Yurkich. But she had not had her theory long enough to make a mental list of suspects. And even if she had, she did not have the ability to speak at the moment. Her mouth would not form any words, no false bravado and no pleas for her own life.

Jenna could see something in Yurkich's eyes, and that was why she could not speak. That was how she knew it would do no good.

She could see the madness.

"I was doing the Lord's work," the big woman said, wading toward Jenna in the water. "They were depraved. Evil men. Our society wasn't going to punish them. They were walking around free, despite their crimes. Despite their *sins*. And they were completely unrepentant."

The water rippled around Yurkich, and the ripples were reflected in the madwoman's eyes, which shone with an ecstatic fervor.

"I saved them. You're a smart girl. I know you understand." A stern look came across the woman's face—the face of The Baptist—and when she continued, it was through gritted teeth. "I made them repent. And then I baptized them, cleansing them of their sins. . . ."

"But Virginia . . . and Jeff . . . what'd *they* do? They were sinners too?"

"I went to your apartment. One girl, home alone. Only it wasn't you, was it? By the time I realized it wasn't you, I was already inside. She saw me. And I'm sure there were plenty of sins staining her heart. As for the boy . . . well, he was stalking you, wasn't he? And what was his punishment for that? Nothing. Little shit didn't even get arrested. Besides, I was keeping an eye on you, watching over you. And if he was doing the same, he was going to get in my way, eventually. It worked out nicely, don't you think? With him missing, they probably still think he's The Baptist. That suits me just fine."

Jenna was sitting on the concrete by then, trying to inch backward, but there was nowhere she could go. Yurkich reached the steps and started up out of the water. "I don't understand," Jenna rasped, shaking her head weakly.

"I grew up in Hell. My mother was a good woman, who gave herself to God. But she was a sinful woman too. A lonely woman. She had a man who would visit her, and when she slept he liked to burn my flesh with his cigarettes, and laugh while I cried. His name was Hank. She tried to stop him, and Hank drowned her in the bath. He told her if she loved God so much, he would help her find Him."

"Why . . . why are you telling me this?" Jenna asked, finally finding her voice.

Yurkich towered above her. "So you'll understand. My mother was a sinner. Hank sent her to God. That was his way to cleanse his own sins, doing the Lord's work. He saved her, and saved himself as well. All my life I prepared for this mission. With the police, I knew I would find the unrepentant. That I would find sin that no law or court would be able to cleanse."

"You baptized them. And then you killed them," Jenna said.

Yurkich paused, and when she smiled, it was beatific. "Of course. They would only have sinned again. Their type always do. I saved them."

"And what about me?" Jenna asked, her voice so tiny, even in her own ears. "What are my sins?"

"I'm sure you have your share. We all do. But your greatest sin is interfering with the Lord's plan."

Her breath came in ragged gasps. Again, Jenna felt as though she might faint. "I . . . I repent," she said.

"Sorry!" Yurkich said brightly. "Too late."

The woman was much faster than Jenna expected. She thrust one hand out and tangled her fingers in Jenna's hair and dragged her down the steps, away from the loose part of the railing. Yurkich's smile, Jenna saw, was gone, and now her face was expressionless again. Her teeth gritted with effort as she pulled Jenna into the water. Then the killer wrapped her hands around Jenna's throat and, staring into her eyes, drove her down into the water.

Jenna screamed. She fought. Her fingers clawed at Yurkich's face, but the woman slapped her hand away. Jenna tried to squirm from her grasp, but the handcuffs would not allow her any room to move. Despite the woman's strength, Jenna would not go under. She staggered to stay on her feet, to stay above the water.

Yurkich grunted "enough." She slid one foot behind Jenna and forced her off balance.

"Mom?" Jenna whispered, as though in her mind she was still a little girl, hoping for her mother to explain how this could be happening.

The word made no sense, even to her, but she was beyond sensibility now.

The Baptist drove her under the water. Jenna's eyes were wide as her air was cut off. Her nose tickled with the chlorine, and she opened her mouth and began to choke on the water.

She began to drown.

Danny could smell the chlorine. A fragment of memory played across his mind, Jenna sneezing, but he pushed it away. Nothing pleasant could be allowed into his head right now. Not with The Baptist here. Not with somebody's life on the line.

*Jenna's life.*

Even shouting, her voice was so familiar to him. Unmistakable.

Together, he and Castillo raced down the wide hall toward the pool entrance. The double glass doors were propped open. They had heard voices as they approached. Now, suddenly, the sounds of a scuffle came to them. A voice crying out. Splashing water.

"Jace," Danny snapped.

Castillo glanced at him. Danny held his gun in a two-handed grip, its barrel pointed toward the ceiling. He motioned forward with it, and Castillo nodded. The Boston detective hurried ahead, back to the wall to minimize his exposure to possible gunfire. When he reached the open doors, his own gun now drawn once again, Castillo blinked, nostrils flaring, then gestured with his weapon for Danny to advance.

But Castillo didn't wait for him.

Danny followed, rushing through the doors, weapon at the ready.

He ground his teeth together, and his eyes narrowed to slits. At the bottom of the stairs of the pool's shallow end, The Baptist was bent over her victim. The only light came from the underwater spots in the pool, and they threw a kind of ghostly flicker up on the ceiling and the walls. But it was enough. Enough for Danny to recognize Yurkich—mental connections firing as he put it all together, her access to the pool, her physical size. They had not ruled out a woman as the perp, but everything in the profile suggested a man.

Under the water her victim thrashed, her single hand splashing, trying to tear at Yurkich's face. Dark hair floated beneath the surface.

In that moment, certain it was Jenna under the water, Danny had forgotten Castillo's presence entirely. Then Castillo began to shout. "Terri! Jesus, Terri, let her up! It's over! You're done!" he snarled.

The next few moments seemed to elapse in a sort of dream time for Danny. The emergency exit door opposite them was flung open, and Audrey came into the room, her own weapon drawn, barrel aimed right at Yurkich. But she wasn't going to take the shot. Danny could see it in her eyes. She thought they could take Yurkich down without firing. And he knew that if Audrey wasn't going to take the shot, Castillo wasn't going to do it. Not on his own partner.

"Terri!" Castillo roared, his throat hoarse. "Let her up or I will fire!"

Yurkich had not even seemed to recognize their presence, but at this she turned and glanced at Castillo, eyes shining with a kind of fever, or perhaps religious fervor. She smiled, and she hauled Jenna up out of the water.

For just a moment, Danny locked eyes with her. Jenna's gaze was filled with a haunting sadness he had never seen before. Not in all his years as a cop. It was the utter, profound certainty that she was about to die. She was limp, eyelids heavy, losing consciousness. Then she started to choke on the water in her lungs.

And Yurkich shoved her under again.

"No!" Audrey cried.

She and Castillo started rushing toward the pool. They would jump Yurkich, one on either side, and wrestle her away from Jenna.

But Audrey and Castillo had not seen Jenna's eyes.

Yurkich was strong. She would fight them. Jenna was handcuffed to the railing on the pool stairs. Under the water. Yurkich needed little time to finish her off, and even if they stopped her from killing Jenna, another few seconds might leave her worse than dead, her brain cut off too long from oxygen.

Jenna was drowning. Danny had seen the despair in her eyes.

He set his feet apart and took aim.

His eyes. Jenna had seen it in Danny's eyes. Darkness was starting to encroach upon her mind, and the terrible truth had hit her: It was over for her now. All the things she had not said or done no longer mattered. She knew this, and in the moment when the killer—her killer—had let her up, as she choked and gasped for breath, dreadful tears in her eyes, Jenna had seen that Danny knew it too.

Over.

The end.

Even so, she did not surrender. She beat at the woman's powerful grip, her own strength failing her. Hooking her fingers into claws, she gouged the flesh of Yurkich's hands, but the woman reacted not at all, holding her under by the hair, and by the throat.

Jenna had to breathe. Her eyes burned. A terrible weight was on her chest. When she blinked, it was a labor to open her eyes, and she did so with terrible slowness.

She meant to keep fighting. Truly, she did. But her hands slipped down to her sides, floating in the water there, and she breathed in.

Breathed the water in.

Her body tried to fight it. She convulsed, forcing the water out, churning it up her throat, but when she inhaled again it was only worse.

Up through the shimmering water she saw the face of Terri Yurkich staring grimly down at her.

She heard a distant, muffled *pop*, and spatters of red rained down on the surface of the pool. Drops of blood that began to spread, sending tendrils of crimson fog into the water around her.

# epilogue

A week and a half later, the world seemed to be desperately attempting to right itself, to return to the natural order of things. Classes were due to start up again shortly. Hunter and Yoshiko were back on campus, and things seemed better than ever between them. Jenna felt incredibly relieved to see them, taking strength and solace from her friends.

Jenna's mother had fussed over her, of course, and after several grim days when she thought her father and Shayna would never leave her alone, they had begun to focus on the small details of their imminent wedding once more. She had been so inundated with people who were concerned for her welfare that she had found little time to deal with her own emotions. And now that more than a week had passed, she felt as though she did not have direct access to those emotions. The moment seemed to have slipped through her fingers where she could have dealt with her fear in a direct and intimate fashion.

Instead, it had slipped into her subconscious, and worked its way beneath her skin.

She dreamed of drowning. Every time she sneezed, she thought of that swimming pool, of chlorine, of the blackness that had encroached upon her vision as she had begun to gulp down water, to choke on it. These nightmares woke her, but not quickly enough. Not before the fear had become terror, and she would have to sit up for fifteen or twenty minutes before she would dare try to go back to sleep. If she drifted down into dreams again too quickly, she would slip right back into that pool.

Often she found herself idly scratching at the new flesh that was healing over the slices on her hand and wrist where the cuffs had bit into her skin. Once upon a time she had liked to take baths, when she had time to soak and read a book. For now, she would only shower.

Memories of that night at Dyson's made her anxious after dark. She nearly always had the television on for company now, even though she was never alone in the house. Not at night. Dyson was all right, and he had wanted her to stay until she could move into Whitney House for the school year. But her father had insisted she stay with him, and Jenna did not have the heart to say no. Beyond that, there was the way Doug looked at her now. He was still as kind as he had always been, but there was a distance in his eyes that made her want to cry. She felt like she had lost him. Dyson had been knocked out, taken fourteen stitches in the scalp, and had his wrist fractured.

It could have been much worse. The Baptist could have killed him. But Jenna felt it would have been cold comfort for her to try to tell Doug that.

*Dyson was all right.*

Jenna felt sure that one day she, too, would be all right. The nightmares would pass. The jumpiness and paranoia would pass. The fear would lessen, though secretly she doubted it would ever go away entirely. Because she would never forget. No matter what happened, she would never forget what it had been like to look up into the face of that lunatic and to know that she was going to die, to become accustomed to the idea. To know that she could not escape.

It tarnished her whole world.

One day, things would shine for her again. But though she spoke of it to no one, Jenna felt sure it was going to take a long time. A very long time.

She had not worked since the incident. They had kept her in the hospital for two days, and then advised rest for a week. With classes starting up again, Dr. Slikowski had made it clear that she was not to even set foot inside the office until the first week of the semester had come and gone. Unless she wanted to talk. She was always welcome for that.

Slick had shown her every kindness. Danny, on the other hand, was MIA.

So, on that Wednesday morning, Jenna was relieved to receive a call from Audrey Gaines. Jenna went out to meet her at Jay's Deli, right on the perimeter of the campus. The coffee at Jay's was terrible, so Jenna knew Audrey was just trying to make it easy for her by picking someplace convenient.

Half an hour later the two were sitting across from each other. Audrey grimaced as she sipped at her coffee. Jenna had not had breakfast, so she smeared cream cheese on a bagel, then let it sit on the plate as if it belonged to someone else.

"How are things going with your firefighter?" Jenna asked.

Audrey blinked, taken aback by the question. Their relationship was not so close that Jenna ordinarily would have asked such a thing. But perhaps they were growing closer. Perhaps this thing with Danny—with his job on the line—was doing that to them. They both cared a great deal about him. It gave them something in common.

"It's going well," Audrey said. A tiny smile ticked at the edges of her mouth and then disappeared. She lowered her gaze.

"He won't talk to me," Jenna ventured, her voice cracking. She gnawed her lower lip. "After all of that, he won't talk to me."

"It isn't you," Audrey assured her. "He cares about you. But he's wrecked right now. He's not talking to anyone. Not even me, and I'm his partner. He's totally cut off."

"That's not fair!" Jenna said, hating how childish it made her sound. She shook her head. "He called me the day I got out of the hospital. I haven't heard from him since, and he doesn't answer his phone. Doesn't respond to e-mail. I thanked him, that one time I talked to him. All he said was that he'd done what he'd had to do. But he . . ."

Jenna took a breath, then let the words tumble out. "Danny killed Yurkich to save *me,* and now his whole career's in jeopardy."

Audrey peered at her, then reached out and lifted her coffee mug. She took another sip. "He's been suspended, Jenna. It really is standard procedure. Yurkich wasn't armed. They have to investigate the shooting. They don't have a choice."

"So you think it'll all just go away?" Jenna asked, hopeful.

But the cloud that passed over Audrey's eyes was answer enough, and her heart sank.

"It's not that simple," the detective said. "Castillo and I are trying to not make it worse, but we can't lie. If we're caught lying, it won't do Danny any good, and then *we're* both screwed as well. I'll do anything to help him. But right now, their attitude is that we could have stopped Yurkich without killing her."

"Not while keeping me alive!" Jenna said.

She was suddenly aware of how loud her response had been and she glanced around, but no one was paying any attention to them.

"That's what the investigation will determine," Audrey said. "I'm sorry, but it's out of our hands. Yours, mine, and Danny's, too. It's all procedure, now. I'm sure what he wants is for you to try to live your life, to get back to classes, and to try to not worry about him. He's dealing with things his own way. I've seen him do it before. He'll brood for a while—not that I'm blaming him—and then he'll surface, and he'll need us all to be there for him."

"I will be. I'll always be there for him," Jenna said.

Audrey smiled. "I know you will."

Turn the page for
a preview of the next
**Body of Evidence** thriller

# THROAT CULTURE

Available April 2005

When the elevator door opened on the third floor of Somerset Medical Center and Jenna stepped out, she felt as though she was in another world. Nothing seemed real. Her skin tingled like she had just stepped from the shower, freshly scrubbed. During the autopsy she had pinned her hair back, though it was much shorter now than it had once been, and she had left the clips in. She was aware it probably looked silly, but she was unconcerned.

*Such a petty thing. How could it matter?*

There was an odd numbness in her feet and her fingers, like her extremities had fallen asleep, or as if she herself had been poisoned. But Jenna had lived through enough trauma to know by now that it was nothing physical. It was the weight upon her heart that made her feel so weak and disconnected.

But she did not let it slow her down. Her arms swinging at her sides, she strode like a martinet along the corridor. A portly nurse, emerging from a patient's room with a clipboard, gave her an appraising glance. Jenna paid her no mind. She wore her SMC ID clipped to her shirt, and even if she hadn't had one, visitors were common in these halls. But Jenna wasn't here only as Shayna's stepdaughter.

*Stepdaughter. I was just starting to get used to the idea.*

She pushed the pessimistic tone of that thought away, unwilling to pursue it. Shayna was going to fine. She had to be.

Jenna's father had not always been good to her. Not that he had been cruel . . . it was more that for much of her childhood, he had not always been there. Often she would see him only three or four times a year. Though he would be wonderful to her, funny and kind, she did not really know him all that well beyond those visits. Frank had not exactly been a stranger to Jenna growing up, but he had not been a *parent* to her either. She was old enough to understand that he had had his own issues to deal with, a life to work out. It had taken her enrollment at Somerset University for the two of them to really get to know one another, and she would be forever grateful for that. He was a sweet man who had never been lucky in love.

Everyone believed that Shayna was going to be the one to change all that. Jenna had never seen her father so happy.

*And now this.*

*It just isn't fair.*

She knew what her friends would say, or her mother. Life wasn't fair. Whoever told you it was? But sometimes that point was hammered home with just a little too much ferocity. Jenna had changed a lot since her freshman year at Somerset, and right now, the most important part of that change was that she had learned self-reliance above all things. Not that she could not depend on others, but that what was important was her own intentions, her own determination. She had learned that her actions could affect the world around her.

That had never seemed more vital to her than right now. If fate had decided to be cruel, she wasn't going to just let it happen, just let it flow. She was going to fight back.

The soles of her shoes squeaked on the linoleum as she hurried down the corridor toward Shayna's room. It seemed to her that she was somehow a little more real than the rest of the world, that the air rippled with her passing. The anger and frustration and sadness in her gave her a furious strength, as though she might reach out and grab hold of the fabric of the world and force it into submission. As crazy as that seemed and as silly as she knew it was, the truth was not so far off.

Jenna had no intention of just waiting for someone else to help Shayna. Not when she had seen bliss dance in her father's eyes at his wedding, and glimpsed the yearning ache in him when she had first arrived at Professor Haverford's autopsy.

She had long since grown used to the smells of the hospital, the way the antiseptic odors of the cleaning products only masked the odors of waste and disease that permeated everything, even the walls and people. Today, though, it churned her stomach to think of

Shayna as one of them, one of the patients whose illness was the source of that smell.

The thought disturbed her so much her step faltered, and she paused there in the corridor, veering off toward the wall.

*Quit it. Just stop.*

Jenna took several deep breaths and then nodded in determination. Yes, Shayna was in bad shape, and Jenna had just helped autopsy a man who was dead because of exposure to the same toxins. But it wasn't going to end up with Shayna's body down on a slab in the cold room, waiting for autopsy. She wasn't going to end up in some drawer in the morgue.

*It's not going to happen.*

A familiar voice drifted down the hall, and she glanced up to see her mother emerging from Shayna's hospital room. April Blake was a beautiful woman whose face revealed too much of her heart. Even from fifteen feet away, Jenna saw tragedy in her mother's expression. She hurried to close the distance between them.

". . . long as she's stable, we have to remain optimistic," April was saying.

"Mom?"

April turned and saw her daughter. A sad smile spread across her face. "Jenna," she said, and opened her arms.

As Jenna went to her mother, she saw her dad standing just inside Shayna's room; but in that moment, it was just the two of them. Mother and daughter, the way it had been for so many years growing up when her father wasn't around. Dad and Shayna might be her family, too, but April was the only one who was ever really her parent. Her mother was everything to her. An errant thought skittered across Jenna's mind: She was glad it was Shayna in that room and not her mother. It made her cringe inwardly with guilt, and she chided herself for it, but that didn't make it any less true. She liked Shayna very much and wanted her father to be happy, of course. But what was happening made her very aware of how much she loved her mother, and so when they hugged, Jenna held her very tightly.

"Hey," April whispered. "It's going to be all right."

"Yeah," Jenna said. "I hope so."

Then she pulled back and regarded her parents carefully, taking a deep breath. "But that's the mom talking. And I think from here on out, I need to talk to the doctor."

April nodded. Then she gestured toward her ex-husband. "I was just saying to your father that Shayna's stable. The doctors are in there with her right now. I spoke with them for a few minutes. At the moment, anyway, she doesn't seem to have any additional symptoms. The paralysis is alarming. It's far more radical than anything I've seen or even heard of with shellfish poisoning . . . assuming that's what we're dealing with. The speed and totality of it is frightening. But as long as she remains stable, they'll keep monitoring her for improvements."

Frank moved over to Jenna and slid his arm around his daughter. She leaned in against him. "What kind of window are we looking at, April? Be honest. What are we looking for?"

Jenna's mother started to say something, then hesitated. She reached up to tuck a lock of auburn hair behind her ear and glanced away briefly, her eyes blinking rapidly. Then she turned and met Frank's gaze steadily. They knew one another all too well, these two. Marriage and divorce, Jenna had observed, seemed to teach people more about each other than they had ever wanted to know.

"We're going to want to see some movement in forty-eight to seventy-two hours," April said. "Anything could happen. If there's no improvement by then, it won't mean the paralysis is permanent. But her odds are much better if we have something by then."

Jenna sighed and reached up to press her fingers against her eyes. She was not especially sleepy, but she felt exhausted. Absolutely drained. Low voices came from Shayna's room—the doctors, examining her again—and she glanced inside. The slender form beneath the hospital sheets seemed so small. So frighteningly still.

"So what do we do now?" she said, without turning around.

"Go home," her father said.

Jenna turned, her brows knitted, and stared at him. "What? I'm not going to just—"

"Shayna's stable," he said. "I appreciate your mother and you coming out here. I know you're worried. I'm . . . I don't even know what to do with myself. Yes, I want company, 'cause I'm not leaving. But you have work and school to attend to, and nothing's changing right this minute. So go. Study if you need to. Work if you need to. Get your mind on something else for a while,

and come back to visit when you can. Maybe later tonight. Your staff ID will get you in whenever you want, right?"

She nodded. "Well, yeah, but . . ."

"I'll be all right. Honest," Frank said, putting a hand on Jenna's shoulder. "I do want you around. I need to see your smile once in a while. But I also need to know that you're tending to other things. Shayna certainly wouldn't want you to screw up the semester because of this. And hey, who knows? Maybe she'll surprise us all and be up in time for dinner."

*Dinner.* The word hit a terribly sour note after the circumstances of Shayna's affliction, and her father looked as though he regretted it the moment it came out of his mouth.

"All right," Jenna replied, pushing past it. "I guess. I mean—I'll come back tonight. Maybe there'll be more news by then. Slick and Dyson have the techs running about a dozen different tests."

"Any guesses so far?" Frank asked.

Jenna grimaced and shook her head. "Dr. Slikowski doesn't guess. Ever."